CURTAIN GOING UP

CURTAIN GOING UP

A Novel

CAROLYN R. SCOTT

A
J<small>oan</small>Kahn
BOOK

ST. MARTIN'S PRESS • NEW YORK

Copyedited by Daniel Otis

Design by Jeremiah B. Lighter

Library of Congress Cataloging-in-Publication Data

Scott, Carolyn R.
  Curtain going up.

  I. Title.
PS3569.C597C88   1988   813'.54   88-1937
ISBN 0-312-01755-3

First Edition

10 9 8 7 6 5 4 3 2 1

For
Jean Mercier
with all my loving thanks
C.R.S.

CURTAIN GOING UP

CHAPTER

1

IT WAS ONE of those May mornings, cloudless, warm, and fragrant: a morning not to be trusted. Sheila Devlin swallowed coffee and caught the nine o'clock typewriter, the only remaining sign of discipline in an otherwise deteriorating life style. She stayed there, lashed to her chair, digging words out of her head, until she saw Will the mailman coming down the road. This was her legitimate mail break. She ran outside and down the driveway, hair flying, as if she and Will were going to meet in a passionate embrace all because she had used the right shampoo. But Will handed over her mail and drove off whistling between his teeth. Will had a beguiling smile. Oh, well.

Sheila flipped through three letters to "Occupant" and a free bar of soap. The next letter was from her agent, Theo Prentiss, who was also her best friend. She ripped it open, expecting a check to flutter to the ground. No check.

Sheila—
Received enclosed statement from your publishers today and I know it will send you into a screaming fit of

depression. But I must point out they gave you a whopping advance on Cage of Larks *and that's the main reason you now have a negative balance, as shown. Besides your books are always slow starters and I'm sure we'll get a paperback sale, which I'm working on with unremitting zeal.*

Call me and come in for lunch soonest. What for did you have to move to the stix? I miss you.

Theo

Plodding back to the house, Sheila read the publisher's statement. Sure enough, a negative balance. They didn't owe her, she owed them. Splendid. Here she was pouring words into a typewriter day after day, broadening her hips, straining her eyes, and humping her shoulders—for what? A negative balance. Why had she chosen to be a writer when she could have been . . . a lepidopterist? . . . a subway pusher in Tokyo? . . . a queen on a very small Polynesian island?

She stalked up the kitchen steps, pulled open the screen door, and poured coffee, some on the counter, some into the cup. "Would that it were hemlock," were the words that passed through her mind. Looking out the window, she saw several large hemlock trees in her own backyard, just standing there waiting. How do you make them into a liquid you can drink? Did Socrates have a Cuisinart? How would the recipe read? "Purée one cup hemlock needles in two cups chicken broth, garnish with ground glass, serve piping hot." She wondered what she could season it with to hide the taste—curry, perhaps?— and her suicidal resolution became sicklied o'er. Her one-time husband used to accuse her of talking herself into and out of everything in the world. "Deliver me from an intellectual woman," were his exact words. And in the fullness of time, she did.

On the counter in front of her, the rest of her letters were drowning in spilled coffee. She dabbed them with paper towels and saw the postmark, "Lawrence, Kansas" . . . a letter from her mother. She loved her mother. Sheila loved her with all the seething rage that most people love their mothers with and she wondered whether Mom might be coming to live with her. If so, she could always move to the sewers of Paris. She slit open the envelope.

Dearest baby Sheila,
I do hope you didn't think I was inviting myself to come and live with you. Good heavens, I wouldn't dream of such a thing! I was only suggesting the tiniest little visit. When my only daughter lives alone in a three-bedroom luxury home in affluent *Westport, Conn. I didn't think she would begrudge me a bed and a bone! But I certainly did receive your message and when you say you are "dubious"—well, least said soonest mended.*
I'm so glad your new book is a big success. I don't care for the title—a Cage of Larks *sounds very depressing to me, but I suppose you know what sells. I can tell you my rental library wouldn't touch it with a barge pole. Anyway, now that you're rolling in $$$, I realize that all the sacrifices your father and I made were not in vain. Of course, I often wonder if your father had not worked so terribly hard those last few years to see his little girl through college, would he still be here by my side? But we won't think about that, will we?*
I hope you're enjoying your single life, even though

3

I'll always consider you made a mistake to divorce that nice man, Spenser. I remember telling you the first time I ever laid eyes on him that he had a weak chin. I feel you should have made him join AA and take up woodworking. Busy hands are happy hands.

I have been thinking about my future and I believe I'll look into a retirement home (even though I'm far too young) where the inmates play auction bridge and the keepers rob them blind. My friend Gwennie said they stole her teeth. *She also said there was a flasher there, seventy-five years old. Said he showed great promise. That Gwennie had a terrible mouth on her, but oh dear I miss her so. The laughs we used to have. There's nobody left to make me laugh now except you, and it's mighty hard to get a chuckle across a continent. But don't misunderstand me. This is not supposed to be a Big Hint. But of course, if you change your mind dot dot dot. And remember you used to like my chicken dumplings, didn't you missy?*

I should think a famous writer might be real glad to have a built-in cook-housekeeper, sober, honest, industrious, and no gentlemen callers in the rooms, ha-ha. (Worse luck.)

You stay away from those caviar cocktail parties and specially those singles bars where you're nothing but meat on the hook. I saw that movie and I had nightmares about you for weeks afterwards. Just remember you are my dear little daughter and how is your little Kerry? I bet you she doesn't love her *mother as much as your* mother *loves you. I'm sending you greetings from the Heartland of the U.S.A. and a bluebird of happiness is flying across the miles from me to you.*

Your loving Mother.

Sheila put the letter down, then picked it up and read it again: masochist that she was, she seemed to enjoy reading that sweet, funny, bone-chilling death sentence over and over. Desperately, she started pacing through her luxury home in affluent Westport, Conn.

It was true the house didn't have mud floors, and there was indeed a chimney to let the smoke out through the roof. But the luxury stopped right there. The original owner was his own architect and, sure enough, had a fool for a client. In the bathroom, there was only one place where you could stand up straight, and that was in front of the hand basin. If a tall man was answering nature's call, he had to crouch leaning forward, as if about to dive into the shallow waters.

One of the three bedrooms would be called a closet if it had a pole. The second bedroom on the other hand had no closet at all. The third bedroom had three doors that opened into each other, forming a vertical coffin, open at the top. For all these reasons, she had been able to afford the house, mortgaged to the ridgepole. Walking now from one room to another, she realized that she loved this house with a fierce and tender love, as a mother loves a handicapped child. It was the first dwelling of any kind she had ever owned and she would defend it with her life. But share it? With her mother? Mind and body lurched as she reeled back into the kitchen for more coffee.

Her mother, that sweet, gabby, cheerful little lady, coming to live with *her?* People always said her mother was cheerful as a bird. Well, if she had wanted a bird, she would have had one long ago. The fact was, her mother was much younger than she was. It was a generation gap, and her mother was the child. Mom had

5

never given five minutes thought to life as it passed by. But this is all there is, Mother, this short journey from howling cradle to weeping grave. Don't you want to understand it, before it's too late? No, she didn't. Busy hands are happy hands. If she had to live with her mother, she would feed them both hemlock purée. Parent and child spend eighteen years of agony outgrowing each other. After that, no power on earth should reunite them.

She picked up the rest of her mail and walked into her bedroom. She fell on her bed in one piece like a tree in the forest and lay there thinking. We meet all the great moments of life in the horizontal position. We are born and give birth horizontally. We make love horizontally. Well, for a start, anyway. We are ill horizontally and die horizontally and are buried horizontally. Perhaps in the horizontal she would find peace and wisdom and a way of coping with life.

She was lying face down three inches from the pile of mail that was teasing her to look. She defied anybody to attain even the most temporary satori in the presence of unopened letters. She slit their throats. Three overdue bills: from Rod the Roofer ("We Top Them All"), from the bookshop at Vassar College *(Beginning Calculus,* used copy), and from her dentist ("We would appreciate your remittance, hopefully in the near future"). Resolving to do a root canal on his grammar at their next meeting, she passed on.

The next letter was addressed with that erratic typewriter she had handed down to her daughter. On the back of the envelope Kerry had written, "DESPERATE

SHORTAGE OF BROWNIES." The look of the sprawling script brought Kerry into the room, leggy, slant-eyed, and husky-voiced. Kerry was the hope of the world. Kerry was a freshman at Vassar College.

Dear Mom,
Every time I start to call you, I know you're working and you'll kill me. Anyway, this is too important for the telephone. And I won't become manic depressive if you say no. But for God's sake, say Yes.

As you know I was all set to go back to camp this summer and teach the little monsters how to swim and speak Italian—(at the same time?). Well, my Art teacher I told you about namely Angelo—he's twenty-four and so sensitive and funny and has this wonderful enthusiasm for painting that's so catching it's like sparks flying around the classroom—Well, anyway Angelo is putting together this trip to Italy, Florence mostly because that's where his parents live and they have a huge house with lions in front. He's taking ten people, co-ed, and I'll be the only freshman. He thinks I have the Big Talent: I have to let him know in one week because we leave June 10. We get to see everything in Florence with side trips to Rome and all CUT RATE. The total damages around $4000 and that includes air fare and all the capuccino I can drink! We do sketches and water-colors every minute we're not seeing MASTERPIECES. I met most of the kids going and it's a NEAT GROUP, nobody on drugs, I figure with the new book such a smash hit you'd feel like investing in my future!!! When I have my first show on 57 Street I'll pay you back! I don't suppose Dad would kick in??? Or is he back in the drying-out place? Anyway, I'm going to call, collect, I'm into deficit spending. My roommate has mono and I have my

crucifixion tomorrow equals calculus exam and I prac-
tically broke my ankle playing shitty game of hockey so
addio bellissima mamma mia and take care of your FAT
self!!!

Loving daughter Kerry

Sheila dropped her head back on the bed, the letter under her cheek. Kerry, Kerry. She loved that crazy child. And then . . . *Italy?* Four thousand dollars worth of Italy? A house with lions? Nobody on drugs? How splendid. The Big Talent? Yes, Sheila thought she had talent. Along with how many thousand American kids pumped full of hope and dreams and spewed out of how many American colleges year after year? To drag their portfolios from gallery to gallery and wind up, if they were lucky, in an ad agency doing layouts. But what if Kerry had real talent, that talent "which is death to hide." How could Sheila say no and for such a stupid, mean little reason? Say no to Kerry? Oh my ducats, oh my daughter.

If she said no this year, could she say yes next year? Fat chance. She was barely managing the child's tuition. Sheila glanced up at the hanging bookshelf over her bed and her four novels in their shiny dust jackets. Surely she could call herself a moderately successful writer. Then why did she never have the ducats? Simple. A handful of writers are rich. The rest of us can't afford a daughter in college, a crazy house in the country, a rusted-out car, and a couple of cavities in our teeth. Writing is a nice way to make a living but you can't live on it.

Despair was sneaking into the room and bringing

his terrible friends, loneliness and panic. The three of them were sneering at her, laying their clammy hands on her face. She could hardly breathe.

What would her father say if he found himself lying here, smothering? He'd say, "I must get out of my lazy bed." He'd heave his great body up, shaggy head on thick torso, and swing his great, tree-trunk legs over the bedside. Her father was larger than life, operatic, with the voice for it too. Sometimes in the evening when Mother had choir practice, Father used to say, "Come along, then. We'll do *Boris Godounov.*" He'd put the record on and sing along with Chaliapin, Sheila squatting on the floor in front of him. When it came time for the Tsar to fall headlong down the palace staircase, Father would stand up on the back of the sofa, swaying and pitching forward, crashing down and rolling across the floor, while Sheila watched in horror and delight. Or when her father sang the last scene of *Othello* to her own silent but trembling Desdemona, he would suffocate her most lovingly. She could see over the pillow how his eyes were glistening with tears. Once when her mother caught them, she scolded Father sharply. "Tom Devlin, you'll make the child morbid!" But Father answered, "Go on out of that! I'll make her a *theater person!*" Then he'd wipe the tears from Sheila's face with the tail of his shirt.

Sheila had a rule. Whenever she used Father, it had to work. She heaved off the bed and went to the kitchen for coffee. Basically, she had a money problem. How simple. With money she could rent a small nest nearby for her birdie mother and avert the threat of matricide. With money she could send Kerry to Italy for

9

this and other summers. With money she could buy a word processor and books would come gushing out of it like water from a faucet. Where to lay hands on money? Work in an office of course, like real people, and write books at night. What office? Theo's office, her best friend. Call Theo for lunch immediately. She put one hand on the phone, her eye on the clock, the other hand into the peanuts. Eating was the one reliable good in a precarious world. Theo said, "Super. Twelve-thirty at Gino's," and Sheila ran to throw on her city rags.

Driving to the train station, she found herself staring right and left. The spring had flung itself across the countryside while she was locked in her house. Veils of sheer green half-hid maple trees, and apple blossoms drifted on the wind. People's gardens could barely contain the milling crowds of tulips and daffodils. Lawns turned green as she passed. Painters on ladders slapped whiter paint on whitest houses in time to the beat of screeching music from their radios. Women in blue jeans swept their sidewalks aerobically. Tree men in cherry pickers swooped, yelling at each other, all of them called Charlie. She felt she was watching the opening scene of a big, Broadway musical. So this was why people lived in the country. She must remember to go outdoors sometimes.

She parked illegally and sprinted for a train that turned out to be twelve minutes late. Finding a window seat, she swore off thinking about the problems. It was spring and she was going to be happy, like her mother. She sat with a vacant smile on her face and watched the conductor punching tickets. This operation littered the floor of the car with tiny white circles of paper that must later be swept up, thereby inducing further railroad bankruptcy. Should she head up a movement called Passengers Against Negligence in Conductors, or P.A.N.I.C.? There you were. She was the only person she knew who could sit for two minutes of happy meditation and arrive at the word PANIC. Basically, her view of the world was cataclysmic, apocalyptic, but always with a fine needle of sunshine piercing the dark brooding clouds, as on a plumber's calendar. The sunshine today was Theo.

With Theo she could be exactly who she was. They had grown up together in Lawrence, Kansas, both their fathers being professors at the university. After college, they had migrated to New York City, but Theo had taken a job with the best literary agent in town and seven years later opened her own shop. Now she handled some of the biggest names in the book world. Theo was successful. She always claimed she had saved lots of time: no marriage, no children, no divorce. Instead, she'd had a string of long-term lovers: Bonesy and Sailor and Magoo and Prewitt and Jasper and Fish and Gordy. Sheila had kept careful track of Theo's men, sometimes reviewing them at night when she couldn't sleep. Theo's list of lovers might sound staggering, but who among us, mused Sheila, would not be surprised if he, or even she, looked back over eighteen years and put down *everybody*, even the most hasty and ill-advised tumble in the sheets?

Theo's alliances had been as happy and wholesome as breakfast cereal and when they were over, each lover

11

had gained from the other, or so they reported. Be it said, Theo was a beautiful girl and an expert skier. You meet a lot of men on the slopes, she said. In any case, Theo had a knack for living. She would understand, and give Sheila a job in her agency. Today Sheila was at the crossroads. Her life was about to take a turn for the much better.

The train crept into the catacombs of Grand Central twenty-five minutes late and Sheila blew her last two dollars and change on a taxi to Gino's. She collided with Gino in the dark little entryway. "Ah, signora—" He kissed her hand and led the way to a table halfway down the long, narrow room, where a young man rose from the banquette.

"Gino, there must be some mistake—"

"No mistake," the young man said. "Theo can't make it. My name's Val Keating and you're Sheila Devlin, right? Will you have lunch with me?"

He gestured to the banquette after wringing her hand. Sheila kept thinking this couldn't be true.

"You mean—Theo's *not coming?*"

"She sent you a note." He held it up as bait. Gino swung the table out—"Please, signora—" and one on each side of her, they pushed her by the elbows to sit down. Like a bagful of bricks, she sat. Gino swung the table toward her, then swung it open at the other end and the young man stooped and folded himself in beside her. He was tall and cadaverous, with bony wrists protruding from frayed cuffs. He had deep-set eyes and a beaky nose.

"I guess you're kind of pissed off."

"You put it so well."

"But we both get a free lunch, right?"

The young man had a beautiful voice. But Theo had let her down. She had been counting on Theo to redeem this real loser of a day. That's how it was. If she'd had a date with Yassir Arafat, you think *he'd* have failed to show? Not a chance. But her best friend, her last hope in this perishing world, had found better things to do. Meanwhile the young man—she remembered his name was Val—seemed to be looking at her in sheer delight. He must be very young or very poor to get so happy over a free lunch. Sheila looked up at the hovering waiter.

"Could I have a double martini straight up with a twist?"

CHAPTER

2

IN LAWRENCE, KANSAS, Muriel Devlin finished her letter to her daughter, Sheila—"The bluebird of happiness flies from me to you!"—and hoped the child would cheer up, for pity's sake. She was turning out to be one of the Black Irish, just like her father. But no time to moon over Sheila today. This was the First Thursday of the month and, according to a custom of several years' standing, Muriel was expecting Sherwood Pell for dinner.

The monthly ritual had begun soon after Tom Devlin's death. Sherwood started dropping by on Thursday evenings to console his best friend's widow. At first Muriel offered him a glass of sherry, a biscuit or two, a tiny hot cheese pastry. But Sherwood was a bachelor and an epicure, and Muriel was an accomplished cook. The conversation had naturally turned to this or that favorite dish, a new recipe, a daring combination of herbs. By now the two were sharing a four-course meal, artfully prepared and splendidly served by Muriel.

She would start several days in advance and clean the entire house. She would set her table with the finest bone china and the Irish linen dinner napkins. She placed the Waterford finger bowls on the sideboard, where they would catch the candlelight, and laid out her dress on the spare-room bed. Tonight she would wear her navy print with the white collar.

She pictured where they would sit before dinner, chatting over their sherry, and then dinner itself, always eaten in a respectful silence, broken only by Sherwood's occasional comments: "An exquisite soup, Muriel, you have surpassed yourself . . . Ah, fresh peas? From your garden? I am indeed a lucky man."

This last was the comment she anticipated hearing tonight. She had been pinching those peas for weeks now, almost praying over them. She planned not to pick them until just before her bath at five, so they'd have this last day to ripen.

The leg of lamb had been marinating for five days, the strawberries Romanoff she would fix this afternoon, when she rose from her nap. A nice nap always brightens the complexion, and besides it would make the day go a little faster. On First Thursdays it always seemed that dinnertime would never come or, as dear Tom used to say, "A watched clock never boils."

The day was proceeding in an orderly fashion until Muriel decided to wash her hair. When the hair drier refused to function, Muriel had to dash next door in rollers to borrow one from Harriet Horton. "My word, don't tell me First Thursday has rolled around again!" Then Muriel spilled a half-bottle of brandy as she was fixing the strawberries Romanoff and washed the kitchen floor three times to get rid of the smell—Sherwood mustn't take her for a brandy-pot!—and suddenly the dragging afternoon had turned into breathless evening. Wasn't that always the way? There was Sherwood Pell standing on her doorstep.

Sherwood was exactly dear Tom's age: he would never see sixty again, but he was trim and casually elegant in his winter tweeds, sparked by a bright silk handkerchief.

"Why Sherwood Pell, if you don't keep yourself fit as a fiddle!"

"An odd expression. Why not trim as a trombone, I wonder. These are for you."

He extended a huge bunch of American Beauty roses, in which a fifty-dollar bill was always concealed. Sherwood knew very well how small was the pension of a music professor's widow, and had even been thoughtful enough to include many cost-of-living increases over the years.

Muriel ushered Sherwood into the front hall— "Enter, dear friend"—left him briefly—"Two shakes of a lamb's tail"—to drop the roses into the waiting vase on the dining-room table and pick up a plate of pastries. She trotted back to him and led him by the elbow to his end of the sofa. She poured their sherry from a crystal decanter and sat on her end of the sofa, smiling up at him. It was First Thursday at last. She raised her glass. "Here's to us, Sherwood, dear."

But it was soon apparent that Sherwood was out of sorts tonight. Muriel found they were not discussing the balmy weather or the wild behavior of the undergrads.

Sherwood said his spring play was due to be presented in three weeks' time and the rehearsals were a disaster. The play had been written by one of Sherwood's drama students, chosen and directed by him. If it should fail, he would look "like a fool, a half-witted, God-damned fool!" "No language, please," said Muriel, but Sherwood ignored her and started stalking the room. Muriel had never seen him like this.

"In fact," Sherwood said, "I should be holding an extra rehearsal right now, tonight, instead of lounging about drinking sherry."

"Now, now, Sherwood. Everything always turns out for the best."

He stopped in his tracks and looked at her. "It does, does it? Everything for the best, eh? In the best of all possible worlds, Dr. Pangloss? Is that it?"

"Dr. who, dear?"

"Could we have dinner now? I have to leave in one hour, or less." He wolfed the crab-filled pastry in his fist, and three tiny crumbs dropped on the carpet.

"Just one itty-bitty second, please." Muriel picked up the crumbs, one by one, and dropped them into the palm of her little pink hand. She went to the scrap basket and brushed them daintily in.

"Now. Shall we dine?"

Usually he offered his arm in mock-stately ritual. Tonight he stood back and examined the ceiling until she preceded him alone.

Sherwood drank his soup darkly, without comment. Muriel tendered a remark on the number of robins she had counted this spring. Sherwood said, "Robins belong on greeting cards," and Muriel bustled off to the kitchen, to return with the leg of lamb.

She set it down on the sideboard and offered Sherwood the carving tools with all the deference of an altar boy. He rose from the table, strode to the sideboard, and began sharpening the knife with long, flashing strokes. He began to carve the lamb. His attack was so vengeful that the roast shied away from him and hit the rose-patterned carpet at their feet with a spattering of juices and a far-flung trail of parsley and tiny new potatoes. They both looked down in shocked silence, then Muriel gave a breathy little laugh.

"Oh well, I'll just wipe it off . . ."

She bent and lifted up the dripping thing. But as she started to replace it, Sherwood intercepted.

"Here! Give me that!"

He grabbed it and crashed it down on the platter and started again to dismember it, plunging the fork into the center and slashing away with the knife as Muriel watched in paralyzed horror. Sherwood was muttering wildly.

"Wipe it off, eh? Oh, no you don't! You'll probably scrub it, if I know you! Disinfect it! Boil it for two days! Nossir, I'm eating this lamb, and I'm going to eat it *dirty!* In my bare hands, like Henry the Eighth, and you're lucky if I don't take your head off when I get through, like Ann Boleyn! *You watch yourself . . .*" He brandished the knife at her and she backed off, terrified.

"Sherwood! Don't! . . . What's happened to you?"

He stopped. It was like a freeze-frame at the

movies. Then he dropped the knife and fork somewhere near the platter and dropped his face in his hands.

"Oh, God! . . . Oh, my *God!*" He lifted his face and looked at her. "Sorry. Overplayed it, didn't I?"

Muriel gave a howl and burst into tears. She ran out of the room and up the stairs. Sherwood shook his head, dazed, staring down at the wreck on the platter. He helped himself to one small nubbin near the bone, licked his fingers, and walked to the foot of the stairs.

"Muriel! Muriel—will you come back . . . please?"

He could hear the muffled sounds of weeping. He climbed the stairs and entered Muriel's bedroom. He had never seen so much pink in all his life. Everything was pink, including the bed where Muriel lay, weeping noisily. He raised his voice so she would hear him over her cries.

"Muriel! . . . I'm sorry! . . . I'm very, very sorry!"

More weeping. Sherwood could not tell whether she had heard him or not. He kept on shouting in spurts, fitting them in between her sobs.

"Don't know what got into me . . . lot of pressure lately . . . those rehearsals . . . shocking, my dear . . . I promise you . . . I am facing public disgrace . . . I shall be pilloried . . . held up to scorn and ridicule . . . ghastly, quite ghastly . . ."

When it was obvious he was making no progress, he slowed to a halt. Muriel spread her fingers to see whether he were still there.

"Please . . . go!" she said.

19

She pointed to the door, in an unfortunate gesture reminiscent of snowstorms and bloodhounds. She sniffed loudly, and he saw that her nose was running. He proferred a box of tissues from the bed table and turned aside while she blew her nose. When he turned back, she seemed somewhat more collected.

"Sherwood, I—" Suddenly, she uttered a piercing cry and fell back on the bed, weeping more loudly than ever.

"Muriel, what is it? What happened?"

"The peas! My beautiful peas! Ruined, all ruined!"

"What peas? Where? Muriel, tell me!"

"On the stove! I put them on to steam while you were carving! Now they'll be ruined, all ruined!"

Sherwood, agile for his years, took off down the stairs. He slammed into the kitchen, lifted the steamer basket, and peered down at the peas. He found a spoon and tasted one, then several more. He dumped the peas into a bowl, remembering to turn off the stove, and puffed back up the stairs again.

"Muriel! These are the finest, I promise you, the most exquisite peas I have ever tasted! Have some!"

Muriel sat up in bed and blew her nose once more. Sherwood held out a spoonful of peas. She looked at him, stony-faced.

"Please, Muriel—"

She opened her mouth and allowed him to tip the spoon between her lips.

"Yes. They're good."

"You see? Have some more."

She shook her head, lips pressed tightly together.

"Well, I'm not letting peas like this go to waste," he said, trying for boyish enthusiasm. He scooped the rest of the peas into his mouth and slid the bowl carefully under the bed.

"Hate to think of that lonely little lamb down there. *Agnus Dei*, you might say . . ."

He looked into her swollen and sullen face and decided the scene wasn't really playing well. He was getting far too long in the tooth for this kind of thing. "The Lovers' Quarrel" and all that. He wished himself a thousand miles away.

"Now see here, Muriel. I've enjoyed our little suppers together—"

"Suppers! You call them *suppers!*"

"Quite right. Dinners. *Banquets*. But on the whole, don't you think perhaps . . . it's time to . . . well, I mean to say . . ." He rose and drifted downstage toward the door. As soon as he could find a good exit line, he would exit, God willing, pack it in. The whole thing had been a foolish mistake from the word go, but no harm done, come to think of it. He braced himself.

"You see, Muriel, I'm thinking of going to London this summer on holiday . . . so this might be a good time to . . . well, make the break, as they say. I mean, nothing lasts forever, right old girl?"

He turned to see how this was going over. Muriel was sitting there motionless on the bed with rivers of tears pouring down her face.

"Oh, Muriel, please don't do that!"

He came to her and held up the tissue box, but she stared straight ahead without moving, those terrible tears flooding her face. He took a tissue and gingerly patted her cheeks, but the tears kept coming. There would not be enough tissues in the world. He did the only thing left to do. He put his arm around her shoulders and kissed her long and hard.

"Oh-h-h, *Sherwood*—" Suddenly she was smiling, and the effect of the childish smile on that tear-stained face was somehow shattering. He cupped her chin in his hand, and kissed her more softly, searchingly. He pushed her gently down on the bed, and undid the front of her dress. Her skin was cool, and white as milk. She lay there, offering neither resistance nor encouragement. She was still smiling slightly, her eyes looking over his head. He managed to undress her, and then himself, without, so to speak, Muriel noticing what was happening.

Her whole body, plump and womanly, was his to command. He found himself lifting her and turning her one way and another, disposing her limbs to suit his desire. She was passive and pliable, showing no desire of her own, but surrendering totally to his. He could feel her small hands resting lightly on his shoulders. Her total compliance increased his passion. She became an object in a dream, feeding his lust even while she satisfied it. At the summit of the act, he wondered if he had ever been so lost in a woman before.

When their love-making was over, they lay side by side without speaking for a few moments. Then Muriel seemed to come to life. She raised herself up and peered down into his face.

"Oh, Sherwood, Sherwood—"

She seemed transformed. She sat up in bed, throwing her head back and caressing the arch of her throat, stretching her rounded arms as luxuriantly as a cat. She bent over him again.

"Oh, Sherwood, do you know what's happened to us? We've become sweethearts!"

Sweethearts. Where did she get these words? He turned on his side. She gave him a playful slap on the buttocks and pulled the sheet over his naked body.

"You naughty, naughty boy!"

She trotted across the room with bouncing breasts, wrapped herself in a pink bathrobe, and returned to plump up the pillows and plant herself regally among them.

"Sherwood, can you imagine what we could do this minute?" He failed to imagine. "We could have those wonderful strawberries I fixed for us! Strawberries in bed! We could feed them to each other, one at a time. That's what sweethearts do, you know."

"I don't feel hungry, Muriel."

"Oh, yes you do! Because you're a bear, and bears are always hungry in the springtime. Now you go down and get the berries—oh, Sherwood, isn't it wonderful? I'm so happy!"

Sherwood hauled himself out of bed. Lose the battle but win the war, he told himself. The business of returning the strawberry dishes to the kitchen would also serve to carry him out the front door, never, never to return. He dressed himself as quickly as possible while Muriel was chirping away.

"When I think of all this time you've been coming

to dinner, and I always wondered how you felt about me. You were always so dignified, such a perfect gentleman. Oh, I like that so much. And of course you were dear Tom's best friend, and I suppose you must have felt awfully funny. I mean about my being his wife. Widow. Isn't that a terrible word: widow? And it's a terrible thing to be, I can tell you. A very lonesome thing to be. I was just writing to my daughter in Connecticut this morning. She's been asking me and begging me to come and live with her. There she is in that beautiful big house all by herself and money to burn. She's a writer, you know, a best seller. Well, I have to admit I was just about getting ready to pack my trunk and go. And now look what's happened. Isn't it just wonderful how your whole life can change in one evening? Oh, Sherwood, would you mind putting the lamb in the refrigerator? We can't take any chances in this warm weather, can we? And you won't forget to bring us two little paper napkins from the drawer beside the dishy-washy—my little Sheila used to call it that, "the dishy-washy"—and come back soon, won't you, Big Bear? I'm just going to miss you, and miss you, and *miss* you—"

She blew him kisses with both hands and he managed a twitch of a smile. Still tucking in his shirt, he started down the stairs. This was really most frightening. Look what you've done, you cretin, you mad, impassioned boy of sixty-one. It was gluttony that got you into this, you know, not to mention lust. And how about sloth? Why didn't you cook your own blasted dinners on First Thursdays? So you've committed three of the seven deadly sins. Would you like to try for the other four?

24

He found the berries in the immaculate refrigerator. Two spoons, two napkins beside the dishy-washy, and all this will soon be over. He trudged up the stairs, somewhat wearied by the recent athletics of the boudoir. At the top, he missed his footing. Holding the strawberries upright in front of him, he fell sideways and backward down three steps and landed with one leg underneath him. The pain was instant and excruciating. He fell back, gasping, against the bannisters.

"Are you coming, Big Bear?"

She came padding out of the bedroom.

"Sherwood! What happened?"

"I—I suppose—Oh, God help me, I suppose . . . I broke my leg . . ."

"Oh, *Sherwood* . . ."

He must have blacked out several times in the next half hour. Muriel didn't allow him to move. She telephoned for an ambulance, she sat beside him and kissed his forehead, she ran to get dressed and find her purse, not forgetting to bring his jacket. She was calm and gentle and soothing.

Two young men lifted him onto the stretcher, and he passed out. Then he was in the ambulance, Muriel right there beside him, holding something cool and wet against his forehead.

"Now don't worry, Sherwood, I'm not going to *allow* you to worry."

He heard a dog whimpering. How did the dog get in the ambulance? No dog. Sherwood, himself. He tried to stop. Now she was talking again.

"I'm a hospital volunteer, you know. I have my

25

twenty-five-year pin. I know all about broken legs. After they set it at the hospital, they'll put on a great big cast, right up to your hip. Oh yes, for six weeks, but it's the only way. You want to have a nice, straight leg that matches the other one, don't you? Oh, I saw how nice they are, believe me."

She gave him a kiss on the forehead.

"Of course, you'll have a wheel chair, and then crutches. Do you have a downstairs bathroom at your house, Sherwood? No? Well, I do. I have a sweet little pink-and-white powder room and I'll put a bed in the dining room and you'll see, everything will be nice as pie."

"No . . . *no* . . ."

"Oh, yes indeedy. Now don't you start fussing and fretting. You're going to be my big, brave Bear and stay at my house where I can take care of you. And if the neighbors start gossiping, why—we'll just tell them we're engaged to be married. Oh, my poor Sherwood, is it hurting just terribly?"

He closed his eyes.

CHAPTER

3

AFTER ORDERING the drinks, the young man called Val turned back to Sheila and said, "Here, you better read this," handing her the note from Theo. It was a scribble on a sheet from a memo pad.

> *Sheila—*
> *I swear I couldn't help it.*
> *Theo*

"Very informative," Sheila said. "What happened?"

"A producer from the Coast called right after you did. Must've had a cancellation. Said he wants to option a property of ours—you know, by one of our writers. Theo had to meet him and set up the deal. She couldn't help it."

Sheila wondered *why* Theo couldn't help it, why she'd never sold any of *her* books to the movies. Self-pity was creeping in, not for the first time today. She began digging her fork into the padded white tablecloth, making a snowstorm of dots between the young man and herself. She wished he would simply disappear, this young man called Val.

"Theo said to be at her flat for drinks at five. I'm supposed to stall you till then. Take you shopping for a mink coat if necessary."

"A full-length mink?"

"Dragging on the ground."

"Not good enough," said Sheila. The drinks arrived and they caught each other's eye with a nod before the first medicinal sip.

"You care if we talk about your books?"

"I can't talk about anything else."

He laughed. Even his teeth were young.

"I want to talk to you and I don't feel like going through all the chicken-shit preliminaries, like what do you eat for breakfast. I mean we could have an earthquake right now or Theo could change her plans and walk in here and I'd never see you again. You follow me?" Sheila nodded. The young man had a beautiful voice. Silvery. She wanted him to keep talking.

"I'm listening."

"Y'see, I've read all your books." He ticked them off on long, knobby fingers. *The Glass Bell, Flowering Tree, Kingdom of the Blind* and uh—the last one." Sheila refused to help him out. "I got it! *Cage of Nightingales!*"

"Larks."

"Right. Now here's the thing of it. Some people have one book in them and they keep writing it forever. Yours are different every time, and better. *Cage* is the best. In my opinion, you're really good."

He took a huge gulp from his drink, then another,

then emptied the glass and ate the olive. Sheila felt the hot, heady liquid of praise going down her throat the way he must be feeling the gin.

"I hate compliments, they embarrass me. Keep going."

"I think—well, I think some day you'll be great. Do you believe that?"

"My God, no!"

"So you don't buy the critics when they say you 'write a shimmering prose' or 'Sheila Devlin knows all the secret places of the human heart.'"

"Critics get paid to say something."

"I knew it! I knew you figured it like that!"

"Really? *How* did you know?"

"Well, actually . . ." He was looking down at the glass in his hand, his hair falling over his forehead and hiding his eyes. "Actually, you're going to have my head on a plate if I tell you."

"I will if you don't!"

"When I found out we were having lunch today, I checked your file. I read your letter to Theo."

"Which one?"

"The one where you said you were going to quit writing."

"I say that every week."

"You said, 'I have only one real talent. I can make a man happy in bed. So I'm going to turn in my typewriter for a silver Rolls and start cruising Park Avenue at twilight.'"

"You bastard! That was private!"

He looked at her intently, solemnly. "Y'see, writing

is one of the things that really matters. And if you're really good at it, you shouldn't kid around about giving it up. Understand?"

"How long have you been lolling around Theo's office reading her personal mail?"

"'Bout a year. Basically I'm a gofer. But I'm learning the business. Sometimes I get to take crabby authors to lunch."

"I'm famous for my sunny disposition! Today . . . I'm making an exception!"

He studied her.

"You're beautiful . . . successful . . . funny . . . I guess you just found out you have terminal cancer."

"If I want to be unhappy, you leave me the hell alone!"

"Sure thing." Cheerfully, he ordered their pasta and turned back to her. "My dad used to get mad at me, too. He said I had three left feet."

"I'm with him!"

"He called me the monster. He said when I walked through a room, you had to have cyclone insurance."

"Sounds like a fun father."

"Best thing in the world for me. When he said that, I signed up for a ballet class. I was the first dancing male swan in Falls City, Nebraska."

"Falls City! I'm from Lawrence, Kansas!"

"I know, I read your bio. We grew up a hundred miles apart." He looked at her as if this had some significance, and perhaps it did. Mainly, she wanted to hear his voice again.

"What else did your father say?"

"He said the way I swam I could drown in a heavy rain. So I signed up for free-style swim and six months later we beat Lincoln High."

"So then he was proud of you."

"No, then I disgraced him. I started acting."

"Acting?"

"In Falls City, a boy who wants to be an actor is better off dead. I was called 'artistic.' My father quit speaking to me."

"Then what?"

"Then I took up hurdle racing and won the four-forty at Falls City Senior High Field Day."

"Then what did he say?"

"He said, 'Son, you think running is going to put bread on the table?'" Sheila laughed and looked again at this young man, Val, with the long face and the shock of no-color hair and had a strange sensation. She must be feeling happy.

Their pasta arrived and they attacked it. By a giant effort of will, Sheila left half the huge serving on her plate. Val finished his, and glanced over at hers.

"No more pasta?"

She shook her head.

"When you're with me you never need a doggie bag."

He switched plates and rapidly emptied hers. She realized he had also devoured all their rolls and butter, all their celery and olives and carrots, and nibbled appreciatively at their parsley. Was it days since he had eaten, or days before he planned to eat again?

He was talking, gossiping about writers they both liked as if they had been mutual friends. The characters in certain books were people to him whose lives continued beyond the last written page. He would shake his head regretfully. "Alfred never should have married Ursula. She's going to be a ball-breaker," or "Don't feel sorry for Georgie, he's going to sleep his way to the top of his wife's class at Wellesley."

Finally, they looked up to see that all the other tables were empty and cleared away. Waiters were starting to hover. Val took a package from his pocket and laid it on the table.

"We're having your favorite thing for dessert. You want to eat them here, or in Central Park while we're walking?"

She looked down at a slightly squashed bag of glazed apricots.

"How'd you know?"

"Theo told me."

"Let's go."

When they walked out into the spring sunshine, he steered her north and west, curbing his long gait to match her own. The sidewalks were clogged with people, pressing and pushing. The city was having its lunch-hour attack of arteriosclerosis.

But the moment they entered the Park, they were in another country, an aimless and amiable place. Pigeons goose-stepped in circles; squirrels scalloped along iron railings, going nowhere; lovers tangled their bodies on benches, accomplishing nothing but pleasure. A scrawny lilac tree had hidden itself in blossoms. Wherever the grass was not beaten down, it was the bravest green.

"The Park looks so beautiful."

"No treat for you, is it, coming from your spread in Connecticut—"

She couldn't tell him she lived in a maximum-security prison, letting herself out on rare occasions.

"Nature in the city is more touching, there's so little of it."

They walked down the Mall to the end and found a bench near the looming statue of Shakespeare. They placed the apricots, carefully nested in their plastic wrap, on the bench between them.

"Go ahead," he said. "Take the biggest one, I dare you." She did, and bit into it. It tasted of the sun that was pouring down on them. She smiled at him, watching her so expectantly.

"Delicious. You take one." He did and they chewed away.

"How come," she asked between bites, "how come you're such a reader? You look like an all-American boy. In this country, women and old men do the reading."

"When I was ten, I had a 'fever of unknown origin.' Stayed in bed for a year, mainlining the books. Guess I never kicked the habit."

"But—you're all right now?"

"As you see, a mountain of muscle. Hey, what's your next book about?"

"People." She was looking over at Shakespeare's statue. "Did you know he was the son of a butcher?"

"Yeah," Suddenly he put on the loud, domineering voice of the angry father.

"Now you listen to me, Will. It's about time you quit all this scribbling and come into the business with me, you hear? You do like I say and you'll always have meat on the table, get me?"

Sheila was laughing and clapping her hands and looking again at this lanky, unpredictable bare-bones of a man.

"Do some more."

He rose and went to the stand beside the statue, leaning against it with a careless grace.

"Oh for a muse of fire, that would ascend
The brightest heaven of invention!
A kingdom for a stage, princes to act,
And monarchs to behold the swelling scene!"

His musical voice carried, even out of doors, and he spoke the lines with a loving intensity that made Sheila nod her head, urging him on.

". . . Can this cockpit hold
The vasty fields of France? Or may we cram
Within this wooden O the very casques
That did afright the air at Agincourt?"

He made the question hang in the air urgently.

"Suppose within the girdle of these walls
Are now confined two mighty monarchies,
Whose high upreared and abutting fronts
The perilous narrow ocean parts asunder."

34

He moved away from the statue and with the barest motion of a hand and look of eye, he conjured up the ocean.

"Think when we talk of horses, that you see them
Printing their proud hoofs i' the receiving earth—"

Suddenly he dropped his hands and came back toward Sheila.

"That's the best, isn't it? Those nags printing their proud hoofs. Will knew about everything, even horses." He threw himself down on the bench beside her and reached for the remaining apricot. A little knot of people had gathered on the walk and now gave Val a spattering of applause. He rose from the bench and bowed deeply in their direction, then held out a hand to Sheila.

"Come on. My pad is right over there." Sheila stood and faced him.

"Val, you're an *actor!* Why are you a gofer in Theo's office?"

"It pays better."

"But Val—you're gifted!"

"Yeah . . . sure . . ."

"I think it's a crime to waste a talent!"

"Talent's a dime a dozen."

"Not like yours!"

"Hey, *get off my case,* okay?"

Angrily, he hooked into her arm and dragged her away. Sheila was stung into silence and walked beside him woodenly. They came to a remodeled brownstone off Central Park West and started climbing the stairs. The walls were a lumpy yellow ochre like peanut brittle. Cooking smells and the screams of children filled the halls. Val kept pulling her on, another flight and another while she wondered miserably why she had come at all. Finally he flung open a door and motioned her in.

His room was clean and spare, all white, with a good window at the far end glowing in the late-afternoon sun. A narrow bed and table stood at her right, one big chair with telephone waited under the window. The surprise was a huge tank of tropical fish against the long wall, as colorful as a garden. Sheila went to watch them, gliding and weaving in their dream world. Val named them off: the Keyhole Cichlid was a shimmering blue and yellow ribbon; the Clown Loch a traffic stopper, and the Emperor Tang had been taught to like spinach. Sheila was hypnotized.

"I want to be a fish."

"Suppose I forget to feed them."

"Don't."

"Sometimes they hurt each other."

"So do we."

"I hurt you a while back, didn't I?" So he did know. "Okay, ask me anything."

"Why are you wasting your life? Why aren't you an actor?"

"You're looking at a graduate of the Yale Drama School, winner of the Carol Dye award, et cetera, et cetera."

"Then what?"

"Then I came to New York. Made my rounds. Answered the cattle calls, sat on the wooden benches. I also waited on table, washed dishes, drove a cab . . . Sheila, I flushed eight years of my life!"

"You never . . . got work—at all?"

"Two walk-ons and a lead in an off-Broadway turkey that lasted three nights."

"It takes persistence!"

"Persistence? Do you want me to tell you about persistence, Sheila? I've seen guys twice my age, living on dog food. They've got persistence. They corner you in washrooms. They grab you on street corners and swarm all over you."

He sidled up to her, a seedy aging deadbeat, wheedling and fawning.

"Listen, ole buddy, I'm up for a reading next week. Producer's a personal friend. Nothing big, y'understand. Cameo part. A real career-builder, y'know? And I'm right for it. Could have been written for me. But they haven't quite got the money together yet, y'see?" He plucked at her dress and crowded her against the wall. "So listen, if you hear of something in the meantime, ole buddy, just remember who your friends are, okay? I'm in the book, y'know. Fired my agent, the blood-sucking bastard, who needs him, right? So give me a blast on the horn, okay?" He was backing away now. "I can play younger, older, you name it. No problem with the wardrobe, anything from banker to bum." He fingered his coat. "Don't judge by appearances, just on my way to the cleaners. See you around the pool, ole buddy, and don't be a stranger, don't forget now, don't be a stranger . . ." He faded away.

"No, Val, no! That couldn't happen to you!"

"Sure it could. Damn near did. You want a Coke or anything?"

She shook her head. He opened double doors to a kitchenette, reached into a tiny fridge for a Coke, and pried off the cap under a drawer pull. He raised the bottle to his lips while his left hand closed one door and his right heel closed the other. The kitchenette disappeared.

"I like what I'm doing. Another three-four years of servitude and I open my own office. Val Keating, literary agent. What's wrong with that?"

He took a long drink and looked at her.

"I guess people always tell you you're beautiful and you get sick of it."

"The people who've told me I'm beautiful in the past year could all get into a telephone booth and each one bring a friend."

"That's a crock." He reached for her hand and led her to his big chair. "Sit down. The light's going to hit your hair and bounce. It's red-gold, isn't it?" He crouched and looked into her face. "Y'know, I've seen tigers that would kill themselves for eyes like yours." Sheila thought he was going to kiss her, but suddenly he stood up. "If you don't hear that in Westport, you better move."

"Val, I—"

"Yeah, you're right. We better call Theo." This had not been her thought, but he gave her the number, which she already knew, and she dialed. Theo was at her apartment, waiting.

In the taxi, they talked about books, and Nebraska,

and why King Lear was so dumb about Cordelia. He left her at the door of Theo's apartment building after a quick kiss on the cheek. She looked over her shoulder and saw him break into a loping run, heading uptown.

Theo came to the door as sleek and polished as her cool and shadowy apartment. They hugged each other and sank into a white sofa piled with clouds of pillows.

"How *are* you," Theo asked. "Tell me everything. Listen, you weren't mad at me for sending Val?"

"Well, *no*, actually Theo, you won't believe this but . . . oh, *Theo* . . ."

"Oh, *Sheilah-h-h!*" Theo screamed and they fell into each other's arms, rocking and laughing. They were both sixteen years old again, and one of them, blissful and bewildered, had fallen in love.

CHAPTER
4

IT WAS THE warmest day of the spring when Muriel brought Sherwood home from the hospital. She had arranged for two of his heftier drama students to meet them on the sidewalk and help Sherwood into his wheelchair, then lift him chair and all up her front steps.

"Now wasn't that smooth as silk?"

The students helped Sherwood into the hospital bed that was waiting for him in the dining room, Muriel having insisted that he travel in his bathrobe. The boys put the bed through its paces with glee. "Geez, Professor, you got it made! Four speeds forward!" Muriel handed each one a folded bill. "Aw, Mrs. D., you don't have to do *that!*" and they sashayed out, stuffing the money into their jeans.

Muriel surveyed him as he lay there with thirty pounds of plaster on his leg. "Now don't you run off anywhere!" and she went to get his lunch. Sherwood was left to examine his new sick room. The dining table had been pushed into a corner, his bed equipped with a fine reading light and television on an extension arm. A hospital table stood ready to swing across his lap, and on it rested a shiny new telephone. Crutches waited against the wall, and an air conditioner—surely not there before?—purred in the window. The room was flooded with spring sunshine, sweetly scented with lilacs. Only the most black-hearted and bad-tempered ingrate could fail to be moved. In a searing flash, Sherwood knew himself to be a black-hearted and bad-tempered ingrate.

He felt beholden. He felt he was piling up an indebtedness he could never repay. He resented this woman for her kindness, her thoughtfulness, her endless little favors. He resented, retroactively, every cup custard she'd brought to the hospital, every plumping of pillows, every soothing of his brow. He felt she was weaving a net, a web of tender little mercies. She would keep on winding this gossamer thread around him until he was totally helpless, trussed up, ready for devouring. He shivered. What about a Great Escape? What if he should throw himself into his wheelchair and go barreling out the door, down the steps, and up the street for home? His home?

At that moment, Muriel entered, bearing his lunch. He surveyed the tray of creamy cold soup resting on a bed of chipped ice, the shrimp and fresh asparagus salad, the lime sorbet with candied lemon peel and sprigs of mint. Freedom could wait, he decided.

After lunch, Sherwood started worrying out loud. While he was lying here, helpless, opening night of the play was hurtling toward him. The student director who was taking rehearsals did not bear thinking about. The pace would be like the movement of a glacier; the cast still carrying books, even though the play had been on its feet for weeks now; the electrician, who wouldn't know a light cue if it bit him in the leg. And when it came to costumes, all Sherwood had ever seen was one hat, one blasted hat. He should have canceled the entire show the night of the accident and, in fact, he would do so right now if he had the brains of an imbecile.

"Nonsense," said Muriel, "you'll do no such thing. I'll go to rehearsal today."

"*You?*"

"I'll report back to you, good, bad, or indifferent."

"Muriel, forgive me, but you're hardly qualified—"

"I might surprise you. Besides, you don't have much choice, do you?" She looked down on him lying there, and he would swear the woman was enjoying herself.

"Now you take a nice nap and mend your bones. Your motorman's friend is here beside you, ice water in your thermos, lots of good soaps on the telly. Ta-ta, Big Bear—" She leaned over and kissed his forehead and he heard the front door close behind her. He groaned. His leg itched under the cast. The house was very still. What was he *doing* here? He could see birds on the lawn outside. Running around, flying away. Free as a bird. He groaned. Eventually, he slept.

Muriel did her grocery shopping and stopped off at a stereo shop, reaching the theater well ahead of rehearsal time, as she had hoped. Wild rock music greeted her as she entered the auditorium. She came down the aisle and mounted the steps to the stage. In the wings, a student wearing headphones was seated at the dimmer panel, twirling dials and thumping one foot. Muriel waved gaily under his nose and he cut the sound and rose, removing his head set.

"Hi."

"You're Bill Boyd, aren't you? Your brother, Mike, always did lighting for my husband, Tom Devlin. I hear you're even better than he was."

"Twice as good." Bill had a crooked grin.

"I knew it! Now Bill, your director has unfortunately broken his leg—"

"Poor ole prof, and he moved in with you, right?"

"That was only an hour ago!"

"Campus tom-toms. Bet you got some kind of patient there, huh?"

"Bill, he's a devil."

"Yeah-h, tell me about it."

"But he's so happy about the play! He says it's going better than his wildest dreams!"

"He says that? You mean he doesn't *know?* Listen, lady, the play's a bomb!" She might as well not have heard him.

"People are saying this is the best play ever done by the drama department. Campus tom-toms."

"You're putting me on."

"After thirty-nine years in the church choir, I don't tell fibs. Of course, it's a heavy show on light cues, but Sherwood says you're handling it like a master."

"Ole Woody said that?"

"So many times! Now Bill, I want to ask you one tiny little favor."

43

"Ask."

"I stopped off and bought a tape recorder. I want you to tangle up your wires and mikes and things so the whole rehearsal today will be on tape for me to take to Sherwood. It'll be the next best thing to his being here! Will you do it, Bill?"

"Sure, give me like a half a day."

"Oh no, half an hour, Bill. But I'll help you! Now let me see, which is the tweeter and which is the woofer?"

"Mrs. Devlin, do me one thing. Please. Get lost. Okay?"

"I leave it completely in your hands, dear boy."

Muriel made her way downstairs. In the costume room, she found several students at sewing machines, surrounded by a confusion of hats and capes, boots and swords.

"Yoo-hoo! . . . Oh, my dear . . . Why, I know you! I'm Muriel Devlin and you're Daisy Cummings. Your mother studied voice with my husband, Tom, and you're as pretty as she was! I was jealous, I can tell you! How are you, my dear?"

"Oh, Mrs. Devlin, *look!* It's a zoo! It's a disaster! I'm going off my track!"

"That's not what I hear! Sherwood Pell is a very dear friend of mine and *I* hear . . ."

"Is it true he *moved in?*"

"Oh, those tom-toms! And Sherwood says your costumes are going to carry this show!"

"Mrs. D., nothing can carry this show."

"And he said thank heaven for Daisy, the miracle girl! I'd be lost without her!"

"He's lost anyhow. The show's a turkey."

"No, Daisy, a blockbuster. I've been on this campus for forty years and I can smell a hit every time. Daisy, this one smells of champagne and roses!"

"Hey—really?"

"And every one of you will be proud as punch to've been associated with the best show ever put on by KU!"

"Geez, I wish."

"Now when is your dress? Next week? Why not throw them a couple of hats and swords today? Give them a lift, you know?"

"Yeah, why not?"

"I'll be out front, and next week they do say the man from *Variety* will be there, too!"

"Wha-at?"

" 'The costumes by Cummings were fresh, inventive, the designs of an authentic talent.' "

"Oh my Gah-h-hd!" Daisy fell into Muriel's warm and motherly hug and waved her out of the room. Upstairs, a few students had drifted in. Bill had acquired several helpers who were stringing cables across the stage and slinging microphones around. Muriel found the student director in the fourth row on the aisle marking up his already illegible script. She sat behind him, and tapped his shoulder.

"Excuse me. Aren't you Virgil Thorndyke? I've read so much about you in the *Record*. I'm Muriel Devlin and Professor Pell is staying with me since his accident."

"Yeah."

"Sherwood was saying how lucky he is to have you to back him up."

"Yeah."

"He feels perfectly comfortable about missing a few rehearsals when you're here."

"Yeah."

"He thinks you're just what the play needs right now. A fresh approach. New blood. A shot in the arm."

"You know what this play needs?" He held up the script by one corner and applied an imaginary match. "Snap, crackle, pop! Look! a bonfire!"

"Virgil, I'm surprised at you!"

"You seen this play, ma'am?" Muriel shook her head. "I've seen it for six weeks and I don't have the faintest, remotest idea what the hell it's about!"

"Well, why don't you?"

"This play is called *Continuum*. That's real sexy to begin with, huh? So the curtain goes up and it's the sixteenth century or something and these two people are in love. So we get some long speeches and a couple of wars, the lights go down to half and the trees get a lot bigger. The lights come up and it's fifty years later and those two actors we just saw are playing their own children. You follow me so far?"

"Certainly."

"So, they're in love, but the guy gets beheaded by the King. His girlfriend makes a speech three pages long, we put a spot on her, and when she gets finished it's the next century. Am I going too fast for you?"

46

"It's . . . different—"

"Hold it. The next time we see these loonies, the man is his own grandson, and he's attending his own funeral!"

"How interesting—"

"Yeah? Maybe you should be sitting here directing instead of me—"

"What a splendid idea!" Muriel reached over and grabbed the script from the young man.

"Hey, wait a minute!"

"You can't sit there and criticize Sherwood's play! I won't have it!" She sprang up and stood in the aisle, glaring down at Virgil, who rose and faced her.

"Now look, ma'am—" He reached for the script, but Muriel whisked it behind her.

"If you don't believe in this play, who will? I think you're a worm in the apple!"

"I didn't say—"

"Indeed you did! And you are no longer the student director! And I speak for Mr. Sherwood Pell himself!"

"Listen, ma'am, I put a lot of time into this turkey—"

"More's the pity!"

"If I quit now it goes on my record. I'm a drama major!"

"Bad luck for the drama department!"

"Look, ma'am, I apologize. I got pissed off—"

"All right, Virgil—"

"Give me back my script, okay?"

"Are you ready to make this play a success, or die trying?"

Virgil raised his right hand. "So help me."

Muriel handed him the script. Virgil took it and started trudging down the aisle, shaking his head and looking back over his shoulder. "Geez . . . I mean . . . I don't *believe* this!" A few students clapped. Muriel smiled politely and sat down. Bill came to stage center, speaking into one of the mikes. "Testing, one, two, three, testing." He tried the other microphones in turn. "Testing, one, two, three. Okay, Mrs. Devlin?"

"Beautiful," said Muriel.

Virgil called into the wings. "I want the curtain down. House lights to half. Stage hands ready? Cast ready. Music cue, please."

The silver voice of a clarinet sang a fragment of melody, and stopped. It started again, and gained momentum. Soon it was joined by other woodwinds. The house went dark, the curtain rose slowly. Muriel shivered. A play was about to begin.

A pair of lovers made their way through several centuries and heaven only knew how many wars, earthquakes, and famines. The rest of the cast consisted of "Friend," who changed sex frequently and seduced one or the other of the lovers—sometimes both!—and a "Mother" and "Father" who often switched roles with each other, sometimes in front of your very eyes! The theater had become very strange indeed, Muriel decided.

The "stagehands" were visible to the audience—a Chinese custom, Muriel had heard. She devoutly hoped this was not a commie play! They wore black body suits

48

and were constantly moving platforms and properties during the action. As the heroine was about to sit down, a chair would slide under her buttocks with split-second timing. When a storm was called for, the stagehands rolled out their thunder-sheet and wind machine and operated both in full view of the audience. Muriel found this amusing, but what ever happened to illusion?

Gradually she became accustomed to the rather odd style and the story drew her in. At the end of the act, Muriel was as confused and delighted as a child at her first circus, and equally exhausted. She collected her tape and sleepwalked out into the world, surprised to find it much the same.

She let herself in the back door and left her groceries in the kitchen, where she could hear Sherwood calling, then bellowing.

"Muriel! . . . *Muriel!*"

Flushed and breathless, she went to him. "Yes, Sherwood, dear?"

"*Well?* Did you see the rehearsal? Was it a disaster? Was it mortifying? Shall I leave town? Tell me, woman!"

Muriel set the tape recorder on his table, taking the tape from her purse.

"There. Hear for yourself."

"What's all this?"

"The first act of your play. *Continuum.*"

"You taped it?"

"Of course."

"By God, that was intelligent!" He picked up the tape and treasured it. "No! It was brilliant! I am grateful,

49

most grateful to you—" He slipped the tape into the player.

"It was nothing, nothing at all," said Muriel airily. "While you're attending the play, I'll fix you a nice dinner." She waltzed into the kitchen while Sherwood started to listen, motionless. Something over an hour later, Muriel returned with his tray.

"It's been so warm today, I've made us a lovely little ham mousse. I thought perhaps—" She broke off at the sight of Sherwood, sitting bolt upright in bed and staring straight ahead of him. "Sherwood, are you all right?"

"All right! I'm so relieved! A weight has been lifted from my shoulders. By you, my dear."

"Oh, how nice—" She set down the tray.

"Suddenly, I have hopes for this play. I find it amusing, even touching. And the cast—they seem to have come alive. What did you say to them, you witch?"

"Why Sherwood, nothing at all!"

"All right, Puss-in-Boots, but I'm not a blithering idiot, you know. Now tell me, what did you think of it?"

"I thought it was very nice. I didn't understand it, of course—" For a moment he was angry again.

"There's nothing *to* understand! It's life!"

"All right, Sherwood."

"I want to hear act two. You'll tape it for me?"

"Of course."

"Go get your tray, so we can eat this delectable dish."

With dinner, Muriel served a delicate May wine. Although Sherwood winced at the strawberry on the rim of his glass, his mood was as jubilant as hers. They ate slowly, watching the twilight creeping into the room. Muriel removed their trays and poured more wine. Sherwood watched her moving about the room. She was a small-boned woman—not one of your Amazons, thank God—with a womanly shape and a womanly walk, and, of course, that still fabulous red-gold hair. Watching her, he felt a surge of desire and cursed his invalid state. He remembered very well how it felt to make love to her.

"Muriel, come and sit beside me."

She came, and he reached for her hand. "I always knew Tom was a lucky man. I envied him."

"You did not. You were perfectly satisfied. You had your occasional fling with a charming little drama student, and you had your two good friends: Tom and Fritz."

"You know, there's some truth in that." She did surprise him sometimes. "Fritz was a handsome devil."

"I can see you now, the three of you, walking across the campus together on a windy day in winter, all of you with scarfs blowing out behind you. You looked as if you were ice-skating, side by side, all in step together, all those long legs and laughing faces."

"I had two friends in the world and lost them both."

"Fritz isn't lost. He's in New York."

"Same thing."

"I hear he's very successful."

"I often wondered—why did Fritz leave town?"

"Oh, heaven knows—" She started to pull away, but he held her hand firmly.

51

"You know, but you're not telling."

"Now Sherwood, that was a thousand years ago!"

"Then it's time to open the tomb. Come on, now—"

"No!"

"Tell me, or I'll—" he reached for a lock of her hair. "Tell!" She let her head fall forward toward him.

"I'll tell! I'll tell!"

She rested her head on the bed and his fingers stroked her hair.

"Fritz and I were locked in the church one night. After choir practice. It was a cold winter night."

"Locked in?"

"By mistake. We were both down in the cloakroom and the sexton thought everybody'd left."

"Go on."

"We stayed there all night. We couldn't get out."

"You couldn't break a window?"

"Those beautiful stained glass windows?"

"Heaven forfend. Go on."

"Tom was in San Francisco but he came home the next morning. The sexton had unlocked the church, so I was home first.

"How fortunate."

"But our furnace had gone out. Remember those old coal burners? You had to stoke up and remove the clinkers."

"Poor Puss, caught by a clinker."

"So I had to tell him I'd been gone all night."

"With handsome Fritz?"

"Tom was very angry."

"Understandably."

"He asked me whether—well, whether we made love."

"In a very cold church, with cushions in all the pews."

"Yes, very cold. Yes, many cushions."

"And you said?"

"I said, if he had to ask me, I would not answer him."

"Oh, come on—"

"Trust is everything."

"And you never did answer him?"

"Never."

"I'll be damed." Pensively, he reached and loosened her hair, so that it spilled across the bed sheet. The fading light caught glints here and there of the red-gold color, as it must have done in the church. "Then what?"

"Then Tom went to Fritz and asked him."

"And Fritz said?"

" 'Don't you trust me, Tom?' "

"Poor Tom."

"So Tom said to Fritz 'I can't live on this campus with you. Either you go, or I go.' "

"So Fritz went."

"Yes."

"Look, it was all a long time ago. Did you, or didn't you?"

Muriel raised her head and looked him straight in the eye.

"If you have to ask, I won't tell you!"

"Why you—" He pulled her by the hair until she

was forced to fall on the bed and bend over him. He was drenched in the warm fragrance of her body. He told himself to slow down. The first time you make love to a woman can always be passed off as an accident, a wild and regrettable impulse. But the second time is far more significant. It is, in fact, some kind of commitment.

But he kept pulling her down, very slowly, until she kissed him. He was sure there was a way to make love while wearing a plaster cast. He was right, too.

CHAPTER

5

SHEILA AND THEO were laughing together on the sofa, catching their breath, and looking each other in the eye.

"You mean it?" asked Theo. "You had lunch with him, and walked in the Park with him, and now you're *in love?*"

"Yes . . . *yes* . . ." Sheila looked defiant and happy.

"It's all my fault," said Theo, "I should have known."

"It's not a disaster, you know."

"You've been sitting up there in cold storage for a year. I tell people to look you up and you don't even answer the phone! I bet you haven't seen a man alone since your divorce."

"You count the mailman?"

"So naturally the first man that offers you a plate of pasta, you fall on his neck!"

"Theo, I can't remember his last name!"

"Keating. Val Keating. Now you can forget it again."

"Val Keating. Is he married?"

"No."

"Gay?"

"I doubt it."

Sheila visibly braced herself. "How old?"

"Thirty."

"Oh, God."

"Yep."

"Are you sure?"

"All in the files."

"That's revolting."

"He'll get older. The trouble is, so will you."

"Thanks, pal."

"Sorry, darling." Theo went to pour their drinks at a little table between the windows. She clinked the ice from the bucket to glasses with quick, deft fingers. She came back to Sheila with her gliding walk and held out a frosty glass. Sheila braced herself again.

"All right, what else do you know about him?"

"Every girl in the office has made a pass at him. The man is unavailable, that's why you fell for him."

"Not true!"

"Oh, yes! Remember Greaseball in fifth grade? Two hundred pounds of lard and you loved him!"

"Greaseball had beautiful eyes!"

"How about Dismal in seventh grade? Always writing suicide notes?"

"Sometimes on my arm." Sheila glanced down as if the ink might still be there.

"Look at Spencer! Sixteen years of your life down the tube. I'm going to save you from yourself this time,

Sheely. I forbid you to see Val Keating ever again! The man is too young and too poor and not for you!" She wagged her finger and pursed her lips.

"You look like my mother!"

"How is your mother, God help us all?"

"She wants to come live with me."

"Never. Find her a wee cottage, not too near."

"Theo, I'm broke! My teeth belong to my dentist, my house belongs to the bank, and Kerry wants to go to Italy! Why don't my books make *money?*"

"You spend it before you get it. You need to be subsidized."

"You mean get the government to pay me not to write books."

"No, marry a man with money. Wait. I didn't say *for* money."

"And what does he marry me for?"

"Sheila! That is a shocking question! What's happened to you anyway? How can you sit there all peaches and cream, with that hair, that skin of an infant, that bod that drives men mad and say what for? By the way, we're not gaining weight, are we?"

"Oh, shut up!"

"And if it's brains they want—my roommate winner of the English prize, history prize, drama prize, not to mention captain of the hockey team—" Theo started chanting and Sheila joined in.

"Rock Chalk, Jay Hawk, K. U.!
Rock Chalk, Jay Hawk, K. U.!
'Cause I'm a Jay, Jay, Jay, Jay,
Jayhawk,

Up at Lawrence on the Kaw!
'Cause I'm a Jay, Jay, Jay, Jay,
  Jayhawk,
With a sis boom, hip hoorah!"

They gave it the big finish and the secret grip, then broke into giggles. Theo was the first to sober up.

"Sheely, I have a man for you. He's attractive, rich as cream, and an old friend of the family."

"Who?"

"Fritz Begley."

"You mean *Uncle Fritz?*"

"He's not your real uncle!"

"My father's best friend? He's got to be sixty!"

"He could pass for forty."

"Not with me, he couldn't."

"Curly brown hair, flat stomach, and loaded with charm."

"I used to get a silver dollar from Uncle Fritz on my birthday!"

"Why stop now?"

"Theo, are you suggesting that I *sell* myself?"

"If the price is right."

"You're disgusting!" Sheila looked sidelong at her friend, with a glint in her eye. "By the way, what is the price?"

"Billions, give or take—"

"I'll take, I'll take!"

"When Fritz left KU and came to New York, he started buying out small corporations. He's been pyramiding ever since. He's only been divorced for a couple of months. He won't keep very long."

58

"You can have him."

"No, I'm younger than you."

"Thirteen days!" This was one of their favorite jokes. "Anyway, I'm not available, at the moment."

Theo told about her new man, well heeled, a scratch golfer, and—would you believe?—a Shakespeare buff. "Come on, Sheely, tell me everything about Shakespeare." They decided this might take time, so they'd go out to dinner.

"Pick a place with disgusting food," said Sheila, "I'm on a diet."

"Since when?"

"Lunchtime."

They went to an expense account place and dined in the "garden," a tiny fenced-in yard banked with spring flowers and twinkling lights. They drifted back into their shared past, lingering over every foolish incident of a time that was—or seemed—light-hearted and innocent. When they returned to Theo's flat, she said, "I'm offering croissants for breakfast." Sheila said, "I'm staying."

Sheila borrowed a diaphanous grown from Theo. "My God, you live well," and they stretched out on cool and satiny sheets. "You too, when you marry Fritz."

"Uncle Fritz. He's too *old!*"

"Bet he's forty. Your father could have a younger friend."

"Where did you see him—in total darkness?"

"Colorado, high noon on a ski slope."

"Have your eyes checked."

"Call your mother and ask her."

"All right, I will!"

Sheila dialed her mother in Kansas. A man's voice answered.

"Hello?" Sheila glanced at the clock. "I was calling 913-261-4562."

"That's correct."

"I'm looking for Mrs. Muriel Devlin."

"Certainly. Who's calling, please?"

"This is her daughter, Sheila."

"My dear, this is your Uncle Sherwood speaking."

"Uncle Woody! Well . . . how are you?"

"Splendid, thank you. I'll put your mother on."

Pause. Then Muriel's voice, breathless and merry.

"Why, Sheila how sweet of you to call! You caught me in the kitchen, washing up."

"Really? It's twelve midnight. Did you have a party?"

"Oh, mercy no! I suppose you're surprised to find your Uncle Sherwood here at this hour, is that it, dear?"

"Just a bit."

"Well, Uncle Woody had a little accident. He fell down stairs!"

"What stairs?"

"My stairs, dear. Sherwood very kindly offered to change my light bulb on the landing—those ceiling fixtures are so difficult, aren't they?—so I gave him that wobbly little step-stool and down came poor Sherwood and fractured his tibia!"

Woody shot Muriel a look of surprised admiration.

"So I just brought him home from the hospital today and I have him all comfy in the dining room. I told him I wasn't going to let dear Tom's oldest friend lie there in the hospital wasting away. He's a good patient, except when he starts fretting about his spring play and gets cross as an old bear, when everybody knows the play will be a masterpiece—"

"What play, mother?"

"It's called *Continuum* and it's sort of a classic, like Shakespeare. I don't understand one word of it, but it's very poetic and goes on for three centuries."

"That's a long play."

"And how is your new book and what are you doing up at this hour, you naughty girl?"

"I just called to say good-night, Mother."

"Well, good-night and sleep tight, dear."

"You too, Mother." Sheila hung up, puzzled.

"Uncle Woody broke his leg."

"Hm?" said Theo.

"He's staying there at Mother's house." No answer. "In a cast to the hip, I suppose." Silence. "Couldn't be any hanky-panky in a plaster case, right? . . . Theo, is that right?"

Theo was asleep, her deep breathing antiphonal to the ticking of the bedside clock.

"Pity," said Sheila out loud to herself. "Maybe he'll marry her, you think? . . . No . . . but wouldn't it be wonderful?"

She'd forgotten to ask her mother how old Uncle Fritz was. As if it made any difference. Uncle Fritz was at this very moment plunging down a ski slope with his curly brown hair, a world-famous beauty on each arm. He did not know or care that pudgy little Sheila Devlin had become a writer (of sorts), married and divorced, and was now standing irresolute at the crossroads of her life. Because, let us face it, nothing had changed since this morning when her situation was fairly desperate. She had come dashing into town to talk to Theo, conceived a feverish attachment for a man with a beaky nose, dined on three thousand calories, and now was lying in a borrowed nightgown, alone, alone, alone. What a wonderful word it was, like the the tolling of a bell. Alone.

Everyone was alone. Nothing worthy of comment there. But married life gave you an illusion of being part of somebody else, of being kept company. Her ex-husband, Spencer, when he was sober, was a convivial man. He laughed loudly. He did everything to the hilt, and then stopped. He would play tennis for seven hours straight and not again for six months. He took "total immersion" Italian lessons and never uttered another *parola*. He never in all his life had one drink.

When Spencer was drinking, she'd been his nurse, his mother, and his unfailing friend. She stood staunchly between him and the world, calling in sick for him, keeping his office and clients at bay, checking him in and out of the clinic that became his home. Half the time, she supported him. My, what a brave little woman she'd been, stout-hearted, and—ah, yes—plucky.

The truth was, of course, she'd been his "enabler." She enabled him to be an alcoholic all those years. Without her, he would have been exposed to himself and the world, forced to admit his disease. She had not been his friend, but his worst enemy. Their divorce a year ago was a victory for them both. How odd that it still tasted like defeat.

She listened to the city noises that drifted in the window: a siren screaming its terror in the distance; a doorman whistling urgently, ardently for a taxi, garbage cans suffering, but not in silence, from the chronic rage of sanitation men.

And now, at last, she allowed herself to think of the latest folly in her unmanageable life. She thought about Val Keating. She saw in her mind's eye his brooding look—"the secret places of the heart where human beings hide from one another"—his open, charming look—"tigers would kill for eyes like yours"—and his dashing look, over one shoulder, as he sauntered away from her . . . forever?

Forever. She would take Theo's advice, smart Theo who knew her better than anybody in this world. She would forget Val Keating who was too young and too poor, put him out of her mind. For once in her life, she would be rational, cool-headed, clear-thinking. Suddenly she sat bolt upright.

"No!"

She turned her face into her pillow to smother her laughter, and Theo didn't stir. Sheila lay there remembering Val, listening to the exact timbre of his voice. She heard him do *King Henry V*. She heard him do the out-of-work actor. But most of all, she heard him do Val Keating, in love with Sheila Devlin.

CHAPTER

6

THE NEXT DAY, after an epicurean lunch, Sherwood had just finished shaving when Muriel came tripping into the room.

"Well, well, well, what have we *here?*" Let me just *look* at you! I'd hardly know you!"

Sherwood shaved every day and Muriel carried on like this every day. She stood at the foot of the hospital bed and stared down at him. She seemed to find him transformed by this daily event. Since he was accepting her hospitality, not to mention other favors, he refrained from asking her for the love of God to spare him this daily performance. Instead, he picked up his electric shaver and brandished it in her direction.

"You call this a razor? This obscene little instrument? No wonder civilization lies everywhere in ruins. We have forgotten the shave as ceremony, a sacrament shared by a man and his face."

Sherwood gazed into the middle distance with narrowed eyes.

"A man takes his fine bristle brush, made from the hairs of cooperative British badgers. He swirls it in a wooden bowl of shaving soap, spicy, aromatic. He applies the winking bubbles to the face in slow, overlapping circles, not unlike the Palmer method of handwriting. When the face is lost in lather, it is allowed to mellow while the razor, like a small sword, pearl-handled and glistening, is honed on a leather strop, sleek and flexible, the color of Honduras mahogany. Six strokes up, six down, and the razor would bisect a falling leaf in midair. The shining blade glides silently down one cheek, then down the other, then caresses the curve of the chin.

"A few short strokes, like grace notes in music, and the dance is done. Splash the face with ice-cold water, bury it in a fluffy towel, and a man looks in his mirror . . . absolved. He and his face have shared the world's purest, most functional art form. That . . . was a shave."

"Why are you using an electric razor?" asked Muriel.

"May God endow me with patience. Because when I came to this house on First Thursday for dinner, my beloved, I did not have the foresight to bring my straight razor, my shaving bowl, and my imported badger brush."

"I see."

"My late unlamented nurse purchased this buzz-saw in the hospital gift shop. I shall return it some day, demanding a refund: half price and I'll throw in the nurse!"

"Sherwood, why don't you give me the key to your house? I'll go and get your razor, your shaving bowl, and your imported badger brush!"

"No, indeed, I wouldn't dream of it!"

"It's no trouble, Sherwood. I'm going to rehearsal, you know, to tape the second act. I'll drop by your house and—"

"Thank you, *no!*"

"Why, Sherwood! Don't you want me to go into your house? Do you think I'm some kind of a *snoop?*"

Since this was exactly what Sherwood did think, he coughed, stalling for time. Nothing came to him— Muriel knew he didn't have a burglar alarm—so he kept on coughing. Muriel made dire predictions about spring colds and sprayed the room with an antiseptic that smelled of moldy gardenias. When she had finished she came back to the subject like a dog who has buried a bone. Muriel would have made a wonderful dog.

"Do let me go, Sherwood! I have your keys right here! I filched them when I sent your jacket to the cleaners!"

She snatched the keys from the left-hand sideboard drawer and shook them in the air until they twinkled as merrily as her eyes. "Say yes, Sherwood! I'm going to find your crazy mother in the attic and the gold bullion in the basement, but think what a lovely shave you'll have!" Sherwood was not an inbecile. He recognized defeat when it laughed in his face.

"Be my guest," he said wearily and turned his face to the window. Muriel kissed him back of his ear. "Bye, bye, old Bear."

She was out the door. If he called a locksmith right now and told him to change the locks before Muriel could get there—forget it. There wasn't a locksmith in this world faster than our Muriel.

Sherwood could see his desk, exactly as he had left it on First Thursday. By custom an orderly man, he had been pressed for time. He had not put anything away. No, not anything. His life was laid out on that desk. His private, secret, intimate world was now at Muriel's mercy. He had a strong suspicion the woman *had no* mercy. He began to run a film in his mind. It showed Muriel entering his front door, glancing left toward his study, stepping left, drawing back, stepping left again. But he knew how the film ended. She marched into his study and cast her all-seeing eye upon his desk.

He fell asleep and dreamed he was on the operating table. The surgeon wore a green mask, but she had red-gold hair. She slit his body from gullet to groin. Then she started taking out his innards, placing them daintily on either side of his helpless body. She was exclaiming, as she picked out one bloody organ after another, "Well, well, well, what have we *here?* Let me *look* at you! I'd hardly *know* you!" and she kept on delving into the bottomless pit that was Sherwood Pell.

In the meantime, Muriel found she was holding Sherwood's car keys and, on a whim, let herself into his jaunty little sports car that stood at the curb and buzzed off down Massachusetts Avenue. She hummed to herself, a little surprised at her own wickedness. This was almost like putting on Sherwood's clothes. And she would see his house, too. If, by any chance, she and Sherwood should decide some day to—well, join their lives, they could choose between her house and his house. This little visit would help Muriel to decide.

As she entered his driveway, she remembered coming here years ago for an eggnog party given by her

67

dear Tom and Fritz and Sherwood. The hosts were dressed as the Three Musketeers and how handsome they were! But that was long ago. She put the key into the front door lock with a real sense of occasion. She was entering, perhaps, her future home.

One of the glass panes in the upper half of the door was cracked. She knew a good glazier. The door squeaked noisily as it swung open. She would bring a drop of oil next time. She stood still and surveyed the entrance hall, so important to a house, like the first page of a book. This one was spacious, perhaps six inches wider than her own, and paneled in oak, my dear, with an impressive staircase to the right. The carpeting was worn, but how simple to drop it down eight inches, so the worn spots would hit the risers. The brass chandelier over her head was nice, but so dusty! What could you expect from a bachelor? To her left was a study, with Sherwood's desk in the window. On the desk was an accordion file, open and stuffed with papers. Muriel stood as still as a bird dog on point.

She took a step to her left, then stepped back. Another step left, and she stopped. Even as a child, Muriel had never in all her life tasted her dessert before finishing her meal. She turned and mounted the stairs.

She found the bathroom, large and ceramic tiled, with a tub on claw feet and a basin on a pedestal. Antique was in. Sherwood's bathroom would make her the envy of the town. She found his shaving articles with ease—how orderly he was—and dropped them all into a laundry bag marked Hotel Savoy.

Muriel threw a quick glance into the bedrooms,

three of them. How nice. Sheila could come and stay and even bring Kerry, now that everyone was talking about *roots*. My word, they would all be a *family*, and Sherwood the father! She walked down the stairs in a haze of domestic images: Sherwood in smoking jacket, greeting his guests; Sherwood at the dining table, carving and making witty remarks; Sherwood in his study doing their accounts, but glancing up, over his shoulder: "Are you there, my dear?" He would always want to know where she was, and if she went out, when she would be home. "I'm here, Sherwood, I'm right here." She floated into his study, the lady of the house.

She stood at his desk and looked down at the open file. She touched nothing, not even leaning on the desk. She saw a small clipping, perhaps from a magazine, taped to the outside of the file. She put down the laundry bag and reached into her purse, extracting a pair of glasses. She bent her torso to one side, dropped her head on one shoulder, and read the clipping:

WITTY, WORLDLY UNIVERSITY PROFESSOR, ANTICIPAT-ING RETIREMENT, SEEKS COMELY COMPANION TO SHARE THEATER, FINE FOOD, MOZART. INDEPENDENT INCOME ESSENTIAL.

Box 453

She straightened and stared blindly out the window. Not believing her eyes, she read the clipping again. Her mind could hardly take it in. Sherwood had done this? Sherwood was seeking a "comely companion"? Of course, this was before his accident, before they had become sweethearts. But she had always known they would some day be "intimate." He had been the secret lover of her dreams for all these years. She had thought she was his. But all that time, he was "seeking." He was dreaming, not of her, but of some stranger he hoped to find. He had betrayed her, an infidelity of the heart and mind. He had been unfaithful. For how long? With how many?

Tears sprang to her eyes as she poked her index finger into the file and pressed the sections apart. There were note papers of every size and color, each one clipped to a typed page in carbon, Sherwood's reply to the stranger no doubt. How methodical he was, even in treachery. Her curiosity by now was almost out of control. She paused only long enough to study the position of the file on the desk and the angle it made with the blotter. Then she pulled up the desk chair, wiped her hands on her handkerchief, and picked up the file, laying it open before her.

She lifted the papers in the first pocket, the one he had hand-lettered "AMANDA." The first letter was dated almost a year ago. Not rushing into anything, were you, Don Juan of Kansas? Was the "independent income" perhaps insufficient? Oh, wicked, villainous man. She read:

Dear Professor,
In some ways I'm the girl of your dreams. I'm not only comely, but sensational. "Theater" checks out, because I'm a retired actress, a star in fact. "Fine food" I adore and can even dish up. Mozart I wouldn't know from a hole in the mud due to a tin ear, but you don't get

70

everything in one package, right? Not to worry about the independent income. I stand to inherit a bundle. Now for the bad news.

My husband has had two strokes and the next one will be his last, Drs. say. Meantime, I don't go out for dinner with another man. This one has been a good friend for eleven years, and I'm going to see him off in style.

So these are the ground rules. Are you interested, Professor? We could be pen-pals and write heavy-breathing letters for as long as it takes. And it might be kind of soon, who knows?"

Box 837

The next page, Muriel found, was a carbon of Sherwood's answer, neatly typed.

My dear Box 837,

Your letter was a delight. A thousand questions leap to mind, but first let me answer yours. Yes, by all means, yes, let us correspond until you are free, whenever that may be.

What is your name, mystery lady? I'm sure I have known and admired your work. You see, I'm retired from the theater too—the Broadway theater that is—and sometimes feel a senseless longing for that frenetic, not to say schizophrenic world. I left it after directing/producing a dozen plays—who counts the ones that close out of town? Here in academe I put on a play with less agony, but of course less ecstasy.

Do you ever think of returning to the stage, fair 837? What a lark if we could make our joint comeback together! Can you picture our two box numbers up there in lights?

Now really you must tell me your name, dear lady, I long to see our correspondence move into the "heavy breathing" stage, but how can I write an impassioned prose to a lady called Box 837? What if Cyrano had cried out to Roxanne "Your name is like a golden bell hung in my heart; and when I think of you, I tremble and the bell swings, and rings—Eight-Thirty-Seven! Eight-Thirty-Seven!"

Write soon, answering all questions of your already besotted

Professor

Muriel snorted. An actress! And Sherwood "besotted!" She flipped the page to find the hussy's reply, then glanced at her watch. She had ten minutes to get to rehearsal. She ached to read on, but tucked the sheaf of letters back into their pocket. After all, she could come back another day. She replaced the file exactly in its original position on the desk. Tight-lipped, she picked up "that man's" shaving things and let herself out of "that man's" house. For Sherwood, in these few minutes, had forfeited his place in Muriel's heart. She considered him no better than an adulterer.

She turned the key in his front door with a vicious wrench. He was a libertine, a rake, a vile seducer, terms she had often read in her romance novels but never expected to find applied in her own life. She flung the door of the car open as if exposing his perfidy to the world. She flounced into the seat and vengefully turned on the ignition, her foot pressed down the accelerator as if it were "that man's" neck. She would never, never forgive him. Not only that, but she would punish him as he deserved. But how?

Threading her way through traffic, Muriel began to

compose herself. Sherwood was indeed a villain, but how fortunate that he did not *know* she had found out. She had been spared that ultimate humiliation.

Entering the auditorium, she showered compliments on Virgil and Bill. Sherwood had sent them his heartfelt thanks for their fine work and would appreciate so much a tape of act two.

As the play unrolled before her and she watched the characters torn apart by their passions, Muriel pitied them. She would not allow her own life to be shipwrecked on the jagged rocks of anger, jealousy, and a tart called Amanda. She applauded the final curtain and graciously thanked the students. She guided Sherwood's little car smoothly back to the house. He was doing a crossword puzzle, not looking up when she entered. She spread his shaving things on the table before him, and topped them off with the second act tape.

"Oh Sherwood, Sherwood, what a lovely home you have! And everything so tidy, so cared for! But I must make my confession. I saw a file on your desk and it was open. I tucked it away in the bookcase. I hope you're not angry with me. I mean, you never know when some policeman might decide to check your house and get very nosy. Tell me you're not angry with me, Big Bear!"

She was looking at him so anxiously, it was really rather pathetic. Her face was the picture of innocence, round eyed and tremulous. The woman was really quite simple. Straightforward.

"Thank you, my dear. Most kind of you, most thoughtful." He patted her hand and breathed an enormous sigh.

73

THE NEXT MORNING, when Sheila awakened in Theo's apartment, she went to stand in the window and look down. Humanity was there, blowing horns and racing engines in a frenzied effort to get to work. There was the real world, the ontological imperative: make a living so you can have food, shelter, and a prepaid funeral. In the cold morning light, her nighttime fantasies seemed ridiculous. Val Keating, very poor and very young, was not for her.

She chewed her croissants, thanked Theo, and caught the 8:07 to Westport. At Port Chester, she took back Val Keating. By the time the train reached Greenwich, she gave him up forever. At Stamford, she could not live without him. At Darien, she renounced him. At Norwalk, she would have Keating or die. As her train pulled into Westport, she realized she was making Hamlet look like a man of firm decision. For the last time, she gave up Val Keating, right now, forever.

She found her car, her house, her coffee percolator and uncovered the machine that usually transferred her ideas from brain to paper. Don't think about Val.

She prided herself on mental discipline. She earned her keep, such as it was, by putting her mind over the jumps. The mind balked. She tried the darkened room, the quiet spirit, free association, but every association led down the forbidden path. Don't think about Val.

She threw open every window in the house. Seductive breezes wafted in. Birds were singing outside in that insistent way. Auditioning. A rabbit loped across the yard, changing direction three times. Not one of your goal-oriented rabbits. The sun poured through tear-stained windows. Don't think about Val.

She decided in cold blood not to work today. She called daughter Kerry and they had a short, unhappy conversation. Sheila could not afford to send Kerry to Italy this summer. Kerry wailed. Sheila would write and explain. They hung up frostily.

Sheila dragged a chair out into the spring sunshine and lay flat out. Waking, she wondered what people did with their time if they didn't write. Was not-thinking-about-Val a truly significant way to spend the rest of her life?

A bird more insistent than the others was sitting on her clothesline, singing, full voice, proclaiming that this entire backyard belonged to him. In the meantime, his wife was flying to the ledge over Sheila's back door, twig in mouth. There was a half-built nest there already, precariously lopping over. The wife fussed, trying to get the twig where it would count. Pavarotti joined her and they fluttered and poked inefficiently. When Sheila felt the need of more coffee and opened the back door, the birds took off in a terrified chattering protest. This was ridiculous.

Sheila watched from the kitchen window and, sure enough, the couple returned to the same nest with more twigs. If they thought they could make Sheila a prisoner in her own house, they could think again. She slammed out the door and the birds took off screeching.

She had never pretended to be a bird fancier. These birds had appropriated her back door, the only one she ever used. Was she supposed to spend the rest of her life apologizing for her goings-out and her comings-in? She stomped down the steps to her deck chair. There came Luciano on the clothesline again, vocalizing.

We are supposed to share this planet with other creatures great and small. Her monthly mortgage payments, drawn from her carotid artery, did not give her supreme right of ownership. Why not? Because birds weren't into money. She drank her coffee. Oh, the hell with it.

She fetched a step-stool from the kitchen and reached up for the nest, ignoring the heartbroken protests from the clothesline. She carried the nest to the garbage can at the foot of the steps, brandished the lid above her head, dropped the nest, and clanged down the cover.

"Get the message? Piss off!"

For good measure, she put a jam pot up there on the ledge. The clothesline was silent, outraged. Guiltily she retreated indoors. She took an indoor walk, picking her way across a floor piled with books and papers. The year of her residence in this house was recorded in layers of geological time. With archeological skill, she dug to the bottom of a pile and extracted a snapshot of Kerry at high school graduation. At that moment, the child called.

She pleaded again for the summer in Italy, her voice rising in pitch and volume, cutting off Sheila's attempts to explain. Finally Sheila swore she had a train to catch. "Letter follows. Bye."

Glancing out the window, Sheila saw the birds were nest-building again, this time on the balustrade around the porch, between two uprights. At a quick count Sheila could see there were twenty-three more spaces, equally desirable, for housing starts. She burst outside, screaming obscenities, and the two small birds disappeared into the hemlocks.

As the beautiful spring day wore on, Sheila alternated periods of hiding in the bedroom with manic forays to the backyard. Countless nests were consigned to the garbage and countless new ones appeared. She asked herself if she could really be doing this. Was it possible that an able-bodied woman was carrying on a war with two learning-disabled birds? Yes. Should she consult a psychiatrist?

She stood on her back porch watching long, wavy shadows creep across the yard. The enemy had retired for the night, leaving an oppressive silence. Then she realized why she felt this terrible loneliness. She missed the birds.

The phone rang.

"Hello?"

"This is Val Keating."

"Oh, hello . . . How are you?"

"I'm okay. How are you?"

"I'm fine, thank you."

"Do you want to hang up now?"

"No. Do you?"

"I thought maybe you're working."

"No, oh no, it's dark here."

"Don't you have electric lights?"

"Oh yes, I mean—it was a nice day today, wasn't it?"

"Yeah, great."

"Have you had dinner yet?"

"No, have you?"

"No."

"I was thinking I might buzz up there. Take you out. Buy you a bun."

"That would be wonderful."

"I could be there in an hour—"

"Wait. I'll get my timetable."

"I'll hitch a ride."

"Oh."

"I'll call you when I get there. You think you could come and pick me up?"

"Yes. Yes, of course."

"I better hang up now, so I can get started."

"Yes, I suppose so."

"Trouble is, I like to hear you talk."

"We can talk when you get here."

"All right. I'm going to hang up now."

"Yes. All right."

"See you."

He hung up. Sheila let out a shriek and danced

away from the phone. She went out on the porch and threw her arms out and her head back and drank in the sky. She took a bath and dressed and made coffee and stared in the mirror to see how she looked when happy. Then the worries. Hitchhiking was illegal. He'd be arrested and thrown in jail. She saw him hopping a tractor trailer, which jackknifed on I-95. His mangled body had no identification. Potter's Field. When the phone rang, she dived at it.

"Hey, this whole town's asleep."

"I'm not. Where are you exactly?"

"I'm at the railroad station, or do you say 'depot'?"

"Which side?"

"Any side. I'm the only living thing around."

"I'm coming, I'm coming."

She found him leaning against a lamppost. He was in his shirt-sleeves, his jacket hooked over one shoulder, the light falling on his jumbled hair and craggy forehead. She knew she would never forget the sight of him. She pulled up alongside and leaned over to open the passenger door.

"Hey—"

"Hey, lady, going my way?"

He piled in, folding up his legs like a carpenter's rule and resting one large hand on each bony knee.

"Take me to your finest fish house." He didn't kiss her, not even on the cheek.

"Everything's closed, except my house." She tried to make it sound more like a fact than an invitation. "Is that okay?"

"Sure thing." He fell silent, and she glanced at

him. He was still motionless, hands stretched on knobby knees. She tried to think what the pose reminded her of. The Lincoln Memorial. The huge bronze figure looking out over the city of Washington. Even Val's expression was the same: brooding and compassionate.

"Sheila—"

"Yes, Val."

"I have a lot of things to say to you. How far is it to your house?"

"Five minutes more."

"I'll wait till we get there. I can't talk when you're driving, you know?"

"I know." She turned on the radio and glutinous music came out. But it was easier to have something to talk against. "Did you work today?"

"Yeah. You?"

"I spent the day having a war with nesting birds on my back porch."

"Purple finches. And you lost."

"Right."

"Good singers, though. Do you still get warblers up here?"

"I wouldn't know."

"I'll teach you. You have any glasses?"

"I might as well come clean. I don't like goddam birds."

"Take it easy. Are we there yet?"

"This is it."

He went out and around the car and had her door open by the time she cut the lights and fumbled for her purse. She led the way to the back door, unlocked it, and held the screen for him. His head just cleared the lintel.

"Hey, it's a real country house. Don't like condos, do you? Nice kitchen. This is where Sheila Devlin lives." He smiled at her and moved into the living room. "Fireplace and everything." He seemed to avoid the books on the floor without even looking. He kept on into the bedroom. "You sleep here, don't you? You see that tree first thing when you open your eyes. I guess the most important thing about a house is seeing out of it." He went into the other bedrooms. She could hear the doors banging together as he trapped himself in the upright coffin. "Hm, interesting, different." He returned to the kitchen, standing a room's length away from her. The moment hung in the air between them like a bubble, and then burst.

"Look, I came to tell you . . . See, I don't want anything between us too complicated to talk about. Do you?"

"No."

"I got to tell you we can never, repeat never, be in love. Make love. I hope to Christ I'm not taking something for granted. Did you feel it, too? Yesterday? Did you want us to make love?"

"Yes."

"Yeah, thank God for that. Well, anyway, we can't. Ever. We can see each other, like eating apricots in the Park. But that's it. You follow me?"

"No."

He turned and stared out the black kitchen window.

"I know people jump in the sack now for nothing. Like saying, 'Hi, how are you?' and jump out again. But that's no good for us. For us, making love would be all the way. Like a transfusion. Your blood for mine, mine for yours. There'd be no part of you that wasn't partly me."

He turned and faced her, hollow-eyed under the light.

"And then, see, when it didn't work out any more— and it wouldn't, believe me—"

"*Who says?*"

"When we have to split, it'll *tear us apart*. We'd be mortally wounded. Mortally, Sheila."

"You don't *know* that!"

"Yes, baby, I do. I've been beating my head on this since yesterday, five-thirty, when I kissed you on the cheek. I knew it then. I know it now." He looked at her across the miles between them. He raised his hands, then dropped them at his sides.

"We just . . . can't make it."

"Val . . . for God's sake . . . kiss me."

He covered the distance in two steps and gathered her in his arms. She turned her face up to his and he tasted her mouth, slowly and tenderly at first, and then wildly, hungrily. Sheila could feel the passion kindling and spreading through her whole body. She clung to him, breathing in his warm, soapy smell.

"Don't leave me . . . just don't leave me."

"Not now. Not a chance."

He pulled her into the shadowy bedroom and stripped off her clothes, hurling them in all directions.

"You're so beautiful . . . You're my girl, my beautiful girl . . . You belong to me, you know it?"

"Yes—"

He pushed her down on the bed and ripped off his clothes, covering her body with his own. He lowered his head until his lips grazed her mouth and whispered a question.

"Tell me, Sheila, *tell* me—"

"I love you, Val."

Her words let loose a torrent. He kissed her hair, her face, her lips while he caressed every inch of her with his searching hands. She felt herself reaching a new level of being, her life force so quickening within her that it seemed her body could no longer contain the storm of her passion. When their bodies joined, they caught their breath at the fulfillment, the longed-for completion. As they moved together, the limits of their two separate selves began melting away. Their single-ness was suspended and two lifelong solitudes mingled into one.

They reached the pinnacle and spiraled down-wards, clinging together lest they be thrown apart, whispering each other's names. They lay side by side, bodies glistening in the warm spring night.

"Oh my love, my love—"

The surprise and wonder of what had happened couldn't be put into words. They twined their hands together and, with their free hands, made shadow figures on the ceiling: two beaked animals that came gently together and kissed. He combed his fingers through her hair. "The color of your hair—it's burnished. That's what it is, burnished . . . Your body's totally female, wonderful dents and hollows, wonderful hills and bubbles. How come you have a bod like this and a big brain too? They must have left out something. You probably have a lousy disposition. Crabby. You kick puppydogs on the street?"

She listened to the teasing, musical voice and felt bewitched. She doted on him. She stroked the straight line of his shoulders, followed the wedge of his torso down to the impossibly narrow pelvis. "You're too thin. You're cadaverous. I could play your ribs like a xylophone. Don't you ever eat anything?" But secretly she admired him for being the very antithesis of her own self. Yin and Yang. When he left the bed to shower, she watched him, as bony as a tree in winter.

They asked each other all the questions. Are you happy? When did you know? How did you know? He asked about her marriage.

"Spencer was an alcoholic."

"The whole time?"

"The last ten years. I'm a slow learner."

"Breaking up is really bad. Like half of you dying."

"Did you—ever?"

"I had one girl ever since drama school. Last winter she married our best friend. Her best friend, my best friend. Wouldn't you know he teaches Greek tragedy?"

"I'm sorry."

"I guess I finally stopped hurting. Maybe yesterday. Maybe about lunchtime."

Sheila put her head in the hollow of Val's shoulder and they slept. When she opened her eyes, Val was awake and she traced the line of his lips with her finger. He bit it.

"Hungry?"

"Oh, man—"

"I'm a terrible cook."

"*Now* she tells me."

He scrambled some eggs while she made mountains of toast and they feasted.

"What's for dessert?" she asked.

"You."

He carried her to bed and they made love, this time with an infinity of tenderness. They slept, bodies entwined, and woke to see the sky outside was flecked with lavender. She reached for him.

"Have you stopped loving me yet?"

"Not for all the days of my life."

"You said we'd split up. When's that?"

"Can't stand happiness, can you?"

"Tell me. I have to know."

"I'll beat you to the shower." They made it in a dead heat and showered together, an ablution, Val said, that could cause the next water shortage.

While Sheila made coffee she glanced at him sitting in her kitchen window, his bare feet under her table. She found herself memorizing the line at the nape of his neck, the jutting chin, the deep-set eyes looking out of that craggy face. A feeling of insatiable longing swept over her. Love-making was not enough. She wanted to seize him, to lock him into her life. She thought if he should ever leave her, she would die.

She poured his cereal and sat opposite him,

inhaling steam from her coffee. He started to wolf his corn flakes, looking up at her between spoonfuls.

"Okay, when are you leaving me?"

"Hm?" His spoon stopped in mid-air.

"You said we'd split up. I want to know when."

"Oh Sheila . . . baby . . . Okay, we'll talk about it—now and then never again, right?"

He finished his cereal in three mouthfuls and took his dish to the sink, poured himself coffee, and came to sit down, taking her hand in his.

"Baby, it's so obvious. How come I have to explain it to you? You're the big brain around here."

"Explain it."

"Sheila, I thumbed my way up here. I got to leave soon and thumb my way back. That's how I live. I have two shirts and this is the good one. I cut my own hair and wash my suit in the bathtub. I eat two meals a day and I make my own fish food. Now let's look at you. Sheila Devlin, established writer, lives in gold-plated Fairfield County. She has a house with purple finches and a car with four wheels. She has a bank account and a fireplace and hardcover books and hot water night and day. Are you following me, beautiful? Do you understand? We live in different countries, a lot more than fifty miles apart. Oh, sure, we'll find ways to be together. I'd crawl up here blindfolded. But sooner or later, see, our countries'll get further apart, we start talking different languages, and then . . . then love's not enough any more."

"You're talking . . . about *money?*

"You bet. Money. Unequal money. She starts

86

treating him to a train ride. He starts snitching very small lumps of sugar from her table." He took three lumps from the bowl in front of him and juggled them in his hand. "He never buys sugar. Doesn't need it. Bad for the teeth. But damn, how he *loves sugar!*" He quietly dropped the lumps back into the bowl and dusted off his hands. "Yes, baby, money. Water can wear away stone, and money, sooner or later, will wear away us."

"This is so ridiculous! I don't know where to begin! My house is mortgaged to the roof! Those books are free, from the publisher! My car has sixty thousand miles on it! Ask anybody! Ask Theo! I'm poor!"

"Honey, there's poor and there's poor, so let's not have a contest. The subject is finished, over and out." He reached and put his finger against her lips. "Hey! Hear that? The birds are back again!"

"Screw the birds!"

"Aw honey, I thought you enjoyed it!" With a leering glance over his shoulder, he slammed out the door and the birds flew away squawking. He reached up for the nest, cradling it in his hands, and spoke softly toward the back of the yard, projecting his voice. "Y'picked a lousy building site. She doesn't like birds. Y'better get smart." He walked off the porch, backing away, to look up at the roof. "I got just the spot for you." He came to Sheila. "Here. Hold this." He climbed onto the porch railing in a crouch and turned, straightening up until his head and torso were out of sight. He raised one foot, stood on tiptoe with the other.

"Now! Boost me up, will you?"

She grabbed one foot and boosted. He vanished.

"Hey, where are you?"

His face appeared, upside down, suspended from the eaves. "Give me the nest, will you?"

She handed it to him. He disappeared again. Sheila ran out on the grass in time to see him settling the nest between two exhaust pipes on the flat porch roof. Suddenly, he turned and started to clamber up the main roof on his hands and bare feet. Sheila caught her breath. He reached the top and straddled the ridgepole, threw back his head, and shouted full voice.

"Now hear this! Sheila . . . Devlin . . . is MY . . . girl!" He turned and faced the other way. "Sheila . . . Devlin . . . is MY . . . girl!" A screen slammed next door at the Terrenzio house and Mrs. Terrenzio, in scarlet bathrobe, shook her clasped hands over her head and yelled "Bravo!" then retired. On the other side Mrs. Granville dropped her roll-up blinds with a clatter. Val climbed down and swung Sheila in his arms.

"I got to go. Drive me to the Merritt."

"Do you know hitchhiking is illegal and danger-ous?"

"I've got somebody to worry about me! Every day I'm going to feel like a soldier going into battle. It's great." He pulled her into the kitchen and sat down to put on his shoes. "Listen, I can't see you tonight. Publisher's dinner. Can I come up tomorrow night?"

"I'll come to town."

"Yeah, we'll have dinner in my bed!" He wrapped her in his arms. "God, I'm going to miss you!" They

kissed and held each other and tried to imagine saying
good-bye.

In the car Sheila chased down a thought that had
been haunting the back of her mind.

"I talked to my mother the other night. She said my
Uncle Woody is putting on a new play at the university.
Woody was a big name on Broadway a few years ago."

"Yeah?"

"The leading man never leaves the stage."

"Y'don't say."

"My mother taped the whole play. Might be
interesting to listen to it."

"No."

"I love your open mind."

"Sheila baby, if you're on a diet, you don't go into a
candy store. I kicked the theater. I don't tease myself."

"Val, don't you even want to *play* with the idea?"

"Sure don't."

"Lots of Broadway plays get started in regional
theaters."

"No fooling."

"A part like that could make a star overnight."

"Just like the movies."

"If we could find a way to bring it to New York—"

"We, white lady?"

"Do it off-Broadway—"

"Quit it right now, honey."

"If it works, move it to Broadway—"

"Baby, you're *crowding* me."

"Oh Val, *think* about it! It's your whole life!"

"Yeah, *my* life."

"And you're wasting it! Publisher's dinners! How dare you! It's wicked and stupid and pig-headed!"

Silence. She had gone too far and she knew it. She glanced across at him, sitting there with that brooding look, the hands on his knees white at the knuckles.

"Do me a favor, Sheila Devlin. Don't ever . . . take me in hand."

They were approaching the parkway where she would drop him off.

"I didn't say all that. Forgive me."

"I'd forgive you if you cut off my head and handed it to me."

"Oh Val, my love—"

"Pull over here, that's a girl. I like to check the bushes for gendarmes. Now listen, baby—" He reached for her hand and held it in his. "Right now, I'm living on half my income. The other half goes in the kitty. Three years from now, I open my own shop. Can you wait?"

"No."

"I love you, Sheeley."

"What shall I do till tomorrow night?"

"Sit by the phone." He gave her a quick kiss on the cheek and jumped out. He waved and walked off.

CHAPTER

8

SHEILA CAME BACK to her house and found it hollow. Val had left traces of himself: puddles of water on the bathroom floor, a tumble of sheets on the bed. But he was gone. Sheila fell into a chair in the living room, dazed, amorous, and bewildered. She was in love as never before, but echoes began to tease her inner ear: "We live in different countries . . . I wash my own suit . . . love's not enough . . . money will wear us away . . ."

Could he be right? She remembered the building where he lived and the reeking smells in the halls. New York poverty was different from the Kansas or the Westport varieties, both of which she had sampled. How often would she make that journey up those smelly stairs? How often would he thumb his way up here to be with her? She had found a man—oh, God what a man—and she wanted more than hurried, passionate nights with him. She wanted to share her life with him. What could she do?

Suppose Val were an actor. She had not the slightest doubt he would be successful. He wouldn't be poor any more. They could live anywhere, be together. They would be happy beyond dreams.

She rocketed out of her chair and into the kitchen to telephone her mother in Kansas.

"Hello, Mother. It's Sheila."

"Sheila, it's six o'clock here!"

"Sorry, I forgot the time difference. Listen, I'll tell you why I called."

"Yes, please do."

"Mother, I have a hunch. Can you tell me a little about Uncle Woody's play?"

"What about it?"

"Is it a good play?"

"I am not a theater critic. I know what I like."

"Did you like it?"

"Well, yes . . . and no."

"Jesus, Mother—"

"Did you call me at this hour to use offensive language?"

"Mother, did the play make you laugh, or cry, or go to sleep?"

"I never sleep in the theater, that would be very rude. It's hard enough to sleep in my own bed when my daughter telephones at dawn, having called last night well past midnight, and starts grilling me about a silly play I happened to mention in passing when I haven't had so much as a *cup of coffee!*" Her mother wound up in a yelp of pain.

"Mother, I'm sorry. Really sorry."

"Not at all."

"I'll call you back in one hour. Have a nice breakfast and give Uncle Woody a big kiss for me."

"Why, Sheila!" Her mother giggled wickedly and they hung up. Sheila made two lists, things to say, things not to say. She watched the clock grow a new hour as slowly as a tree grows a new branch.

"Hello, Mother. Did you have a nice breakfast?"

"Yes, and I'm upstairs in case we might have to say something—you know, confidential."

"I'm glad, because I wanted to tell you I have a new beau."

"A beau! Why, that's wonderful! Is he handsome?"

"No. Homely."

"What church, dear?"

"Nondenominational."

"I see. What does he do?"

"He's an actor." Pause.

"Are you playing a joke on me?"

"No. He's an actor, Mother. You know, like Lord Laurence Olivier."

"Oh. What's his name?"

"Val Keating."

"I never heard of him."

"You will."

"This is nothing serious, is it dear? You've been working too hard and you went to a play and got a crush on this man. Did you go to the stage door, or how did you meet him?"

"Actually, Mother, he's an out-of-work actor."

"How . . . very . . . unfortunate."

"That's why I'm calling you, Mother. When you mentioned Uncle Woody's play, I was curious. Tell me something about it. Anything. I'm asking you to help me, Mother."

"Of course I'll help you. You're my only child. Didn't I always tell you I'd get you the moon with a pink ribbon on it?"

"Mother, tell me about the play, hm?"

"I took down a few lines at rehearsal. You know how your father always admired my shorthand. I was going to ask Sherwood what they mean."

"Mother, read them to me. Right now."

"Yes, dear. I'll get my pocketbook." Sheila could hear the click of the purse, the rustle of paper. "It goes like this, dear. The man is talking. Are you ready?"

"Yes, Mother."

"'Lady, I take my leave of you. I pry myself from the sweet sovereignty of your embrace. Are you well gratified by the stamp your love has left on me? See how you made a roaring lion into a household cat. You harnessed me to small ambitions. You schooled me to domestic tricks. Like a pretty puppet I danced for you. But now the dance is done, my lady. We are unwed, disjoined, and put asunder. *Exultate, jubilate.* I leave you one breath before your last.' That's when he almost chokes her, but he doesn't. 'I wish you a man of puissance to come after me, to smother between your thighs. Unman him, degrade him, use him up. But do it quickly, for he will surely plunge a dagger between those ripe and bursting breasts of yours, his steely point

94

making my point for me. Then, in that last little snip of time, you'll know . . . how I detested you.'"

"Ah, it's a love story!"

"I find it most unpleasant!"

"Mother, I want to hear the rest."

"I can't imagine why."

"You said you'd help."

"I will, dear, but—"

"I want you to get hold of those tapes, and take them somewhere to be copied."

"Uncle Woody'd never allow it!"

"Then don't tell him! Does he tell you everything?"

"Indeed he does not!"

"All right, then. And I want you to mail me the tapes by overnight mail. I'll pay for everything. Oh Muddy, will you do it for me?"

"Certainly."

"I'll never forget this. I'll find you an elephant's egg."

"You naughty girl, you remember all my foolishness."

"Bye, Mother."

"Good-bye, my baby girl."

Sheila put herself back to work to preserve her sanity. Val called twice from the office, hurried and constrained. Sheila went out in the afternoon and bought a tape recorder. The next morning, she awoke to a driving rain, but the tapes arrived. She shook the package and squeezed it, but no more. By late afternoon, it was still raining. She packed tapes and recorder and her best nightgown in a briefcase and put on her high-school raincoat. She wore her ugliest shoes and a bilious yellow rain hat. She looked in the mirror and asked herself the question, "Can romantic love survive?"

At Grand Central Station, people stood in knots on the sidewalk, twenty hands flashing in the air for every taxi that passed, most of them smugly proclaiming "Off Duty." Sheila reminded herself that she was a country person now and a little spring rain never hurt anybody.

She walked to Val's West Side address through a lashing torrent. She folded up her useless umbrella and slogged onward, ever onward, buoyed by the thought of Val's admiration and a hot cup of anything. She rang his bell. After three rings it became apparent that Val was not at home. Tenants were coming into the narrow entryway, throwing her suspicious glances, and slamming the inner door behind them. She walked up and down the block.

The briefcase grew heavier. Her shoes squelched. Her hair was plastered to her forehead. She was cold and hungry. If she went to a coffee shop, she would sit there in a puddle of wet clothes, and besides, she wanted to know exactly how late Val was going to be. She kept on pacing the block and he was, it turned out, very late indeed. He grabbed her from behind, tipping her hat over her face.

"Oh baby—how long have you been here?"

"Several . . . centuries."

"Theo had a client that wouldn't quit. I had to stay and lock up."

"What are you? Her office boy?"

"That's right." He leaned down to kiss her, but at the touch of her cold, hard mouth, grabbed her briefcase and pulled her after him.

"Come on. We can fight upstairs." He led her into the entry, glancing over his shoulder as he fiddled with his key, as if she might run out on him. They started the long climb.

"You have a good day? Two good days?"

"Simply glorious."

"What's in the briefcase?"

"A pearl-handled revolver."

After this, they maintained a trudging silence. He let them in, dropping her briefcase on the bed and going quickly to make coffee. She whipped off her sodden clothes, slipped into her nightgown, and wrapped herself in his bedspread. By the time he returned, she had a tape rolling and she pointed.

"This is it."

"So I see." Now his face was stiff, too.

"We'll listen to the first act. You don't have to sign something in blood, you know."

"Splendid. Just how I hoped we'd spend the evening."

He handed her a cup of coffee and sat down as far away as four walls permitted. Shouts and squeaks came from the tape, then a student's voice. "Did you turn on the tape, shit-head?" "Yeah, shit-head." A heavy object fell. "All right, who's on the book?" "Dutch, but he's in the can." "Well, Chrissake, get him out. Who's on curtain?" "Frankie, but he went to get a Coke." "Jesus, why'd I get into this screwin' mess?" "Because it's a gut course, 'Drama Production, One-thirty-three.'" Grunts followed, then muffled laughter, then the magic word, "Curtain!"

At first it was hard to get oriented in this freeform play, especially through the sense of hearing alone. Sheila stole glances at Val and found him looking skeptical. She struggled to get her bearings.

A man and a girl were threading their way, in different guises, from the far distant past to the present. In scenes that layered over one another like transparencies, the reality of one time shifted into the coloration of the next. Soon, Sheila began to accept the idiom as if she were learning a new language at top speed. She saw Val shift his position and lean forward, closer to the disembodied voices. His face and body became a listening instrument. Finally, he came to sit beside her on the bed and took her hand.

Toward the end of the first act, a battle was taking place off-stage. They heard neighing horses and pounding hooves, the clash of lances against breastplates, the shouts and cries of soldiers. A silence, and then a girl's voice, sweet and clear.

"Can this be the place? My true love said he would meet me close by the fountain (gurgle of a fountain) if he were not killed in battle (sounds of battle). He said I must come to the deserted garden (cry of a loon) and wait for him beside the fountain (gurgle). He told me to come through the silver gate (silver music) into the deserted garden (loon's cry) and wait for him beside the fountain. (gurgle). So I'll sit here beside the fountain (gurgle) in

98

this lonely deserted garden (no loon's cry—she raises her voice) in this lonely deserted garden (loon's cry very loud) with the silver gate (silvery music) and my love will surely come to me."

Sound of galloping hooves and a neighing horse. "Ah, my love! He comes to me! And how magnificent he is, mounted on his white charger, whose name is Balthazar!" (Neighing sounds.)

A man's voice. "Stop, Balthazar! Stop, you fiery steed!" (A squeaking of wheels that slows and stops.) Sheila pictured a huge wooden horse on wheels, complete with armored rider. "Ah, my fairest fair! At last I see the face that haunts my dreams!"

"It is indeed my face, grown old and ugly waiting for you!"

"If this is ugly, this porcelain perfection, why then I've lost my eyesight in the battle." (Sounds of battle.)

"My love, dismount I beg you. Hold me! Embrace me!"

"My fairest love, I cannot!"

"But I must feel your touch. Embrace me my lord, or I shall surely die!"

"Oh my beloved, if I should come to earth with this hundredweight of armor (clanking of the armor) then would I be unhorsed. Then would I indeed be naked to mine enemies."

"But I have waited so long!"

"Reach me your hand, beloved. I'll cover it with such kisses that will travel in the blood to every part of you and make you hot with my desire."

"Yes, take my hand! Tell each finger of your love!"

"When I kiss this first finger, my beloved, I kiss your shuttered eyes, and taste the salty lids, and tease the lashes upward with my tongue."

"Oh yes, and then?"

"And when I kiss the next, imagine that I press my mouth against your throat and find your heartbeat with my lips, and match my own to yours, till we have one heart between us, beating like a captive bird."

"Oh yes, I feel it—"

"I kiss the third and fourth fingers and you must think I kiss your breasts, first one and then the other, and hold the sweet fullness of them in my hands."

"Sweet love, go on—"

"When I kiss this last, small finger, I bury my face in your belly, seeking the navel as a honeybee seeks the center of a flower."

"Ah love, I shall swoon."

"Give me the other hand, my love, for it shall be to me that warm and secret place in you, that wellspring of my felicity, that patch of paradise—"

"Yes, tell me—"

"Wait. Is the darkness growing darker?"

"No, no, lighter, closer to the dawn—"

"But, my beautiful . . . I can . . . no longer . . . see you."

"But, what is it? You are so pale! Your face is whiter than the moon! Oh God in heaven, there's blood on my hand! My lord, you're bleeding! A trickle of blood comes down your breastplate! You've been wounded in the battle! You didn't tell me!"

"It was . . . the merest scratch . . . I'd never die . . . of such a paltry wound . . . If I should die . . . then I would die . . . and gladly die . . . of love for you."

There is a crash of metal armor falling to the ground. The girl cries out.

"Oh no, come . . . put your head against my breast. I'll comfort you . . . I'll make you well again. . . ." Long pause. "His heart has stopped. My own true love has left me. I shall never be happy again . . . Perhaps I'll take my life. Indeed, I have nothing now to live for . . . The fountain is beautiful tonight. All those splinters of glass, rising and falling, rising and falling . . . I wonder if it will do that forever? Is it possible I've just discovered eternity? . . . Perhaps I shan't die this instant. Perhaps I'll sit here by the fountain, (gurgle) in the deserted garden (loon's cry) with the silver gate (silvery music) and perhaps . . . I'll find out . . . about eternity. . . ."

Swoosh of the curtain closing. Sheila and Val stared at each other.

"I'll be damned," Val said.

"Me, too."

"That might be one hell of a play."

"Knocked me out."

Val got up and paced.

"Who wrote that thing?"

"No idea."

"Sounds like a blockbuster."

"Val, will you try for it?"

101

"Hey, wait a minute—"

"If I could put a production together—get Uncle Woody—bring it to New York—"

"Now hold everything. I told you, the theater and I are finished, washed up—"

"This is different! It's falling in your lap!"

"Look, I work as a literary agent. Not a big operator, but I get by. I like it. What are you rocking the boat for? It's *my boat,* baby!"

"Will you do one thing? Will you come to Kansas with me and see the play? We fly out, we fly back. One weekend, my treat. Goddam it Val, what can you lose?"

"What are you trying to do, rape me little by little?"

"Val, I *know you can do this!*"

"Yeah, and who asked you? You think because we love each other, we have one heartbeat between us, and it's in your throat? That was the old days. We have two lives, yours and mine. I like mine. I got it all laid out. If you're ashamed of having an office boy around, dump me. But don't help me, Sheila, don't shape me up. *Get off my case!*"

Sheila, wrapped in the bedspread, fell face down on the bed. Val put a hand on her shoulder.

"Are you crying?"

"Only inside."

"I don't know what to say."

"Skip it."

"Baby, I want to skip the whole frigging thing!"

Sheila raised her head. "We can't! I can't."

"Why the Christ not?"

She faced away from him. "You think I want to do this for you. Not so. I want to do it for me."

"Oh, sure."

"This year, since the divorce, has been my little hell. I sit up there in the country and run newsclips of my life. I try to make me look better. The fact is, I'm a loser."

"You? Come on—"

"Oh, I can write books. In real life, I do everything wrong. I married Spencer and got to be part of his disease. I used up half his life."

"*Who* used up *who*?"

"I'm a loser with my mother. When I was a kid I loved her. But I never found the bridge to being grown-up people with her. My mother irritates the hell out of me! And I probably break her heart!"

"Parents are a pain."

"My daughter Kerry—we're great friends, 'just like sisters' as they say. But I'm supposed to stake her to a college education and a fancy trip to Italy. What if I can't do it? You think we'll still be sisters after a kick in the teeth like that?"

"No—"

"Val, I was scraping the bottom when I met you. My God, was it only three days ago? You could turn my whole life around. If I could do this one thing for you, but really for me—Val, let me bring you luck! You'll be rich and famous and doing what you were born to do!"

He gave her one long, grave look, then lunged away from her.

"You have no goddam right to ask me! This is *my*

life you're kicking around! Jesus, why can't you leave me alone?"

"I will. You watch me."

She squirmed off the bed and stomped over to her pile of sodden clothes. She picked them up, clutching them and the bedspread to her bosom, then came to a halt.

"Oh God, you don't have a bathroom!"

"Actors don't have bathrooms, either. Lucky to have a pot to pee in."

"Well, where *is* it?"

"Down the hall and hang a right." She started for the door. "I share it with seven people. It's occupied right now. Heard the door slam."

Sheila whimpered with frustration and moved to a corner of the small room.

"Have the decency to turn your back."

"If I close my eyes, I can see you naked. I do it all the time. So what's the difference? Say, are you a bit bandy-legged?"

"You're a brutish sort, aren't you?"

"Yeah. I wonder why you thought you liked me."

"Because you were young and vigorous and brutish." She was yanking on her clothes.

"Oh, I was frantic at first, afraid I might be too old for you. Now I realize you're far too old for me. You are *calcified!* Your mind is factory sealed against new ideas!" She pointed an angry finger at Val and dropped the bedspread. She let it lie there. "No power on earth can penetrate your skull. No opportunity that comes once in a lifetime—" She was struggling to put on her soggy shoes. "Oh, my God, why have you deserted me? A man who doesn't have a bathroom certainly wouldn't have a shoehorn, am I right?"

"Let me help you—"

He came to her as she raised up. Her elbow clipped him in the nose. He staggered back. She continued to struggle with the shoes. "I wish you all the luck in the world, all you deserve, that is." Shoes on, she faced him. "You will enjoy your dull little life, won't you? Remember, *never take a chance!*" She tried to steady her voice, but it broke. "You big . . . dumb . . . ox!" She turned and made for the door. Val followed her and stood close behind her while she fiddled with the chain lock. She could hear him breathing. Suddenly, she heard his beautiful, soft voice.

" 'When I kiss this finger, imagine that I kiss your shuttered eyes . . . and taste your salty lids . . . and tease the lashes upward with my tongue.' "

Her hand froze on the chain.

" 'I press my lips against your throat to find your heartbeat and match it with my own . . . one heart between us, beating like a captured bird.' "

She turned toward him to read his eyes. He started unbuttoning her shirt.

" 'I kiss your breasts, first one and then the other . . . holding the sweet fullness of them in my hands.' " He unzipped her skirt and let it fall to the floor. He pushed her down on the bed.

" 'I bury my face in your belly, like a honeybee searching for the center of a flower—' "

He did so.

"'And then that warm and secret place in you, that wellspring of felicity, that paradise—'"

"'Ah my love, I shall swoon.'"

They made love that night and in the morning Sheila telephoned her mother while Val was striking actorish poses at the other end of the room.

"Mother, we're coming out to see you, Val Keating and I."

"Why that's lovely, dear. Does Mr. Keating enjoy a leg of lamb?"

CHAPTER

9

O N THE FOLLOWING afternoon, Sheila covered her typewriter, locked up her house, and persuaded Mrs. Terenzio next door to take her to the Connecticut limousine for La Guardia Airport, where she would meet Val Keating. Sheila could not remember the last time she had taken a trip anywhere, and found herself fidgeting. But she caught herself, and resolved to be composed, relaxed, the image of the seasoned traveler.

She checked her airline ticket three times before the limo reached Stamford. She dropped her reading glasses between the seats, tore a Kleenex into confetti, and narrowly missed choking to death on a cough drop. Finally, she decided to permit herself a state of excitement. After all, she was engaged in an impassioned elopement with the love of her life. Why shouldn't she be grasping a paperback with blanched thumbs? Of course, the only trouble with the elopement theory was that she was fleeing toward her family homestead and not away from it, and that she had bullied Val unmercifully into coming with her. Gradually, this entire excursion began to take on a jaundiced color.

She was dragging a man she hardly knew—well, had known for less than a week—dragging him halfway across the continent for some purpose that had seemed valid, in fact urgent, and now began to seem mildly insane. She watched the other passengers boarding the limo at various stops, and envied them their clearcut, legitimate purposes: a brace of parents heading for their son's graduation; two high-school girls wearing no-nuke buttons pointed toward their congressman in Washington. But here sat Sheila Devlin, running out on her work with a deadline coming up, squandering money on airline tickets, barreling off to Lawrence, Kansas, with Val Keating soon to be shackled to her side—for what? To see a play. An incomprehensible play that nobody ever heard of, written by God knows whom, acted by a bunch of college kids, directed by her so-called Uncle Woody, the Stuffed Shirt of the Western World, and presented in a city from which she had long since made her thankful escape. Yes, she thought, her entire life had been a series of unfortunate decisions. This one, though, was without a doubt, the most idiotic, the most intensely embarassing. Sheila could feel the blood rushing to her cheeks and pictured the limo sideswiping a utility pole with only one fatality: herself.

When they pulled into the airport, Sheila brushed past the skycap at the curb and hauled her bag to the Braniff counter, where Val was waiting with his matchless grin. Sheila faced him without a word of greeting.

"Look, we're not going. Chuck it. Listen, I made a mistake. Stop staring, will you? Come on, we'll send the bags to Kansas and go to the movies. It'll be another first. Bags arrive, passengers lost. What do you say?"

He stared down at her, and then his great laughter poured over her. "Are you off your *hinges?*"

He folded her in his arms and kissed her, grabbed her bag, and checked them into their flight. "Come on. We got almost an hour. You want to eat? I'm buying. We'll have cheese Danish and I got us a giant Hershey, and they give us a snack on the plane, I checked."

"Val, it's only a three-hour flight!"

"Who cares? How often do you think I elope with a sexpot novelist to Lawrence, Kansas? I'm going to pig my way out, and pig it back!"

Sheila noticed a certain confusion in his appetites. She herself would have preferred a night flight, in an empty plane on automatic pilot. But sitting here in the cafeteria, all chrome and purple plush, surrounded by the din of clattering trays and the smell of thick, brown gravy, she was unaccountably happy. Val was wolfing his Danish and growling like a lion at feeding time.

"Come on, eat up. Clean plate, or you don't get any Hershey's."

"Val, I have to tell you something. You and I are incompatible. Your entire life is dedicated to the next time you're going to eat. Mine is dedicated to the next time I can avoid eating. I think we'd better split, right now, and you get custody of the Hershey."

"What's wrong, you think you're fat? Corpulent?

Obese? Sheila, honey, you're not fat. Believe me. If anybody in this world is an expert on your beautiful, voluptuous bod it is me. Am I right?"

He was leaning across the table toward her, and projecting that soft, silver voice so it could be heard ten tables away.

"Val, shut up, will you?"

He reached for her shoulders and pulled her toward him. "Is there one square inch of this milk-white instrument of joy that I have not seen and touched and smothered with my kisses? Am I blind? Is it possible that you have concealed from me some imperfection? Are you—God forgive me for the word—are by any chance . . . *flabby?*"

Sheila hissed at him. "You shut up or I'm leaving!"

"Sure, honey, eat your Danish," he said in his most everyday voice. When she looked up at him, his deep-set eyes were fixed on hers and one of them winked.

They dawdled toward their boarding gate, doing a flash forward. "Y'know," Val said, "if we like this play as much as we think, if there's a chance in hell of getting it to Broadway, there's nothing I wouldn't do to get the part, I mean nothing. The idea of being an actor again. When I think about it, I get the shakes! Look!" He held out a rake of a hand, and indeed it was trembling.

Sheila felt a glow of admiration. Here was a man who could do a one-eighty turn. On him it looked good.

They strolled past live lobsters barely moving in their holding tank to the holding tank for Kansas City passengers, also barely moving. Like obedient children they fell in with the small rituals of air travel: single-filing on board, listening while flight attendants explained with balletic gestures the unlikely need for flotation cushions and falling oxygen masks; nodding when the captain included them in his flight plan. Val held her hand across six states, when he was not eating, and bent his shaggy head down close to hers. Sheila wanted to freeze time.

The Kansas City Airport was so clean and quiet compared to any on the eastern seaboard that Val said, "Hey, is this still planet Earth?" They were standing in a huge, circular building, open at the far end. The floor was polished to a glassy shine, innocent of gum wrappers. They picked their luggage from a silent carousel without a single elbow jab from other passengers. They rented a car from a smiling attendant apparently enamored of his fellow man. Driving westward toward Lawrence, they tried to remember why they had left this spacious, friendly landscape known as the Middle West.

"Of course, it *is* flat."

"You can't send out for Chinese."

The attendant who handed them their ticket for the turnpike said it was "some evening," and twinkled.

"They're all on drugs," said Sheila.

Sheila smiled to see again the undulating Indian names: Oscaloosa, Wakarusa, and Osawatomie.

When they saw a sign, DENTURES—ONE DAY SERVICE, Sheila knew this was truly the *obliging* part of America. This was a country where people expect everything to work out fine. The faces in other cars were cheerful, without a sign of the *rigor mortis* of the

111

highway. She reminded herself that she herself was a native of this land of Oz, and probably suffering from the same idiotic optimism. She had come out here to find a play that would make Val a star and herself a happy woman. They crossed two rivers, the "Mighty Mo"— muddy as ever—and the good old "Kaw" for Kansas, and soon it would be too late to turn back. She would be revealed as a silly, romantic female who never should have left her typewriter.

"Val, let's turn around." He knew her by now.

"It's all going to work out, baby. My bones tell me."

They drew up to the house, a middle-sized, middle-aged house, two stories with a front porch and dormer windows. It looked anonymous, the replica of so many others, and yet Sheila had spent almost half her life in it. A woman came out on the porch, plump and pretty in a frilly apron, shielding her eyes in the setting sun, smiling and waving her handkerchief.

"She's pretty. Looks like you."

They all met on the sidewalk, with embraces and handshakes.

"Is this your first visit to Kansas, Mr. Keating?"

"Val is from Nebraska, Mother."

"Falls City, Ma'am, last stop on the Underground Railway. Civil War, y'know?"

"It was Lawrence, Kansas, that sent you your runaway slaves, Mr. Keating, or you wouldn't have had any, would you?" and she smiled up at him, supremacy established.

"Mother, can we go in now?"

"Of course, dear." Muriel led the way, and Val

cocked his head at her departing figure. "Feisty, huh?" he whispered. Muriel stepped into the house and turned to hold the screen door open.

"You are most welcome, Mr. Keating."

"It's an honor, Mrs. Devlin." Sheila hoped all this elegance would soon wear itself out.

"Welcome home, Sheila dear."

"Thanks, Mom. It looks . . . really nice." And it did. The tacky morning glories were still climbing endlessly up the stairwell and the sun was forever setting over the watercolored Grand Canal of Venice. In the living room she glimpsed the upright piano where her mother would approximate "Clair de Lune" and the plush sofa that had tormented her bare legs. But the house had a sweetness to it, and, of course, it was immaculate.

"Now you must come and meet Sherwood."

They filed into the dining room where Sherwood sat bolt upright in his hospital bed by the window, wearing a Noel Coward dressing gown and looking urbane. They skirted the dining table, set with the best lace cloth, and squeezed awkwardly between bed and table.

"Sherwood, you have visitors. Sheila is here, and her friend Mr. Keating."

"Uncle Woody!"

"Well, well, little Sheila Devlin."

They shook hands.

"Sorry about your tibia."

"My dear, the merest trivia."

"This is my friend, Val Keating."

Val shook hands.

"It's an honor to meet you, sir."

"Do I hear you're one of those dreamers that call themselves *actors?*"

"We dream of having Sherwood Pell for a director."

"My dear chap, no honeyed words, I beg you. You're far too young to've heard my name, even *in utero.*"

"I read the critics: Atkinson, Kerr, Barnes. Somebody said Pell could get a performance out of a bag of dirty laundry."

"My word, how unsavory," said Sherwood, but he was chuckling and patently pleased.

"Come along now, children, and I'll show you your rooms." Muriel led the way up the stairs. Sheila remembered how she'd been taught never to step in the middle of the stair carpet, for fear of wearing it out, but to walk spread-eagled with one foot on each outside edge. Now she planted her feet defiantly dead center and hoped her mother would notice.

"This will be your room, Mr. Keating, and Sheila will be at the end of the hall. I do hope you won't mind sharing the bathroom."

"In Nebraska, Ma'am, we just started tearing down the privies."

"Oh, Mr. Keating, my dear husband would have liked you! Now come and see your room, Sheila. I've kept it just the same."

Sheila was touched to see the rosebuds strewn across the walls and the tattered books on the shelves. Muriel closed the door behind them.

"Sheila, your young man is so attractive! How old is he?"

"Oh, thirty or so."

"Oh my—quite young, isn't he?"

"Ten years younger than I am. Do you find that frightfully important?"

"Of course not, dear. Do tell me . . . are you sweethearts?"

"Yes. We hold hands all the time." She kept her face deadpan.

"How nice." Muriel moved the bedspread a quarter-inch to the left. "I suppose you're having a relationship? Everybody does nowadays. But I must tell you one thing. *Not under my roof.* Do you understand?"

"Mother, I'm in love with him! I'm crazy about him! It's not some kind of a sin!"

"I'll be the judge of what's sinful in my house!"

"Okay, I take a vow of chastity! I will not have carnal relations with Val in this house, unless, of course, he rapes me!"

"Sheila!"

"And, if he does, I promise not to enjoy it!"

"Oh-h." Muriel turned away with a cry, her lacy handkerchief to her mouth. "If you knew how you hurt me! Making fun of everything! I thought this time it would be different!"

"It will! I swear it will!" Sheila came to her mother and hugged her. "Come on, Muddy, please—I was kidding. Do you really like him?"

"He's charming. Very handsome. Of course, all actors are handsome."

"He's a fine actor, Mother. He's talented."

"A full-grown man, play-acting!"

Sheila froze. "Yes, like Father."

"Your father was, in his youth, an opera singer."

"That's acting!"

"Until I persauded him—"

"Bullied him!"

". . . to become a voice teacher at the finest university in the Middle West!"

"So we'd all be *respectable!*"

"And live in a house instead of a costume trunk!"

"To Father's eternal regret!"

"Sheila, how *can* you? After all these years?" The handkerchief approached the face once more and Sheila wondered how she could have fallen into the old, old trap again.

"Mother, I'm sorry. Let's be friends."

"My daugher is my best friend in this whole world." Her mother smiled bravely and Sheila kissed her cheek.

"When can we see the play?"

"I believe there's a run-through at eight-thirty."

"*Tonight!* Oh, my God!" She was pounding on the bathroom door. "Val! Hurry up! There's a run-through at eight-thirty! Let's eat!"

Val emerged, hair slicked down, face shining, wearing his other shirt. Muriel was tripping down the stairs.

"Sherwood cannot possibly carve in his bed. I hope you'll do the honors, Mr. Keating?"

Over his shoulder, she threw him the glance of a born coquette. Val bowed.

"Honored, Madame."

When Muriel was out of sight, Val folded Sheila in his arms.

"She's a sexpot like you."

"A *what?*"

"Very sexy lady. The kind that used to topple empires. Come on, I'll show you." He pulled her toward his room.

"Val, we can't!" Instead, she led him down the stairs and into the dining room. "Talk to Uncle Woody and I'll help Mother."

The women scurried in and out of the kitchen while Val stood at the foot of Sherwood's bed.

"Do you ever miss Broadway, Mr. Pell?"

"Miss that dogfight, that massacre of the innocents?"

"I call it the survival of the shittiest."

"Why, Mr. Keating!" Muriel stood frozen in her tracks with a platter of asparagus.

"I get my bad language from Sheila."

"It's true, it's true. He's pure as a beaten biscuit," Sheila said, peering into one to see if it was buttered.

While Muriel poured icewater from a frosted silver pitcher, Val carved the lamb and Sheila contemplated her mother's uncurdled Hollandaise sauce.

"Why didn't you teach me to cook?"

"You said cooking was a waste of time."

"Do you remember anything *good* about me?"

"You were a sweet, beautiful child, but you grew up."

"I had to, didn't I?"

"Of course, dear. Now take Uncle Woody his tray, please, and be careful not to spill."

Sheila managed. Muriel sat at one end of the table, Val at the other, Sheila between them, with Uncle Woody dominating the scene from his raised bed.

"Will you say grace, Mr. Keating?" Muriel asked.

They bowed their heads, and Sheila heard Val's chameleon voice raised in prayer, not reverent perhaps, but certainly respectful.

" 'Oh, Lord, please bless our daily bread. We hope it will make us strong and well. Thanks a lot. Amen.' I made that up when I was nine. Is it all right?"

"That was very nice. Thank you."

The silence that followed was punctuated by the scraping of knife against plate and the song of birds outside.

"Bet you keep your cardinals and goldfinches all winter," said Val.

"We do, Mr. Keating, we do indeed. So colorful. If flowers could fly, they'd be cardinals and goldfinches, wouldn't they?"

"You know it!" said Val, and they laughed together. "Your warblers been back for long?"

"The first to return, the very first!" They seemed to be naming off old friends they'd discovered in common.

"And then the grosbeaks and the thrashers, right?"

"And then those noisy, wicked birds—oh, you know . . ."

"Grackles."

"Who were surely sent to try us. Mind you,

118

Lawrence is at the crossing of the flyways. We get egrets and blue herons and bald eagles, all passing through." She waved her shapely arms in their lines of flight. Val was leaning toward her mother and speaking softly, as if they were alone.

"Mrs. Devlin, Sheila never told me your first name."

"It's Muriel. It means bittersweet."

"Mine's Val, and I think you're one nifty lady."

"Why thank you, thank you so much." She blushed a little, looked down at her plate, then at Val sideways through rather long eyelashes. Sheila turned to Sherwood.

"Shall we dance, Uncle Woody?"

"If you give me six weeks, young lady. . . ."

"Six months, more likely," said Muriel brightly. "And you haven't danced since the bunny-hop. You're hopeless on the dance floor. You always were."

"Perfidious woman! Have I not suffered your tedious ministrations without a whimper for seven interminable days and brightened your humdrum existence with flashes of wit and wisdom? I'll have another morsel of that lamb, young man, and I'm partial to the nubbin."

Muriel gasped in outrage, but Val soothed her ruffled feathers while somehow, at the same time, letting Woody know that he found him amusing and clever. The crosscurrents continued through the meal. Sheila watched and listened and wished she could hold Val's hand. She had thought his charm existed only for her.

119

But obviously it radiated from him like rays from the sun. She should be glad that other people could feel the warmth. But she was not glad. A love affair is the most private thing on earth, she reflected. Is he carrying on a love affair with the entire world? Now he was naming off plays that Uncle Woody had directed and asking perceptive questions about the theater before he himself was born, at the same time dropping a few names: the Yale Drama School, the Actor's Studio. But surely they had come here to charm Uncle Woody, among other things. All right, enough already.

Sheila rose and filled Val's water glass to the brim and beyond, while her hand rested on his shoulder. When the icy trickle reached his lap, he leapt up shuddering.

"We have to go now, Mother."

"But I've made a strawberry shortcake!"

"We'll have it afterwards."

"Take notes for me, young man."

"Disgusting meal, Muriel." Val kissed her cheek as if he'd been doing it for years.

"Drive carefully."

"Come straight home now."

" 'Night everybody."

"Good-night, children."

Sheila drove through Lawrence toward the university campus and found herself pleased to be back in her home town. She pointed out to Val the broad streets and the neat geometry of square green lawns outlined by round-domed trees.

"This town lives close to its past. The streets are

named after the states, in the order of their admittance to the Union. Locals are expected to know the order. Visitors carry history books."

Val played the game with her, trying to anticipate the next street name.

"As for the Civil War, it might have happened yesterday. This town was the abolitionist heart of abolitionist Kansas, and paid for it dearly. You ever hear of Quantrill's raid?"

"Never."

"The smallest child in Lawrence can tell you about Quantrill's Raid."

"You tell me."

"The year was 1863, high summertime. William Quantrill came galloping into town with his three hundred outlaws. It was five in the morning and the whole town was asleep. They massacred two hundred people and burned and looted for four hours. My mother's great-great-grandmother was one of the survivors."

"How about her husband?"

"She hid him under a manure pile. One of the raiders put a gun to her head and asked where her husband was. She took him down in the cellar and made love to him. At the height of his passion, she shot him in the head with his own pistol."

Val whistled through his teeth. "You come from a long line of hellcats. I'm afraid to meet your daughter, she'll probably deck me."

Sheila looked over at this big man with the knotty hands spread on his knees.

"I'll protect you."

She showed him some of the fine Victorian houses as the passed, houses like castles, towered and turreted, adorned with a lacy white gingerbread that glistened in the last rays of the setting sun.

"Some stage set you have here. Who does your lighting?"

Sheila was thankful for the chatter, because it covered her suspense. They were minutes away from the play they had come to see. Was it going to change their whole lives? Or was this an expensive, brainless, wild goose chase? Who wanted a tame goose anyway?"

They walked into the nearly empty theater and slipped into seats toward the back. The Crafton-Pryer auditorium looked as if it would seat nearly a thousand, with a large semicircular balcony and fine sight lines. They watched the organized confusion of an assistant director shouting orders and a light man adjusting his spots. Suddenly, the house lights dimmed. Sheila and Val grabbed hands and suspended breathing.

After the final curtain, they rose unnoticed and left the theater. In the darkened car, they drove along in silence. Finally, Sheila spoke.

"Well?"

"Well?"

"Okay, we'll have a secret ballot. Put your hand behind your back. One finger sticking out is yes, two for no. You ready?"

"Ready."

"One, two, *three!*"

Each one extended a hand toward the other. Each one held out one finger. They both yelled "Yes!" in unison, and both started talking at once.

"It's a strange play."

"Man, is that a part! I can taste it!"

"That girl—she's lovely."

"I could work with her."

"Hope you never do."

"Some of those speeches."

"I've been *sluiced* with words. Lovely feeling."

"Yeah. What do they mean?"

"I think it's about how men and women will never, never live in peace together."

"You and I could."

It was the most serious thing he'd ever said to her.

"Yes, we could."

"Baby, we need this play. We *need* it."

"I know."

They burst into the house, to find Muriel reading aloud to Sherwood—a novel of Sheila's in paperback.

"The play's a blockbuster, sir," said Val.

"Uncle Woody, it's brilliant."

"Found it tolerable, did you?"

"Who wrote it?"

"A student in my drama class. Helped him with rewrites, of course. I'll tell him he's been praised by a fine novelist." He tapped her book with a patrician finger.

"It must have been a difficult play on paper. How did you know it would work onstage? That was gutsy."

123

"My dear, I've spent my life learning to be gutsy. Now, young man, do you have some notes for me?"

Val dug out an old envelope with scribbles on the back. "You're running two hours and forty minutes playing time. You might want to cut three minutes . . . That's all, sir."

"That's all! What do you mean, 'That's all?' I've been lying here paralyzed for a week while my play gets torn to ribbons and the Yale Drama School has nothing to say but 'cut three minutes!' Mother of God, speak up, man!"

"I'm not a theater critic, sir. Theater critics make me puke, picking and pinching like old ladies at a fruit stand. The play I saw tonight is an event in the theater, directed by Sherwood Pell. All I have to say is . . . congratulations, sir."

Sheila was so touched that she turned away. Sherwood himself was for once without words. Muriel arrived with a pitcher of lemonade and set it in front of Sherwood, who busied himself pouring it out.

"You see, Sherwood," said Muriel, "didn't I tell you? You should be proud of those students. They learned every single word of that play!"

Sherwood shot a look at Muriel as she leaned over him. The look was a pellet of hatred, thinly coated with pity. Sheila wondered how they had both survived for a week. She lunged forward and clutched at two glasses, handing them to her mother and Val.

"Mother's lemonade recipe is in all the time capsules."

"No kiddin'? What's in it?" Val asked.

"Uh—lemon juice, sugar, and water."

"Oh, Sheila, you silly child!" They all drank to the play.

"To the play . . . *Continuum!* . . . May it run forever!"

"Here in the heartland of America we do three weekends and close the show."

"God, what a waste."

"This is a college campus. Small risks, small rewards."

Sheila breathed deeply and asked Woody the heavy question in what she hoped was a light, even casual tone.

"Would you consider bringing the play to Broadway?"

"Surely you jest."

"With your name, we could raise the money."

"Do you realize how *much* money?"

"The money's unimportant." Woody looked at her, but she kept her face straight. "The question is, would you be interested, Uncle Woody?"

"Is she hallucinating?"

"You're joking, aren't you dear? She always had such a sense of humor . . . she and her father . . . full of pranks . . ." Muriel's voice faded away, like somebody sinking under water. Sheila went on.

"Val would play lead, of course. He has an enormous talent. You'd be discovering a star, *and* a new playwright! You'd be continuing your Broadway career right where you never should have broken it off!"

Sheila watched him closely as she spoke. He was

125

shaking his head and smiling, and yet . . . and yet . . . there was a lift to his chin and a look in his eye. Uncle Woody hankered for Broadway. She was sure of it.

"So you have powers of persuasion inherited from your father, do you? I'll have to watch out for you, Sheila Devlin."

"My father always said you were too big for this campus, 'like a lion in a birdcage.'"

"Tom said that?" Uncle Woody made circles on the frosty side of his glass.

"Dear Tom always exaggerated so," said Muriel with a sniff.

Sheila rose and put herself between Muriel and Sherwood. "Uncle Woody, you have a Broadway opening in the palm of your hand, a beautiful play, and a leading man. Val happens to be 'at liberty.'"

Val came in on the next beat.

"I'd like to read for you tomorrow, sir, if I could borrow a script overnight?"

"Of course, of course, right there on that table." Val made a dive for it. "But I'm warning you, if you read like the new Olivier, I'm a college professor these days. Teach four courses and do a play every semester. I might add, just between us, I'm up for a deanship at the moment."

"Sherwood, you didn't tell me!" It was a cry of pain from Muriel.

"I beg you, don't noise it abroad." He turned back to Val. "So you see, young man, I've settled into academia. Broadway will have to putter along."

"But why didn't you *tell* me?" Muriel pulled at his sleeve like a child. Sheila took her arm.

"Mother, will you come upstairs for a minute? I brought you a present."

"A present? Why, that's lovely but . . ." She was backing away from Sherwood reluctantly, pulled by her daughter.

"You see, it won't keep. It's something alive."

"Alive! Oh, good Heavens, I do not want another puppy, Sheila. I'll give it right back to you!"

As they climbed the stairs, Sheila reflected that her mother made quick recoveries. She seemed to tuck away the hurts of life in some attic of her mind, and carry on.

In her room, Sheila produced from her suitcase a gossamer scarf in flowery colors and swirled it in the air.

"It *is* alive!" Her mother took it, let it glide from hand to hand, floated it over her head and spiraled it around the room.

"Oh, my dear . . . I never had . . . anything . . . so beautiful."

"I'm glad. It's nice on your hair."

Muriel sat down on the bed, the scarf adorning her, and stole glances at herself in the long mirror opposite.

"Uncle Woody's nice. Much nicer than I remembered."

"You think so?"

"Well, don't you?"

"Sherwood has disappointed me . . . terribly. He has been, well, he has been untrue to me."

"Really? How?"

"Another woman. I don't wish to talk about it."

She paused, eager to talk about it.

"Somebody here? On campus?"

"No, no. Off campus."

Funny how the old habit came back: the world was divided into two parts—on campus and off campus.

"Of course, I don't wish to imply that there has ever been anything *between* Sherwood and me."

"Then how could he be 'untrue' to you?"

"We had an *understanding*. For all these years. Ever since your father died. Now I find out that he has been looking elsewhere. *Searching* elsewhere!"

"Mother, *searching* is not *finding*."

"Never mind. I have not let him know that I know. It would be too embarassing, humiliating. But when his leg is better, Sherwood Pell is leaving this house and I shall never, never speak to him again."

She touched her handkerchief to her eyes and Sheila put her arm around her mother, eager to put a stop to what her father used to call "the waterworks."

"That's a shame, Mother. Woody's such an *attractive* man. Respected on campus. A friend of Father's, an escort anywhere you might want to go. I wonder how many million women would snap at Uncle Woody?"

"They're more than welcome."

"Of course, he'll be rich as cream."

"*Sherwood?*"

"When he takes this play to New York."

"Nonsense, child!"

"Mother, it's going to happen. Believe me."

"You're dreaming, child, as always."

"After his big success, Woody will probably marry.

His wife will have everything her heart desires. If it's you," Muriel was shaking her head, "if it should *happen* to be you, I wonder what you'd do with all that money. Apart from lifetime security and a sable coat, I think you'd give a stained-glass window to the church, in memory of Father."

"Oh, my dear," Muriel looked up, seeing the window. "If you knew how I've always wanted—"

"Yes. I also know you're a real Christian. You're not going to throw Woody out on the street. You have too much charity. Also, too much horse sense."

The two women looked at each other. Muriel reached for Sheila's hand and held it.

"It's so long since we've had a talk. I'm going to remember everything you've said. And I'm so glad you came."

"I'm glad, too. And Mother, will you help me?"

"How do you mean, dear?"

"Val's going to read for Woody tomorrow. If Woody thinks Val's a flaming genius, will you think so, too?"

"Sheila, what do I know?"

"More than you think. Mother, promise me. Be on my side. Help me."

"Oh, my dear. Your father died. My friend Gwennie died. You're all I have left. I'd walk on hot coals for you."

Sheila hugged her mother and felt the firm suppleness of her body. She was plump, but there were no bulges. She looked into her mother's face, pink-cheeked and bright-eyed, and suddenly felt very tired.

"Let's go to bed, Mother."

They went downstairs, where the men had switched to Scotch and soda and Sherwood was telling Val why he would never, under any circumstances, return to Broadway. A good sign, thought Sheila. They all said their good-nights, leaving Muriel to "put Sherwood to bed."

When Sheila had changed into nightgown and robe, she crept silently down the hall and opened Val's creaking door. He was stretched out on the bed in his shorts, clutching the script and devouring it with his eyes. He did not look up. This was either fanatical concentration, or an actor's fine facsimile. Sheila closed the door and retreated to her room.

Who got hold of that script for him, anyway? Why was she always shooting herself in the foot? She crawled into her childhood bed, alone again.

CHAPTER

10

SHEILA HAD BARELY sunk into sleep when she heard her door creaking open. Val must have finished the script. She raised herself on one elbow and turned on the bedside lamp. The figure in the doorway was tall, wearing jeans, and had long, pale hair. Not Val. The figure whispered.

"Mom?"

"Kerry!"

The child came to the bed, shrugged off a backpack, and wrapped Sheila in a giggling, smothering hug.

"S'prise! S'prise!"

"Kerry, I can't believe—how did you—Kerry, what are you *doing* here?"

"Talking to you. Listen, it's easier to talk to the Pope. How are you anyway?"

"Kerry, how did you know I was *here?*"

"Couldn't get you on phone, called Mrs. Terenzio. She said you were making a *visita* to the *madre*. Caught the next flight after yours!"

"You could have called me!"

"I had enough of those phone calls. The ones where

you'll tell me everything later. I never felt so rejected in my whole life. Mom, you've practically been hanging up on me!"

"I'm sorry, I—"

"That's okay, I'm here, we can talk."

"*Talk* about *what?*"

"Mother! You're having a major life crisis. I can tell. I'm having a major life crisis. We need to *talk*. What do we have airplanes for?"

"But Kerry," Sheila looked up at this flaxen-haired child sitting on her bed and gasped for words. "I'm glad to see you, but Kerry—I'm not *ready* for this!"

"No hurry. We've got all weekend. Geez, is it ever hot in Kansas!" She was stripping off her shirt and slithering out of her jeans. In bra and panties, she flopped down on the narrow bed beside Sheila and propped her eager face against one childish hand.

"You're not sleepy, are you? I'm revved up like you wouldn't believe. Listen, how's Grammy? You think she'll make popovers for breakfast? I mean I actually *dream* about Gammy's popovers. You realize I haven't been here since I was eight years old and *teething?* I think that's terrible. I mean, I believe in ancestors and roots and all that crap. I think you should have brought me out here every year. 'Dashing through the snow, to Gammy's house we go!' And cookies baking and big brown turkeys and cranberries that *pop* when you bite them! You think I'm a belly slave? Listen, you look practically anorexic. All right. Now you go first and tell me what you came out here for. Yeah, to see a play. Like there's not fifty plays on Broadway one hour from your house. So after you clear that up, I get to talk about Italy this summer and Angelo, you know, my art teacher. Okay, you go first. Mother, *talk*. Tell me you're not mad at me for coming. Mom, *talk* to me!"

"Oh, Kerry." Sheila embraced the child and smoothed back her hair and kissed her forehead, then fell back to stare at the ceiling. "I'm not mad at you. I just want to break your neck."

"*Why*, Mom?"

"Kerry, I came out here for a reason. I'm here . . . well, on business."

"You mean—*your* business . . . is none of *my* business?" The child looked shattered.

"Oh, Kerry, no! Don't you see, I . . ."

Kerry clutched her mother's arm and whispered. "Mom! Listen! Somebody's there!"

They stared, as a man's shaggy head came around the creaking door.

"Sheila?"

Val wore only briefest briefs, gleaming white in the dim light. Sheila covered Kerry's mouth just before the inevitable scream. Val approached the bed and stopped when he saw two figures side by side, motionless. There was an endless pause.

"I need a good line here," said Val.

Sheila struggled from the bed, covering Kerry with the sheet. She tried to push Val toward the door, gave up and moved away.

"You've got to be Kerry," said Val, peering down at the bed.

"Yeah. Who're you?"

"Val Keating." He went to the bed, Kerry sat up, and they shook hands. "I'm very glad to meet you."

"Yeah," said Kerry dully. Val backed away smiling and turned toward Sheila.

"Guess I should have knocked. Afraid of waking Muriel."

"Kerry . . . just . . . dropped in."

"Uh-huh. Me, too." He smiled at them both. Sheila glanced from Val, nearly naked, to Kerry in small, pink triangles to her own unchaste garment, and all in her mother's house.

"Val, get lost."

"Yes, Ma'am."

He turned, and with what Sheila considered an excess of protocol, shook hands again with Kerry.

"It's been—significant."

He went to Sheila and kissed her forehead.

"That's one dynamite daughter." And he was gone.

"*Moth-er!*" Kerry's eyes were huge and glittering.

"That's the one! I told you about him!"

"You told me you had lunch! Walked in the Park!"

"Kerry, sh-h-h, you'll wake Gammy!"

"You didn't tell me you were bringing him to Kansas! Stark naked!" It came out as a shrieking whisper.

"Darling, I wanted to tell you. It all happened so fast." Why did she have to fall into clichés?

"I mean *fast!* You only met him on Monday!" Like her father, Kerry always remembered days and dates.

"Kerry, I'm in love. Crazy in love."

"After *five days?* You're having a thing with that man and you've known him for *five days?*"

"I guess we weren't counting. Kerry, that's why I couldn't tell you on the phone. I knew you'd be shocked. But Kerry, it's *real.*" Sheila wondered what quirk of fate had brought her to this point of apologizing to her daughter for this natural wonder, this gust of happiness that had blown into her life.

"Kerry, we saw Uncle Woody's play tonight and it's a winner. If I can get him to bring it to New York, it will make Val a star. Oh, Kerry, be happy for me!" She hugged her daughter.

"I think it's great, Mom. Really great."

With their heads touching, Sheila could almost feel the thoughts whirring through Kerry's brain. In the half-dark, she could see a new set to the young face. Slowly, she pulled back from her daughter and waited.

"Now maybe you'll understand about Angelo."

"I do understand."

"I'm in love, too. Angelo and I have been lovers since December thirteenth. At midnight."

"Oh, Kerry," Sheila touched the smooth face and turned it toward her own. "Kerry, baby."

"Now you see why I have to go to Italy this summer. I can't live for two months without Angelo. I would die."

"I know, darling."

"I mean really die. Do you believe me?"

"Some part of you will die. But Kerry, he'll come back."

"I have to go, Mother. I spent my camp money to

135

come out here and ask you. Beg you. Give me four thousand bucks. Please."

Sheila could not bear the urgency of the outstretched hands, the trembling mouth. She rose and walked to the window.

"Kerry, I *can't!* We don't *have* that kind of money!"

"You don't *have* it! Don't kid me, Mom. You flew out here with him, didn't you? Your treat, I'll bet. And what else is your treat? If you take this dumb play to New York, it'll cost you plenty, right? You going to chuck your work or what? You going to retire, while you promote *him?* Don't tell me you don't have money! You have money for *him* but not for me!"

"Kerry, I told you on the phone." But the child was angry beyond reach. She flung herself from the bed, her long-legged runner's body a head taller than her mother's. Her angry face looked down into Sheila's and it belonged to a stranger.

"And it 'all happened so fast' says you." She imitated her dreamy tone. "And you're the one that always told me, 'Make a friend, *then* make love,'" She walked to the bowl of pansies, plucked one out, and crushed it. "So I did. I dated Angelo for months and months. We were climbing the walls, but we got to be friends, *before* we hit the sack. What about you? One week of making out with this unemployed actor and you're ready to trade me in for him! Me! My whole life! My happiness! For him and his crappy play!"

Sheila reached for her, but Kerry pulled away, with tears in her eyes.

"I'm your daughter! Remember me? Nah, what's a daughter compared to a big hunk of *stud?*"

Sheila trembled with the need to hit the child. Her hands were clenched together, tearing against each other. She stared at this brutal young girl. Where had she come from?

"I'll never, never trust you again."

Kerry threw herself down on the bed, sobbing. Sheila moved slowly to sit beside here. Now she was a child again, weeping, needing comfort. Sheila petted her, kissing her shoulder, smoothing the hair back from her cheek. Several times, Sheila started to speak . . . to say what? That she would give up Val and his play? . . . *Not . . . bloody . . . likely.*

She stroked her daughter's shoulders and back, slowly, rhythmically. She heard the sobs catch in Kerry's throat, with longer intervals of quiet. Finally, she heard the breathing become deeper. She turned out the light and lay down slowly beside her sleeping daughter.

CHAPTER
11

I N THE MORNING, Sheila returned from the bathroom to find Kerry sitting up in bed, hugging her knees. She searched the child's face for a sign.

"Hi, Beany."

"Let's go home, right after breakfast."

"No, Kerry. I'm committed to this. Shall we talk about it?"

"What's to talk? I'm asking you. Drop the whole stinking, shitty idea."

"No, darling, I can't."

"All right. I'm going to trash it for you."

Sheila looked once more at the hostile, stranger's face. She struggled to find an attitude, a way to meet this new and unimagined hurt and gave up.

"I can't fight before breakfast."

Sheila found Woody sipping fresh orange juice, the table set, and Muriel prancing in from the yard with Val in tow.

"This crazy boy! He wants my home-grown lettuce for breakfast!" She brushed the bright green leaves against his cheek. "I only hope he isn't staying long!

Eating me out of house and home like this!" She kissed
Sheila gaily and trotted back and forth with steaming
coffee and plates of pancakes, chattering nonstop about
the weather, the birds breakfasting on her strawberry
bed, and the range-fed chicken's eggs she would be
happy to fix for everybody. Val was standing beside
Woody's bed, the rolled-up script in his hand, and
caught Sheila's eye with the look of lovers who know, all
evidence to the contrary notwithstanding, that the world
is a resplendent place. Then Kerry stood in the doorway.

Muriel gave a gasp of surprise, put one hand to her
bosom. "Why, *Kerry*, how did you *get* here? Sheila, you
wicked child, you didn't *tell* me!" She embraced her
granddaughter, clucking and chirping. "So tall, so
strong, the image of her grandfather, of course."

Val and Kerry were introduced, as if for the first
time ever, and a place was set for Kerry next to Val.
Finally, with sighs and flutters, Muriel came to rest at
the head of the table and surveyed them all.

"Well! This *is* a surprise! My grandmother always
knew when company was coming. The grass on the
plains was eight feet tall in those days. She would look
out from the back porch over the valley and call out to
Grandpa, 'Poppa! Company's coming! I can see the grass
waving,' and sure enough, after a spell, along would
come a horse and rider, parting their way through the
grass." Her small hands parted the air in front of her.
"But, of course, nobody's company here today. I have my
very own granddaughter, and my dear daughter, and her
very dear and very *talented* friend." She beamed at them
all and Sheila recognized gratefully that the first blow

had been struck, no matter how ingenuously, for the cause. She flashed her mother a smile and her mother bridled and dimpled. This was a woman, thought Sheila, who should have had a huge family growing up around her, instead of one crabby and distant daughter.

Kerry began quizzing Val on his schools, his jobs, his sports.

"I was a natural for running. No wind resistance."

"What did you run?"

"The four-forty hurdles."

"Me, too."

"No foolin'. What's your best time?"

"I can beat you silly." She smiled at him, the slanted eyes gleaming.

"I wouldn't take candy from a baby." Val was grinning, too. But they used the jeering tone of children, and Sheila felt an unaccountable chill.

"Want to bet?"

"Not on a sure thing."

"Let's see the color of your money." Kerry sounded almost grotesquely tough, street smart.

Val dug in his pocket and produced a bill, slapped it down on the table. Kerry dug into her jeans and covered the bill with two of her own.

"See you and raise you."

"Kerry, don't be silly," Sheila said. "Val is ten years out of college!" She kept her voice casual as she embellished the truth by a year or two. Val did not take his eyes off Kerry, but he sounded equally casual.

"Not to worry, lamb chop."

"Val, she's on the varsity track team. She runs like a bullet!"

"Lay off, Mother." To Val, "Hey, stud. Are you going to cover my bet, or not?"

Val peeled off another bill and slapped it down. Then he handed the money to Muriel.

"Will you hold the stakes, Muriel?" But Muriel caught Sheila's look.

"Certainly not. I don't approve of gambling." She returned the bills to Val, who tucked them into the appleblossoms of the centerpiece. Kerry snatched the bills out and Val snatched them back from her, both uttering cries of "Oh, no you don't!" and "Hey, give me that!" The others watched the by-play in silence, until Woody spoke up with Olympian authority.

"I find the war between the sexes inappropriate at the breakfast table. After all, we are present at the birth of a day. Mornings should be greeted in a mood of quiet, but not excessive, anticipation."

Kerry threw back her head and let out a peal of laughter. "Uncle Woody, you're a panic! Does your play sound like that?"

"Yes," Val said, "and you won't understand it, brat. But it'll be good for you to try." Before Kerry could reply, Val turned to Woody. "You said I could read for you today, sir."

"I look forward to it."

"I'd like to read onstage."

"My dear boy, I am, as you see, immobilized."

"No sweat. I'll pick you up like a crate of eggs, put

you in your wheelchair, drive you to the theater—trust me." Woody sized up the young, gaunt figure. Val had risen from the table and was standing behind his chair, in an exaggerated body-builder pose.

"If you drop me, I'll burn your Equity card."

"Never lost a director yet," said Val cheerfully. "I want to read with the little English girl we saw last night. Piper York. Sheila, can you con her into it?"

Sheila had never seen this take-charge side of Val before. Suddenly, breakfast was over, Muriel was clearing the table, Val bringing Woody his shaving things. Sheila telephoned from Muriel's ruffled pink bedroom and located Piper York's residence hall. She found Kerry face down on their bed.

"I'm going to find Piper York. Want to come with me?"

"Try and stop me."

"Kerry, I know how you feel, but you're mistaken. The play is not stopping you from going to Italy. I am. I think you should wait at least another year."

"I always thought you were a 'liberated mother.' Was I ever wrong. You're narrow-minded and mean . . . You're my enemy."

Sheila tried not to feel the scalding words. She turned away and jerked a comb through her hair, then turned back to the tall young person she had loved so well.

"We'll be friends again. In the meantime . . ." How long would the meantime be? "In the meantime, you are one rotten kid!"

Sheila ran down the stairs and Kerry followed. They

drove to the university in silence. Sheila chose to park the car at the Alumni Center so that they would walk across campus together, the campus where Sheila had once been a student, also young, also poor. She showed her daughter the Oread bookstore, where she had worked all through her undergraduate years. At the Student Union, they picked up the *University Daily Kansan*, on which Sheila had once been a "paid" staff writer. The pay, Sheila added, was microscopic, so she also slammed trays around in the cafeteria.

"So you had two jobs, big deal. You realize I hung seven student shows for Angelo this semester and posed for life class and mucked out the locker room for track? Besides, you were living off-campus with Daddy the last couple of years, riding around in a convertible. So tell me about poverty, Mom, I bet it was rough."

Sheila was stung and fell into silence, knowing she had joined the ranks of ponderous parents at last, telling her offspring of the hardships she had endured. She had become a MOTHER, that figurehead, that law-giver who says, "Try to be more like me." She had been Kerry's friend, protector, older sister, but that was a delusion. It was impossible, in the nature of things, to have an honest, loving friendship—between equals—with one's own beloved child.

Sheila gazed around her at the sublime spring morning. As she walked beside Kerry, the warmth of the sun fell on their heads like a blessing they were not in a state of grace to receive. They were following an ample walkway that wound past clipped lawns and some of the fine old campus buildings. Flags snapped gaily on top of

143

Frazer Hall. Even the Jay Hawk, that ugly mythical bird in front of Administration, was looking at them benignly. Redbud and flowering fruit trees tumbled down green slopes and students passed by laughing in their careless, summery clothes. How could so much felicity parade before her eyes and leave Sheila's heart so somber?

She noted all the old landmarks, each one bringing back a cluster of memories. In front of Wescoe Hall the students still lounged on "Wescoe Beach," a series of low concrete walls where you could hang out and work on your tan. Nearby, Sheila noticed six or eight students gathered loosely in a circle and bouncing a small, leather ball from foot, to knee, to leg and on to the next player. The game was played so casually, so effortlessly that it hardly seemed to be happening at all, yet obviously required considerable skill. While Sheila watched, not one player let the ball escape him. The angular figures simply stood there, cooly and quietly, with a bend of the knee and a slip of the foot passing the ball, no hands, around the circle. This was surely the most laid back occupation ever invented. Sheila asked the inevitable question.

"What's it called?"

"Hacky Sack," said Kerry, in a tone that proclaimed her mother's appalling ignorance.

"I should have known," said Sheila. She could feel Kerry's sidelong glance and the unspoken question, "Are you putting me on, Mother?" but Sheila gave no sign.

They passed the campanile tower, always affectionately called "the Tooth," and Sheila heard it chime the hour. As the silvery notes floated down around them, and out across Potter Lake shimmering in the hollow below, Sheila wondered whether Kerry heard the sweetness. She wanted to ask, but bit back the words. Weren't mothers forever asking "Do you hear it? Do you see it? Isn't it *beautiful?* Aren't you having a wonderful time?" Then, too, she supposed there was always the implied question: "Aren't you glad I gave myself all that trouble and brought you into the world?"

The chimes fell silent, and the moment went unremarked. As they came to the lake, Sheila watched a cloud reflection drift toward the shore and playfully bump the mirror image of an apple tree, itself a cloud of blossoms, an encounter filled with mystery and delight. But Sheila would die on the rack before she would mention it to this big, surly child who used to be her friend.

Not a moment too soon, they arrived at the residence where Piper York was living. They walked up stairways and down corridors cacophonous with Saturday morning stereos. As they knocked on her door, Piper herself padded up behind them, her head wrapped in one towel, her small body in another. After apologies and introductions, Piper led them into her chaotic room.

At first the child seemed very small offstage, very usual. She could have been any one of the healthy, pleasant young things gathered into this "people factory" to spend four years "becoming." But as she whirled about the room, flipping the bedspread and tossing pillows, there was a magic in her fluid movements and darting, weightless hoverings. She motioned them to be seated and lit on the corner of her desk. A dragonfly could not have been more hypnotic to the eye. Sheila said she had seen the play and admired Piper's performance.

"Thank you *so* much. At first I didn't *understand* the play, you see. I thought it was all bits and pieces, like a jumble sale. But I do think it's *starting* to come together, as Professor Pell kept promising it would, and I'm *quite* enjoying it. I do hope you'll come and see us again on opening night?"

She spoke in a light, British voice with darting flights and a rising inflection. Sheila explained why they had come.

"So Val is going to audition right now and he's hoping you'll read with him. Will you . . . please?"

"Now? At the theater? Oh, I say, what a lark!"

Sheila blessed the spontaneous lives of the young, as Piper ducked into a dress, raked her hair, chomped an apple, and stood beckoning to them at the door.

Kerry, quiet but watchful up till now, fell in beside Piper on the stairs. Outside, on the paths across campus, two could walk abreast more easily than three. Sheila followed the girls, while snatches of their chatter floated back to her.

"Mummy's a famous model, she was, you see, and then she married Daddy. So now it's all tea in the drawing room and shall we sell off great-grandfather by Romney or open the place to the barbarians. That's the Americans, I'm afraid . . . frightfully boring for Mummy. So I really must be a huge success as an actress, as I don't doubt I shall be. Your mother's divorced, isn't she? I can always tell, she *looks*

146

divorced . . . of course, one misses the horses and dogs. And the younger brother Alfie, just *oozing* out of the painful stage. But I shall *die* to leave America, though everyone has vowed to come and stay, and you must come, too, please say you will . . ."

Kerry's tall athletic body curved slightly toward Piper's tiny figure beside her. Piper's cropped head was tilted up to Kerry, who had shortened her stride so they walked in step. When they parted to let other students pass, and came back together again, they were still in stride. They broke into each other's sentences and overlapped each other's thoughts. They might have been friends since the cradle.

"But you'll *adore* Italy! You'll adore Florence! *Firenze e bellissima!*"

Kerry responded in Italian, sounding surprisingly fluent. Her voice was pitched lower, but clearly the dialogue had arrived at Angelo.

"Ah, Angelo! *Che bel nome!* . . . *Dovresti vedere che bel ragazzo è . . . ed è anche molto simpatico . . . É una bella fortuna per te . . . devi esserne molto felice!*"

But for Piper's love life they reverted to English. "My dear, I haven't any! Truly! I shall be the bride of the theater! No, a concubine, passed from play to play!"

"Not to Uncle Woody, I hope!"

"Oh, mercy no!" Piper giggled. "That *dear* old gentleman!"

Kerry broke in, "Listen, you watch out . . . I'm telling you—a crackpot, nutty as a fruitcake . . ." She had lowered her voice, so that Sheila caught only

147

snatches. "My mother, you know . . . as for the boy-friend . . . No, honestly, I *swear* to you . . . listen, I'll tell you later. . . ."

The two girls piled into the back seat together so that "Mom could have the air conditioner to herself. She gets all red and puffy when it's hot."

Sheila drove to the theater, teeth clenched. They entered and found Woody parked in his wheelchair in the center aisle down front. Val was onstage, pacing. Sheila took a seat near Woody and Kerry slammed down a seat several rows behind them. Piper skimmed up the stage, stage right, and crossed to shake hands with Val. They could be heard murmuring their names, Val thanking her for coming, Piper shaking her head as she touched his bare forearm with the lightest possible tap.

A bare work light hung from the flies at center stage, washing the two young faces in a cold, flat light and leaving the corners of the bare stage dark with shadow. Now the actors were opening and leafing through their two black-bound play scripts, searching for a scene to use for the audition. They stood side by side, the top of Piper's head barely reaching Val's shoulder. They conferred in whispers.

"When you're ready, people!" Woody's voice was sharp and businesslike.

"We'll take it from the top, sir." Val disappeared into the wings and Piper ran to perch on the edge of a platform, a lost young maiden.

Val made his entrance on "horseback," supplying the hoofbeats himself. He made his way through a "forest" whose invisible "brambles" caught at his clothes. He forded a "stream" that filled his boots with water on the bone-dry stage. Hearing the sound of weeping, he dismounted and came downstage to speak to Piper. Hearing his voice again, Sheila felt a shock of pleasure, and saw Woody give a quick, small lift of his head and then sit very still.

They went through the whole first act, hardly glancing at their scripts, quickly learning each other's timing and falling into the give-and-take, the sheer fun of play-acting. Piper seemed to mature as the strange story unfolded, bringing more weight to the role. In a tragic scene where the lovers are torn apart, she seemed to catch Val's intensity and move with him beyond her well-bred English limits. She lacked Val's technique, but there was a reserve of passion inside her small, young person.

When the act was finished, no curtain fell and no lights flared up. Actors and audience were left beached, stranded. Sheila burst into a solitary salvo of applause, and felt foolish. Val and Piper grinned and mockingly took their bows, then quickly hugged each other and left the stage together, arms around waists. For one stinging second, Sheila wished they would both drop dead.

But Val came straight to where she sat and kissed her, then went to stand in front of Woody's wheelchair, grinning down at him.

"I want a run-of-the-play contract and I'll work for Equity minimum. Okay?"

But Woody wrenched at the wheels of his chair, spun it around, and started himself up the aisle.

"Did you have to give me the whole, blasted act?

It's an hour past lunchtime and not a breath of air in this confounded theater!" He was struggling to roll his chair up the incline. "Push the blasted thing, will you?" Val got behind and pushed. "You, Piper York, join us for lunch—if you're so inclined."

They all looked at each other in the wake of his wrath. As they filed out, Kerry whispered to Piper. "See? I told you! He's a loony! The food'll be good, anyway."

The two cars arrived at Muriel's house in tandem and Muriel ran to to greet them. While Val was lifting Woody from car to wheelchair, the invalid kept up a scathing commentary.

"You'll never make it as an orderly, young man. I know several hospitals that would pay you to stay away. You have the touch of a charging bull. When this unfortunate incident is over, I shall probably be forced to have my leg broken and reset. Do you realize you are cutting off the blood supply to my left arm and gangrene is setting in? Oh, God help me, he's broken my neck. Muriel, I want you to expel this man from your house. Have him arrested for criminal negligence. Ah, merciful God, she's brought the coat-hanger."

Muriel unhooked from the belt of her apron a wire coat-hanger, straightened it, and handed it to Woody, now in his chair. Whimpering with anticipation, he inserted the coat-hanger between his leg and the cast, moving it slowly up and down, with little cries of muted ecstasy.

"It's the hot weather," said Muriel. "His cast gets itchy, doesn't it, dear?"

They lifted him up on the porch, where Muriel had

set out huge platters of thin sandwiches and pitchers of ice-cold drinks. Woody soon had Piper fetching and carrying for him. "No, no, not the cucumber! Don't you know that cucumber sandwiches were the downfall of the British Empire? Endow me with curried egg. Bestow on me the beef. And spare not the gleaming slices of love-apple, which the groundlings call to-*mah*-toes."

Then, suddenly, he turned on Val.

"All right, Val Keating, where were you twelve years ago when I needed you?"

"I was . . . I was at Falls City, Nebraska, Junior High School."

"I could kill you for that, Keating. I needed you desperately that year. I was heartbroken by the whore-house they call 'Broadway.' If you had come to me then, I would have stayed and fought it out." He paused and looked out toward the street. "I think you have the biggest talent since the young Olivier. I think you are supremely gifted. There is no limit to what you can do." Now his look came back to Val, and his voice was barely controlled. "But damn you, Keating, damn you to hell! You've *come* . . . *too* . . . late!"

Nobody spoke. Woody picked up a sandwich and looked at it as if he'd never seen a sandwich before. One could not be sure, on the shadowy porch, whether it was tears that made his eyes shine so.

12

AFTER WOODY'S OUTBURST, the talk swirled around his bitter silence. When lunch was over, Kerry and Piper said they would walk to the stadium to see a track meet. Sheila offered to pick up Kerry afterward, but Kerry preferred to walk back, barefoot over hot coals being the implication.

As Muriel started to clear the dishes, Sheila and Val slipped into chairs on either side of Woody. Val spoke first.

"I wish I'd been there fifteen years ago. Over my dead body you'd have walked out on Broadway."

"How vivid, how touching," came the glacial reply.

"Fact is, I was late getting born. I apologize."

"I implore you, don't get whimsical, Keating."

"But now," said Val, impervious, "I'm here and you're here. Are we going to sit around and bitch—or shall we get the show on the road?"

Woody sent him a look that would drill through stone, and then closed his eyes in pain. "Shall we cut this lugubrious conversation to the bone? You can't do this play because I don't have the rights. The author has gone to Greece for the summer, address unknown. Am I clear?"

"Hell, I can find the guy in Greece! Small country, bright sunshine." He opened his script, never far from his hand, to the title page and read the author's name, " 'Jason Pelias,' huh? Sheila, pack for Athens!"

Woody roared at him. "Back off, Keating! You want me to tell you every last reason why this half-witted scheme of yours won't work? All right. I'm up for dean of fine arts this year, and I expect to make it! You think I'm going to toss away twelve years of grueling labor in this Midwestern backwater to make you a star on Broadway? You and who else, Keating? Do you have an established, first-magnitude costar in mind? Don't you know it takes at least one big name today, and I mean a household word, before you can book a theater? With your name I couldn't book a phone booth!"

"But I'm available." Val smiled his wide, disarming smile, but Woody was not disarmed.

"There are many other reasons why I cannot take this play to New York, but I find this conversation has all the fun and frolic of beating a dead horse. Keating, it has been a useless experience to meet you, and a painful one to witness your idle and wasted talent. Muriel, I shall return to my bed and receive no visitors."

"Of course, dear." Muriel hastened to wheel him in. While Val held the screen door open, she chattered on, "So very warm for May, isn't it? I think we'll take our bed-bath now and get into our nice, cool pajamas. Won't that be nice?"

"And I won't have that young man admitted to my sickroom. Suffering has its privileges, however small."

Val and Sheila shared a look, and without another word, ran silently upstairs and into Val's bedroom. He shut the door and fell back against it, pulling Sheila to him and holding her, running his hands over her back and buttocks, kissing her lips and cheeks and eyes.

"Geez, I didn't know we were coming out here for the celibate life, I'd have shaved my head." He was opening her shirt and drawing her toward the bed.

"Val, wait, we can't."

"Why not?"

"My mother."

"You're kidding." He sat her down on the bed, went to the door, turned the long black key in the lock, and came back to her. "Okay? Mummy can't come in."

"But she'll *know!*"

"So what?"

"She told me." Sheila started to giggle in spite of herself. "She said . . . 'not under her roof.'"

"Now look, honey."

"Val, we *need* her!"

"Baby, I need you!" He reached for her, but she sprang off the bed and stood behind a wicker rocking chair, her hands clutching the back.

"Val, please, listen. I can't make her angry. She's got to help us, this is going to be hard! Tonight, after she's asleep, I'll come."

"You swear to me?"

"I swear."

Their eyes held each other for a minute, then Val

fell back full length on the bed, arms wide, face staring up.

"Is this *real?* We're together. We're alone. And we *can't?* I don't *believe* this!"

"Val, I've been dying for you."

"I almost pulled you under the dining-room table!"

"You look sexy in New York and Connecticut, but in Kansas—in Kansas, you make my arms ache."

They yearned toward each other, he on the bed and she barricaded behind the chair. For one long instant, Sheila was pulled between two desires, and then, "You were so good this morning, and I was so proud of you. Val, I want you to do this play."

"Me, too."

"Uncle Woody's our problem."

"Problem! He's set in concrete!"

"But what is he really saying?"

"I think I heard the word 'no.'"

Sheila came around the chair to sit down and start rocking slowly, meditatively.

"He's saying three things. First, he doesn't have an option on the play. Do you believe that?"

Val glanced at her face and quickly responded, "No."

"Right. I don't know why, but no."

Val moved his long body imperceptibly sideways across the bed toward Sheila, like a sidewinder in slow motion. Sheila went on. "Second, he might be appointed dean of fine arts. We'll have to check that out."

"How?" Val moved another imperceptible fraction.

"My mother's a bird dog," said Sheila.

"Hey, pup." He moved a fraction closer.

"The third thing is, he wants a big name. That's a tough one."

"I want little Piper York."

"Val, if we can *get* a big name, we will!"

"Oh, sure, sure." Val was by now almost at the edge of his bed. Sheila, rocking away, head thrown back to gaze at the ceiling, was intent on the problem.

"So we have to knock out his three reasons, before the weekend is over. Val, this is Saturday afternoon! *How are we going to do it?*"

"Why not the same old way?"

"What?"

Val gave a roar, lunged from his bed, planted one foot on the tip of the rocker, and stamped. Sheila was flung forward and into his arms. He threw her on the bed and stood grinning down at her where she lay, helpless with laughter. With one knee on the bed, he ran his hand under her skirt and up along her thigh. Sheila could feel her purpose dissolving, until nothing existed except a craving for him, a hunger that remembered the joining of their bodies and obssessed her totally until they were joined again.

To Sheila, every time they made love was different. This time Val seemed to be reaching for some inner part of her, something he would not allow her to deny him. "Don't think . . . don't go away from me . . . You're all mine, you hear? I want you sexy and hot, *right here, right now.*" How could she be anywhere else when every nerve in her body was taut with longing for him? She embraced him fiercely, losing all sense of time and place and self, becoming totally her desire.

And yet, when they had climbed this mountain of passion and tumbled slowly, dreamlike, down the other side, Sheila had a dim perception of a truth quite different from his. They would be separated, if they ever were, not by anything she might withhold from him, but because Val inhabited a country where she could not follow him, a country where joy was an element he breathed, his customary climate. This man lived on the edge of laughter, almost immune to pain, a man who found the world made perfectly to his measure. In all her life, Sheila had never known anyone with such a gift for happiness. She lay quietly next to him, and wished she were not so far away, in her own, more desolate country.

They dressed quickly. When Muriel came, she found the door wide open, and Sheila primly rocking.

"I hope I'm not intruding."

"We've been waiting for you," said Val, all smiles.

"Mother, we need you."

"Of course, dear."

"You and I are going out this afternoon. Val will stay here and take care of Woody."

"But Sherwood can't *abide* Val! Excuse me, my dear, it's certainly not your fault, but he says you should have had better timing! He never wants to see you again!"

"He'll see him," said Sheila. "Val will wait in the living room. Shall we go, Mother?"

Val followed them downstairs and stood in the hall, listening. Sheila pushed her mother out the front door, then stepped into the dining room.

"Uncle Woody, Mother and I are leaving I'm afraid. She's had an emergency call from the hospital, and I'll be working at the library. But Val is here if you need him."

"*I do not need Val Keating!*"

"Right. See you later, Uncle Woody!"

As she left, Sheila passed Val the precious coat-hanger. With a quick kiss, she was gone. According to later reports, Woody endured for one hour before he called to Val.

"*Keating, you get in here!*"

Val came tripping along in a perfect imitation of Muriel, hands fluttering and bosom heaving.

"Oh, Sherwood, I thought you'd *never* call!"

Woody broke up, Val handed him the coat-hanger, and they spent the afternoon reviling Broadway.

Sheila and her mother took Muriel's car, Muriel chattering away about her neighbor's drier that must have broken down again because there was her laundry out on the line, not that God's own sunshine wasn't the best drier after all.

"Mother, this isn't going to be easy."

"What, dear?"

"We're here to get hold of a play."

"Yes, of course. We'll just get down to business."

This expression of her mother's had always covered everything from putting up tomatoes to getting a dry law through the state legislature. Her mother lived in a wash of optimism.

"All right, Mother, can you get us a Broadway star?"

"No, but Sherwood can."

"Wha-at?"

"I'll show you. When I pick you up, we'll go to Sherwood's house."

"What for?"

"Ask me no questions, I'll tell you no lies." It was sayings like this that had made Sheila an old woman at the age of six.

"Do you think Woody will be appointed dean of fine arts?"

"How should I know, dear? But I can certainly find out."

"Tonight?"

"Tonight! Good heavens, child!"

"Mother, we're leaving tomorrow afternoon. Val has to get back to work. So do I."

"Rome was not built in a day." Sheila clenched her teeth. "Can't you work right here in Lawrence? You could use your father's study and finish your book in no time!"

"*No*, Mother!" Sheila heard a note of panic in her own voice. "No, thank you. When Val leaves, I leave."

"How sweet."

Sheila was shaken. If they failed to persuade Woody, she could accept that. Separation from Val, she could not. "I . . . am . . . leaving here . . . tomorrow." The sentence came out like so many blows of a sledgehammer.

"Very well, dear."

Muriel dropped Sheila at the Watson Library and picked her up exactly an hour later. Woody's house turned out to be a Victorian confection, with towers and turrets rising from shadowy porches. Slender columns were connected by arches of glistening white lace. Windows wore elegantly raised "eyebrows," and every balcony was outlined by a frill of balustrade. Sheila thought how like Woody to live in a perfect stageset.

"How does he paint it?"

"With a toothbrush," her mother tartly replied.

Inside, Sheila found a house perfectly suited to a "theater person." Crimson draperies fell dramatically from high ceilings to dark, gleaming floors. The furniture was sparse, the paintings few and cleverly lit. Polished tables held one fine porcelain, one silver goblet. To Sheila, thinking of her own bombed-out ruin of a house, it was a room of maddening discipline. She was thankful to find Woody's study an inviting mess, programs and play scripts stacked everywhere, curling snapshots tucked into bookcases. The two rooms spoke of a public and a private Sherwood Pell: an elegant, austere man, and a rather dear, muddle-through type like the rest of us.

Muriel sat Sheila down at Woody's desk and showed her Woody's "personal": a "witty and worldly professor" who was seeking a "comely companion."

"*Woody?*"

"Not only that, my dear. Look at these letters!"

Muriel took a packet of Amanda's letters and Woody's responses from the file and plunked them down in front of Sheila. "Read them!"

"Mother, I can't! They're private! Did *you* read them?"

"I *skimmed* them." A little bit pregnant, thought Sheila. "Her name is Amanda."

"Amanda Hapgood?"

"Possibly."

"Mother, she's a major star!"

"Why do you think I brought you here?" said the cat who had swallowed a quart of cream.

Sheila paused. Did the end ever justify the means? Could she bring herself to read other peoples' letters, for Val's sake? Don't be a hypocrite. For her own sake? Could she really, against her lifelong principles, do anything so sneaky, so underhanded? She could.

The letters were very moving, very personal. They showed Woody's arrogance dissolving as he queried the world out there for his "comely companion," and with each letter taking one more step toward the intimacy he feared and desired; Amanda, the pragmatist, gradually lowering her guard, amused and piqued by this theater-person-turned-professor.

When Sheila had read the last letter, she slammed down the packet in frustration. Amanda's "friend" had not died, and Amanda was not yet ready to return to the stage. Life, as usual, was inconclusive and tantalizing. Sheila had compromised her principles for nothing. She heard Muriel's dust cloth being snapped out the window in the living room.

"Mother!"

"Yes, dear?" She came trotting in proudly. "Aren't you pleased?"

"No. I should not have read those letters and I hate myself."

"Oh, dear."

"Amanda is not available."

"But perhaps, very soon?"

"Soon is too late. Shall we go?"

"I haven't finished my dusting. Just a few tiny minutes?" and she bustled off.

Sheila glanced at Woody's bookshelves: mostly plays, some poetry, and many scrapbooks. Having no honor left to lose, she started leafing through the old photos and news clippings. Woody had been in every school play since the age of five, in parts ranging from Christmas Wise Man to Greek warrior, with cardboard shield on one arm and woolly dog tucked under the other. As director, Woody had filled five scrapbooks in his rise from neighborhood home movies with megaphone to winner of several Broadway Tony Awards.

Then, increasingly, photographs showed Woody with a beautiful actress, Adorée di Carlo. She clung to him as they boarded the Concorde, she gazed at him as they dined in a five-forks restaurant—and Adorée was a girl who knew how to cling, not to mention gaze. The more Sheila saw of that long, indolent body and that perfect, expressionless face, the more she began to fear for Woody. There was a girl with a stone for every finger and another one for a heart. Oh, Woody, be careful.

Turning the page, she realized she had come to the end of the last scrapbook. She read:

> Adorée di Carlo has signed to do *Hedda Gabler* next season with, of course, Sherwood Pell directing. We always said Adorée would be a classy dame for the classics. Go git 'em, kids.

And then,

> Further cast changes coming up in the di Carlo-Pell production of *Hedda Gabler*, now playing to the ushers

in Boston. Word is *la belle* Adorée is writing herself a few temper tantrums Ibsen never did.

Followed by,

A beleaguered *Hedda Gabler* has limped into the Golden. Adorée di Carlo indisposed last night—What, again?—and tix refunded at B.O. They do say she's dreaming of a Raj with a Taj! To Woody Pell, director/producer, our deepest sympathy.

And finally,

Sad to report, the di Carlo-Pell *Hedda Gabler* is no more. Closing notice went up Saturday. *La belle* Adorée and her Raj are private-jetting to New Delhi, where he will toss her a half-million acres of rice for a wedding present.

Sheila put the scrapbook away. Poor Woody. No wonder he had chosen the safety of a university town and theater-without-risk. But now, twelve years later, was he satisfied with his bargain?

Muriel appeared in the doorway.

"Ready to go home, dear? I heard some news at the hospital. Guess who will be admitted there tonight?" Muriel was locking Woody's door behind them.

"I give up."

"The chancellor of the university. For surgery on Monday morning. And, of course, since the chancellor is a very old friend, I shall stop by and see him tonight. You see, the chancellor knows *everything*."

"Such as?"

"Such as who's to be the next dean of fine arts."

"You can't *ask* him!"

"Certainly not. He'll inquire for Woody's leg and I'll say it's much better and I *hear* he's to be the next dean. If the mustache twitches, I'm right."

"Sometimes you surprise me."

Sheila looked at her mother's small hands on the steering wheel and remembered it was she who had taught Sheila to ride a bike. It was summertime, a broiling Kansas summer, and her mother would run alongside the bicycle, one hand on the back of the seat, one hand guiding the handlebars.

"I'm glad I know how to ride a bike."

"That's nice, dear," said Muriel absently.

They arrived home to find Val had dished up his famous tomato omelet for Woody's supper.

"Frankly, it looked like a street accident."

"I noticed you pigging out."

Muriel and Sheila nibbled and Muriel left for the hospital. Upstairs, Sheila and Val met briefly in the hall. He grabbed her and kissed her hungrily.

"Where you been? Are we winning?"

"We're trying. I even cheated."

"How?"

"I read Woody's mail."

"Any clues?"

"Why would a Greek warrior carry a woolly dog?"

"Dog was tired?"

They went down to Woody and sat on either side of his bed. "In grade school, you were an *actor*."

"Oh, indeed. Wise man, scarecrow, Greek warrior."

Sheila tried to speak casually.

"What was the warrior's name?"

"Jason."

"The one who went after the Golden Fleece?"

"The very same."

"Where did you get a fleece in second grade?"

"I had a woolly dog. Better than talent any day."

"Oh, Woody, I knew it! The minute I looked at that picture! Val, remember how Jason found the Golden Fleece? He harnessed two fire-breathing bulls! He sowed the dragon's teeth, and every tooth came up an armed warrior! And then he snatched the Fleece from the serpent's jaws! Oh, Val, don't you remember?"

"No."

"Neither did I, actually, but I went to the library this afternoon." Sheila turned to Woody in triumph. "You *are* Jason! Broadway was loaded with fire-breathing bulls and dragon's teeth but you captured the Golden Fleece—and here it is!"

Sheila snatched up the script where it lay beside Woody and brandished it over her head. "Oh, Sherwood Pell, I'm so *proud* of you!" She leaned over and planted a kiss on his forehead and fell back laughing into her chair.

"My dear child, you're having delusions!"

"Val, look!" She held up the title page. " '*Continuum* by Jay Pelias.' Jay stands for Jason, that's easy. King Pelias was Jason's uncle, who sent him to find the Fleece. The first syllable of Pelias is Pel—as in

Sherwood Pell, so everything fits! Val, I give you Sherwood Pell, playwright!"

"I'll be totally damned," said Val. Woody snatched the script away from Sheila.

"So you've been spying on me, prying into my past—don't break a leg, Keating, these women will examine your back teeth!"

"I knew you wrote it anyway! I'm a writer, Woody. It takes one to know one. I recognized your style. Also, I remembered King Pelias from school, because he was boiled in oil."

"He never forgot it either," said Woody, flicking an eyebrow.

"Woody, why did you use a pen name?"

"Ah, Sheila, you know campus life. Suppose this play's a screaming disaster. It'd hang around my neck forever. 'There goes Pell, wrote that dreadful piece of trash.' And if you ever breathe one word—"

"I promise."

"Say, writing's a dog's life, isn't it?"

"Lonely, grueling, slave's wages."

They started to talk shop, who typed and who used a word processor. Val strolled out the door, muttering that he used smoke signals. The other two chatted on, Woody declaring by next Friday he would have the verdict. Perhaps the KU audience would be lenient, like sharks that is.

Suddenly, Kerry and Val streaked into the room and both touched Woody's bed in a dead heat.

"Who won?" Kerry, panting, appealed to Woody, "*You* say, not Mother, who?"

"Dead heat," said Woody.

"So what?" said Kerry. "It was only a warm-up. Tomorrow's the race." She turned to her mother. "And you know what's first prize?"

"An airline ticket home," said Sheila, quite cleverly she thought.

"The play! To be or not to be!"

"How do you mean?" Sheila asked.

"If he wins, you keep trying to do this dumb-ass play. But if *I* win, he gives up! He goes back to his dumb-ass job! Isn't that right, stud?"

"That's right, brat."

"You heard him, Mother. And you're a witness, Uncle Woody. If I win tomorrow, he goes back where my mother found him and stays there! You going to shake on it, stud?"

They shook hands.

"Hah!" Kerry shouted, leering into her mother's face. She punched the air and ran from the room. Sheila turned to Val and said, "She's kidding."

"Hell, no. We shook on it."

"But Val . . . suppose she wins?"

"I'll win."

"She's a runner! She's young! Val, *how can you take a chance like that?*"

" 'Out of this nettle danger, we pluck this flower safety.' Hotspur. One of my *great* roles."

"Val, answer me!"

"I did."

Sheila turned, ran from the room and up the stairs. She couldn't go to her own room, Kerry might be there.

Not to Val's room, not her mother's. She went into her father's study, opened a door at the far end, and climbed to the attic.

It was hot and musty, but at least she could be alone. She picked her way past boxes and trunks, broken lampshades, and twenty-five years of *National Geographic*s. She slumped onto a chaise longue left over from her father's first heart attack ("Makes me feel like a passionate pasha") and lay there suffering an almost physical pain. She heard footsteps, and realized she had left doors open behind her. The psychiatrists say we do nothing by accident. Val loomed in the doorway, got his bearings in the dusk, and came toward her. He sat on a trunk across from her, and waited. Sheila heard her own voice, and it was shaking.

"You're committed to nothing in this world. Not to this play, not to me, not to your own talent. Living is for *fun*, right?"

He did not answer. She could not tell whether he was even looking at her.

"We came here to try for a wonderful play. But now the play is going to be first prize in a silly little race. Maybe you'll win. Maybe my spiteful little daughter will win. But oh, Val, how could you make us both . . . so *trivial?*"

He looked at her dumbly, rose, and walked to the door. She thought, if he left her, she would stop breathing. Suddenly he kicked a box into the air, and it fell open, spilling out its contents. He stooped and retrieved a long, dark cloak and a hat with a trailing white plume. It was her father's *Cyrano* hat. Val swirled the cape around himself, pulled the hat over his thatch of hair. He spoke softly, in the silver voice that melted Sheila's bones.

> " 'Night, making all things dimly beautiful,
> One veil over us both—You only see
> The darkness of a long cloak in the gloom,
> And I the whiteness of a summer gown—
> You are all light—I am all shadow!
> How can you know what this moment means to me?
> If I was ever eloquent—You have never heard till now
> My own heart speaking!' "

He paused, and Cyrano fell away from him. He came to sit down on the trunk, the hat in hand, the long plume grazing the floor.

"I'm not committed? I don't know . . . I'm committed to this minute. *Now.* If it's a race, I run it. If it's a play, I'll act the hell out of it. And if it's love . . . if it's love, Sheila, I feel it up and down my body like a fire. . . ."

Sheila knew the tears were coming into her eyes. Val dropped to one knee in front of her and wiped her cheek with his finger. He raised his arm and lifted the cloak, so that it covered them both, in one dark, sudden night. She could see nothing, but she could sense his face coming closer to hers, and waited for his searching, peace-making kiss.

CHAPTER

13

LIGHT SHAFTED in the half-round attic window.
Sheila found herself crumpled on the chaise longue,
with tangled vertebrae. Val was stretched out on the floor
beside her like an overgrown dog. She massaged her
neck, and willed his eyes to open, which they did. It had
been a night of magical love-making, and she was sure
that at last they understood each other.

"No race today, right?"

"I thought we had that all squared away, honey," he
drawled, with his disarming smile.

"You mean you're going to *do* it?"

"I sure . . . as hell . . . am."

"I hope . . . you break . . . your neck."

She pulled her disarrayed clothing around her, and
stomped down the stairs. Finding Kerry sprawled diago-
nally across the bed, Sheila curled up in a chair. She was
dozing when she heard her mother whispering in the
doorway.

"Sheila . . . come."

Her mother led Sheila into the pink bedroom and
sat her down.

"I have something to confess to you." She giggled. "Now you mustn't be cross with me. You promise?"

"I'm cross already."

"When I showed you Sherwood's letters yesterday, there was one more that I forgot. It came—let me see—on Friday, and I decided to hold it till you arrived."

"*Hold* it?"

"Yes! And here it is!" She plucked a letter from her bureau drawer, the flap unglued and slightly wavy.

"Mother! You opened it!"

"You asked me to help you, didn't you, dear? How could I tell whether it was a good letter or a bad letter, until I opened it? Sheila, it's a *good* letter! Read it and you'll see!"

"Mother, I can't!"

"Why not? You read all the others! What's one more?"

Sheila turned the letter over and saw that it was shaking slightly in her hands. So this was the road to perdition, a very gradual downhill slide.

"No." She handed the letter back.

"All right, then I'll tell you what it says. It's from Amanda and it says—"

"That's enough, Mother." Sheila took back the letter. Muriel patted her daughter's shoulder. "Much simpler, dear," and moved away.

Sheila read:

Dear Professor,
Your letters were a big help the last few weeks. It's been kind of dismal around here. My best friend is on his way out. The

Drs. don't think he'll make it through the summer. So I'll be heading for N.Y.C. by fall at the latest.

When it happens, I'm going to put the word out— Amanda's available! But you'll be top of the list, Professor! Here's hoping you have a part for me with bells on! And keep those letters coming!

Amanda

Sheila put down the letter and closed her eyes. Amanda Hapgood available? With a name like that you could raise money and book the Garden.

"Isn't that good news, dear?"

"Yes, indeedy, good news. Mother, how could you hold Woody's mail? When do you plan to give him this letter?"

"Why, today, if you think so."

"Sunday?"

"I'll tell him it came yesterday and I've been very careless."

"He'll eat you alive!"

"Oh, ish-ka-bibble!" Her mother burst into laughter and hugged Sheila girlishly. "Come down to my laboratory!"

While Sheila started the coffee, she watched out of the corner of her eye as her mother applied a cool iron to the back of the envelope, followed by two quick dabs of paste.

"There! Nobody will ever know!"

Sheila wondered how many years of practice had led to this expertise, deciding she'd rather not know.

At breakfast the tension was palpable. Muriel had given Woody his letter, but good manners forbade him to open it in company. He fingered it, and fumed. Kerry wanted to race with Val immediately, but Val said they must find a track and make their own hurdles. When Kerry accused him of stalling, he suggested they put on the gloves instead. Muriel wanted her daughter and granddaughter to go to church with her, as she had always dreamed they would. Sheila hoped she had spent her last night on a chaise longue. Ever.

After breakfast, Woody called Sheila in from the kitchen. He had read the letter and was turning it end-for-end in his fingers. His eyes were dancing.

"I don't want you to think, just because you *unveiled* me last night, that I'm bringing my play to New York."

"Certainly not, Woody."

"Even if we *had* a major star," he said, tapping the edge of the letter on his tray table, "we'd still have to raise the money. Untold millions, my dear." He stretched for the coat-hanger, lying just beyond his reach. Sheila handed it over. He scratched luxuriantly. "You realize I'm fantasizing. A man has to do *something*, lying here on the rack."

"Fulton broke his leg, gave us the steam engine," Sheila invented.

"Besides, this play has never had an audience. After all, what do you know, or Keating either? You're both disqualified. Conflict of interest. Next Friday night the play will have an audience, a Lawrence, Kansas, audience, but they're not cretins, you know."

"This play will be a hit, here, on Broadway, in London, Paris, Vladivostock."

"Will you stay till Friday, my opening night?"

Sheila was taken by surprise.

"Oh, Woody, I have to go! Tonight!"

"Let Keating go. You stay—a week—"

She knew instinctively how rarely Woody asked anything of anybody. "I wish I could. I mean, I . . ." His eyes were still asking her, as if she had not spoken. She rose and moved away. "I'm sorry. I . . ."

Muriel came in, hatted and gloved for church, and started laying out Woody's shaving things.

"We'll be leaving soon, dear, and the good Lord would not appreciate you in blue jeans." Sheila remembered well the good Lord's strong opinions on wearing apparel and went upstairs to change.

When her mother drove them into the church parking lot, she cut the ignition and paused.

"Before I go into the Lord's house, I always tell him the bad things I did during the week." If the list were long, the car would soon be an oven.

"Tell him when we get in, okay?"

"No, dear, now. You see, dear, I did not really and truly *forget* Woody's letter. I mean there *wasn't* any letter."

"How do you mean?"

"I wrote that last letter myself."

"Oh, Mother, you're joking."

"I thought it might be helpful, and it was! Sherwood was very cheerful, wasn't he?"

"Mother, are you telling me that letter was a *forgery?*"

"Indeed, I am. Now I feel much, much better. Shall we go in?"

"Mother—you wouldn't! That's lying! It's cheating! Don't you understand—it's *wrong!*"

"Oh, Sheila, you always take everything so *seriously!* It was a tiny little trespass, and nobody but us will ever know!"

"Moth-*er!*"

"I was careful to use the typewriter at the hospital and I changed the postmark on the envelope *skillfully!* Oh, Sheila, I thought you'd be so proud of me!"

"Proud! Mother, you did a terrible thing! A dishonorable thing!"

"Dishonorable? Oh, Sheila, how can you speak that way?" Her mother was starting to cry, and took a small, lace-edged handkerchief from her purse. "I tried so hard to help you, and now you turn on me! Oh, Sheila, you don't love me! No matter what I do, I can never, never make you love me!" She turned her face toward her daughter, the great eyes swimming with tears and the soft lips trembling.

"Mother, please don't. Of course I love you. But don't you see, *that's nothing to do with it!*" Immediately, her mother rallied, dabbed at her eyes, and put her hand on the door.

"Oh, my dear child, my dear little girl. I'm so glad you're not angry with me!" She gave Sheila a quick kiss. "Now we must go in. I'm *never* late to church." Her mother was swinging her legs out, but Sheila grabbed her arm and spoke with rigid control.

"Mother, we've done a bad thing. It was my fault, because I asked you to help me. But now, you see, I'll have to tell Woody, tell him the letter's a forgery."

"Oh, no indeed! My own darling daughter would never put me to shame, disgrace me, oh no. . . ."

"Mother, Woody *believes* that letter. He'll answer it!"

"My dear, I mail Woody's letters. Unless of course . . ." she gave Sheila a sidelong glance and a dimpled smile, "unless of course I forget. And I'm very forgetful."

"*No*, Mother."

"Come along now, dear. So many friends for you to meet." They crossed the parking lot under a blazing sun, and Sheila was introduced to several coveys of her mother's friends. "My daughter from New York who writes all those best-sellers you naughty girls are always reading." And Sheila, stunned, mumbled their names.

They sat in a fourth-row pew and Sheila cast a dazed look around her. The whiteness of the church was dazzling to the eye. Set into the walls on either side, were tall, stained-glass windows, red-blue-green-purple, as brilliant as crushed jewels flung against the light. On the altar, between trembling candle flames, stood a huge gold cross, focusing the mind on the meaning of this place: Jesus died on the cross for us.

This was her mother's other home. All this splendor of soaring windows, gold cross, and trembling flames belonged to her. All these clean, respectable people pouring into the church were her mother's friends, her supporters. To the last man they would swear to the integrity of Muriel Devlin. If Sheila stood up now and announced that her mother had committed forgery, she, the daughter, would be stoned out of town. She must decide what to do.

She must tell Woody the moment she returned, though she dreaded the sight of his face. This would mean confessing she had read the other letters, quite different from glancing through his scrapbooks. She would also be "putting her mother to shame," surely another betrayal.

But if she said nothing, she would be as guilty as her mother, who would proceed to "hold" Woody's letters to Amanda, or perhaps forge a whole correspondence between them, later to be published and have a movie sale!

Sheila was losing her grip. An almost sleepless night, followed by all this sanctity and stained glass, had left her in a state of vertigo. What was happening to her life? She had fallen in love, and set herself to bring a play to Broadway. Since then, her daughter had turned against her and called her "the enemy." Her mother had started lying and cheating. The man who caused all this, whom she loved to the point of folly and perhaps beyond, remained unscathed, dedicating himself to hurdle racing. She asked herself the inevitable question, "How now, brown cow?"

Sheila leaned toward her mother to whisper in her ear. Mother, frowning, put a finger to her lips. Sheila clutched at a paper and pencil in her purse and wrote, "Promise me you will *never* help me again. Sign here." She passed the paper to her mother, who smiled, made an "X" and returned it. For now, Sheila could do no more.

The service proceeded in its time-honored way, with half-remembered prayers and stately hymns. Sheila had not for years been in the presence of three hundred people all praising God. Her mother's soprano soared, so innocent, so pure. Sheila felt herself to be in two realities at once: in one she was comforted, in the other sore beset.

As they drove home, Sheila tried once more to reach her mother, keeping it very simple. "You see, Mother, you lied to me. You told me a letter had *arrived* for Woody."

"Of course. If I'd told you I *wrote* the letter, you wouldn't have let me give it to him."

"Mother."

"But *now* I've told you, so everything's fine, isn't it, dear?"

Sheila wondered if a moral sense could be missing from an otherwise normal person. Was it like being colorblind?

They arrived home to find the racetrack almost finished. In a vacant lot next door, Val had scythed and sickled a circular track and set up five pairs of hurdles. Slender branches rested horizontally between cleft sticks stuck in the ground, the forward part of the cleft cut short: a runner touching the hurdle would not be thrown. Every hurdle was fringed with many-colored Christmas ribbons from Muriel's attic. No runner could fail to see the jumps. Val, stripped to his shorts and glistening with sweat, was making a final inspection of the track. This insane hurdle race was about to happen, and if Val lost, there would be no play. Sheila, in a last-ditch effort at ridicule, asked if she could have the popcorn concession. But Val leaned down to her with a grin. "Not to worry, baby. I'll win," and he went into the house to get Woody. Kerry, in running shorts and T-shirt, faced her mother belligerently.

"You could stop him if you wanted to."

"You know what? I can't."

"I'm going to win. And then—no play."

"Yes, dear." She looked over this strapping girl. "I'm wishing you bad luck."

"Thanks, pal."

Val wheeled Woody out and stationed him at the finish line, which was a knotted rainbow of ribbons. He put Muriel at the starting line, where he had dug holes in the ground for the takeoff. He instructed Muriel gravely on the spacing of the words: "On your marks . . . set . . . go!"

Then, with an unerring sense of anticlimax, the two runners started doing their warmups. Seated on the ground, they doubled themselves over one leg, and then the other. Using the porch railing as a barre, they bent and stretched and flexed. They worked out their "stride plan," Kerry taking eight steps from starting line to first hurdle, Val seven. It was high noon under the Kansas sun, and Woody was cursing vividly. Muriel trotted into the house and returned with a huge black umbrella for Woody, a small red one for Sheila, and a fan and ruffled parasol for herself. Sheila wondered if the fate of a Broadway play could truly be decided in a Kansas meadow at high noon with homemade hurdles and people wielding umbrellas and fans.

179

"You ready, brat?"

"Try me."

"On your marks!" caroled Muriel.

The runners dropped to the track, settled their feet into place, hands bridged on the ground in front of them.

"Set!"

Both runners were resting on toes and fingertips like spiders.

"Go!"

Kerry exploded out of the "starting block," springing from her trailing foot. A good "raise." The arms were pumping, the knees high, and the eyes riveted on the first hurdle. But Val was motionless at the starting line. *Why?*

Kerry reached the first hurdle, raised the lead leg, straightened it, and bent forward. A good kick. She sailed over, with the snap that gets the lead foot down on the track fast, while the trailing foot skims the bar. She was running smooth and strong. Sheila had watched her for years, but today the kid was floating. Before she remembered, she was proud of her.

Finally, Val started, one hurdle's handicap behind Kerry. She'd kill him for this. He ran powerfully, a leopard to Kerry's gazelle. But they took the second and third jumps with the same gap between them. Val wasn't gaining on her, only holding his own. Sheila heard a shout, and realized it came from her own throat, "Val!"

Then, by agonizing inches, Val started closing the gap. They reached the fourth jump and he was closer. At the fifth and last jump, he had almost overtaken her, but Kerry, with a glance over her shoulder, accelerated. Now they were on the home stretch, fifteen yards to the finish line. Val was level with Kerry's heels, and gaining on her. As they came to the finish line, they ran abreast. Kerry leaned into the tape, leaning too far and a split second too soon. She lost her balance and plunged forward, skidding along the rough stubble on her chest and belly. It was Val who snapped the tape.

SHEILA KNELT ON the ground beside Kerry, as Muriel came running and Val turned back. They grouped around Kerry's prone figure.

"Kerry, are you all right?" Slowly, painfully, the child pulled herself back on her haunches.

"Yeah. I'm okay."

Muriel and Sheila helped her to her feet. Val bent to examine her bruised knees and elbows, patted her shoulder.

"Good race, kid."

Sheila watched Kerry's face, caked with dust and sweat, one cheek bruised and one eye starting to swell. Years of training in sportsmanship suddenly paid off. The child held out a trembling hand to Val. "Get you next time."

"Bet you will," said Val.

"I'm going to fix you an herbal bath," said Muriel, "from the roots of my comfrey plant and some of the leaves, too. It's magic, you'll see."

She trotted off to the kitchen leaving Val and Sheila to help Kerry into the house, over Woody's loud protests.

"You're going to leave me here to *rot?*" But he wheeled himself into the shade. Val offered to carry Kerry upstairs. "Screw that," she replied, and winced at the first step. Sheila and Val formed a basket chair, hands grasping wrists, and carried her between them. Sheila sat beside Kerry's bed with basin and cloth, cleaning the child's bruises.

"Does that hurt? Tell me if I'm hurting you."

"I guess *I* mostly hurt *you.*"

"Oh, well."

"But I'm not taking anything back."

"You mean, we're going to stay mad—*forever?*"

"I just wish it never happened, never, never, *never.*"

Kerry turned her face away, sobbing. Sheila leaned down, her lips close to Kerry's ear.

"Me, too, baby."

They were silent, thinking of words spoken, never to be unspoken. In the long emptiness that followed, it was too soon for healing.

They heard Muriel on the stairs, her footsteps heavy with the weight of the large cauldron she carried. She emptied it into the bathtub, added warm water, and helped Kerry to undress and sit in the tub. Sheila, looking at the slimy infusion, remembered its miraculous properties. The liquid was shallow, but Muriel scooped it up in her hands and poured it gently over Kerry's knees and elbows, crooning and clucking the mother animal sounds that Sheila remembered from her own childhood. Kerry lay back in the tub and allowed her grandmother to fuss over her. They both ignored

Sheila, standing in the doorway. She felt the sting of being totally superfluous.

She went downstairs, where Val and Woody were lapping up a velvety vichyssoise and wondered if Muriel cooked in her sleep. Woody, "exhausted from all this ridiculous foot-racing," settled in for his nap. Muriel came down to say Kerry was sleeping soundly. Muriel would take her mending and sit with her. Thankfully, Sheila and Val escaped. They drove to the Kaw River, left the car to watch the fishermen at the dam, then walked on along the river road and picked up a wooded trail.

Sheila told Val that Kerry had become her "enemy," that Muriel had forged a letter to Woody. "We're getting in very deep, aren't we?" Val's shoulders seemed to droop as he listened, his great strides losing their spring. When they reached a picnic table, Val lay down full length upon it. He was staring up at the sky, squinting into the filtered sunlight, shadows playing across his craggy face.

"I'm the world's longest hot dog," he said.

Sheila sat down on the bench beside him.

"Val, I'm trying to tell you . . ."

"I know. You're telling me forget the play. It's cost you a lot of grief already, hasn't it? My fault, too." Then he spoke in sepulchral tones. "The play is dead. Long live the play!" He raised a bony finger to heaven, and let it fall with a thud to his side.

"Val, I'm sorry."

"Listen, honey," he raised his head to stare into her face, "I never came so close . . . to glory." He let his head fall back on the table but his face was turned to her and smiling. Sheila couldn't speak. "So close to glory." The bitterest regret flooded over her. How could she come this far and lose her nerve? More than anything in all her life, she loved this man lying beside her, this long, cadaverous, quirky, life-enhancing man. He was all she wanted in this terrible, magnificent world. She sprang to her feet.

"Come on! Curtain going up!"

They raced back to the car, Val pretending to stumble and fall, calling for water from a parched throat, tearing up "edible roots" and offering them to her in trembling, clawlike hands. At the car, he snatched the keys from her and drove home singing like a madman.

They found Woody reading *Variety*, and Kerry still asleep, but where was Muriel?

"She went to the hospital," said Woody.

"To the hospital? Oh, my God!" Without another word, Sheila took off. She drove to the hospital, asked for the chancellor's room number, and stood in his open doorway glaring at her mother. Muriel was arranging pink tulips in a vase while she chattered happily to the chancellor.

". . . but what do I know about the theater? To me, it's children playing games, and other children coming to watch. Don't you agree, Chancellor?"

Sheila knocked loudly on the open door.

"Mother, this is an emergency! You have to come home!"

"Why, Sheila! Chancellor, this is—"

"*Right now*, Mother!" Sheila took a stride into the

room and grabbed her mother in mid-tulip and swung her out the door. In the elevator, Muriel was all innocence.

"Sheila, dear, what happened?"

"*Not now*, Mother!" said Sheila, as a patient on the stretcher rolled his eyes from mother to daughter and back. The women marched to the car in lock step and took their seats in silence.

"*Now*. Tell me *exactly* what you told the chancellor."

"Why, I told him Sherwood was doing nicely."

"Then what?"

"Oh, campus gossip—you know, dear."

"Does the chancellor like the theater?"

"My, no, he's far too intelligent."

"Then why is he coming to the New York opening?"

"Because I invited him!" Then Muriel gasped and clapped her hand to her mouth. "You trapped me, you naughty girl!"

"All right, let's have it."

"Sheila, you asked me to help you. I thought, instead of just finding out whether Sherwood had the deanship, I'd make sure he *didn't* get it! Now wasn't that more tidy?"

"So you said—he'd be taking the play to New York?"

"And applying any day for a sabbatical."

"Jesus . . . wept."

Sheila started the car for home.

"Now Sheila, you can't have it both ways. If you want Val to do this play on Broadway, then Sherwood's not going to be dean of fine arts and you can't make an omelet without breaking eggs. I hope you're not going to carry on as if I've done something wrong when I was only trying to help!"

The handkerchief was coming out.

"Mother, please don't cry. It was my fault. I did ask you to help. I forgot about your moral code."

"My moral code is . . ."

"Flexible, Mother, flexible. Now I want you to help me just one more time." Sheila glanced at her watch. "Val and I have a plane to catch. I want you to throw my stuff into my bag and get Kerry up and dressed and packed. I'm going to talk to Woody, alone and without interruption. Is that clear?"

"Of course, dear, and remember, nothing is ever as bad as it looks." Sheila had often thought if she disemboweled herself in her mother's presence, her comment would be "Nothing is ever as bad as it looks." She drove along in a state of misery. By her own stupidity, she had caused Woody to lose his deanship, if indeed he might have had it. There was the turn of the screw. She would never know, would she?

They came home to a quiet house, Woody in bed, and Val having left to say good-bye to Piper. Sheila remembered the sliding doors of the dining room (closed only on Christmas mornings before the opening of presents) and she closed them now.

"Woody, I have something bad to tell you."

"They're going to amputate."

"No, it's worse."

She told him that she and her mother had read his

private correspondence, had forged a letter, and had ruined whatever chances he might have had for dean of fine arts.

"It was all my fault. Mother did it, but I *know* her. She's *my mother*. I should have *known*—Look, I didn't come here to wreck your life, but I guess the innocent betrayal's the worst, isn't it? Oh, Woody." She struggled to control herself. "I'm sorry. Of all the useless, pointless things to say, I'm sorry."

She flung herself out of her chair and roamed the room, then stood at the foot of his bed trying to read his unreadable face. He was staring out the window, tapping the coat-hanger against his cast. Then he started to chuckle softly, his face creasing into smiling lines.

"Oh, Sheila, my child . . . it's all so . . . utterly . . . ridiculous. Don't y'see, my whole life has turned into a black comedy, the theater of the absurd!" He caught his breath. "A week ago, your mother and I had one of our little dinners. Everything proper, everything delicious, precisely like the last seven years of little dinners. Then, God help me, the scene wasn't playing any more. All of a sudden your mother was weeping and I was consoling. Well, how many ways are there to console a woman?"

"You mean—you and Mother?"

"Precisely. We became lovers. 'Sweethearts.' So I locked myself into eternal bliss with a woman—forgive me—a good woman, a fine woman, but a woman who could drive a man to drink. To suicide. To murder."

Sheila was nodding. "Yes . . . *yes* . . ."

"And so, immediately after the—uh—consummation, I broke my leg on those confounded stairs! For one week I have been driven to the edge of madness by a woman who feeds me and washes me like a mewling infant. I have been lacerated by equal portions of guilt and gratitude. Now you tell me this woman reads my mail, no, she *writes* it! And she's wrecked my chances for the deanship, if ever I had any. Ah, Sheila, it's funny! Laugh with me. I need your company."

"*I can't laugh.*"

"Now see here, child. This was not your doing. You must stop making yourself responsible for your mother. You did not give birth to her, nor raise her, and you're not accountable for her sins."

Sheila was so struck by this insight, and so relieved by the absolution it implied that she could only stare at the man she had thought was almost a stranger to her.

"Now, what does a civilized man do under such circumstances? He does not go crying 'Foul!' to the chancellor. Useless and undignified. I accept that I'll never be dean of fine arts at this university. My academic career will remain forever preserved in aspic, commendable but not exceptional. I am at liberty to remain here the rest of my days: comfortable, respected, the acknowledged wit of the Wednesday night faculty meeting. I shall continue to initiate into the mysteries of the drama an endless procession of young men and women who see the stage as a multiple mirror for their vanity, or a leap to fame and fortune, but never as a holy place where a man looks deeply into his own soul. Did you know the theater is a church, Sheila?"

"Yes."

"I thought you did. Your father knew it. And I'm talking about the wicked old Broadway theater, too, y'know."

"I know."

"Do you miss him, girl?"

"Till the day I die."

He nodded, reaching for her hand and turning it in his. A knock came on the dining room doors, followed by Muriel's voice calling anxiously.

"Sheila, dear, you have a plane to catch!"

"All right, Mother . . . I have to go, Woody."

"Don't go."

"We have to. Val will be fired!" They were speaking softly, almost intimately, as if the closed doors had cut them off from the world.

"Let Val go. You stay here. Stay for my opening Friday night."

"Oh, Woody, I wish . . ."

Muriel's voice came again. "Sheila, do you hear me? You must leave now, this very minute, dear." Woody went on quietly, urgently.

"If the audience likes the play, we'll draft a few letters. I still have my list of investors, y'know. They can't all be dead after ten years!"

Val's voice boomed through the door.

"This is your captain speaking! We are passing over Cleveland, Ohio!"

Woody continued. "We could fire off a few scripts. Get some feedback! Perhaps this is the script that will save Broadway!" He was talking rapidly, his eyes alive and shining. "What do you think, childy?" He had used her father's word.

"Mother, are you coming or not?" Kerry yelled outside the door.

Sheila pulled back, but Woody held her wrist. She could feel his energy flowing into her own body. But to stay here, to let Val go without her? She didn't think she could bear it. Woody spoke again, and this time he let go her wrist in a theatrical gesture of setting her free. The choice was hers.

"You've got me believing in this play. *Are you going to run out on me now, Devlin's daughter?*"

For a long moment, they stared at each other, then Sheila ran to unlock the doors and fling them open. Val and Mother and Kerry were facing her in the flight-or-fight positions. Sheila went straight to Val.

"I'm not coming. I'm staying here for the opening Friday night. You take Kerry, she can use my ticket." While Sheila burrowed in her purse for the ticket, everybody spoke at once.

"You're *not coming?*" from Val.

"You're staying? How lovely!" from Muriel.

"Let's go, beanpole," and Kerry snatched the ticket.

Val strode into the dining room.

"You're taking the play to New York?"

"I'm toying with that preposterous idea."

Val grabbed Woody's hand and pumped it, struggling for words. "God almighty . . . Oh, my God . . . Well, break a leg, sir." He backed off, and turned to Sheila.

191

"You did it!"

"We did it."

"I can't leave you. But I'm going to." He kissed her. "Come home soon." He laid his great hand against her cheek, then turned to hoist Kerry's backpack and his own. He brushed Muriel's cheek with his. "Take care of her, y'hear?" and he snatched Kerry's hand and lunged out the door.

Now they were in the car, waving and calling, and now they were gone. Sheila stood on the sidewalk, watching them out of sight. "Be careful what you wish for," she told herself, "you might get it." She and Val had come one giant step closer to their heart's desire, but Val was gone. Gone. Why was it always like this? Because the rule is "jam tomorrow and jam yesterday— but never jam today." She fixed her mind firmly on jam tomorrow—fame and fortune for Val, everlasting happiness for them both—and returned to her mother's house.

CHAPTER

15

Sheila Devlin to Val Keating
Lawrence, Kansas—May 15

Val,

    No call from you for three nights. I have dialed you until fingers bleeding. But here in Siberia, nicknamed Kansas, we need to hear from loved ones at home. Are you out of town? Caught in a subway door riding up and down Lexington? Lying in Bellevue brain dead?

    Opening night went well, and thanks for sending all those telegrams and red, red roses. Pity they didn't arrive. The audience was polite, puzzled, and pleased. Now Woody and I are shooting off letters to potential backers, xeroxing and collating Continuum *ad infinitum. If I do not hear from you by tomorrow, plan to pile all copies into gigantic bonfire and commit suttee. Oh, Val, my darling, where are you?*
S.

Sheila Devlin to Val Keating
Lawrence, Kansas—May 20

Val,

    I am sending this letter to your office in hopes that one of your co-workers will have the decency to forward

it to whatever jail, hospital, morgue in which you now reside. I've tried Theo who does not return my calls. Your own telephone has gone from no answer to "not in service at this time." Actors' Equity does not carry you on their roster and points out helpfully that you may be delinquent. I spoke to a Mr. Keating in Falls City, Nebraska, who said he didn't know any Val Keating and didn't want to. I feel exactly the same.
S.

Sheila Devlin to Val Keating
Lawrence, Kansas—May 25

Val,
I have enclosed self-addressed, stamped postcard. Drop it on the street. Somebody will mail it. Check one: I have dumped S.D.; I have dumped the play; I have dumped both. I hope you died, but not painlessly.
S.

Val Keating to Sheila Devlin
London, England—May 31

Concubine of the Western Plains,
As you'll see from postmark, boss-lady sent me to London on two hour's notice and what a blast. I hang out in pubs and pick up young and talented writers (male & female) sign them up for boss-lady to represent them in the U.S. She gave me some letters to established authors, but the others are more fun.
Three letters from you in today's post forwarded (eventually) by my subtenant. He's a Zen Buddhist doing I-am-the-world and he always pulls the phone out by the roots. Also, Theo promised to call you but left for L.A. in a cloud of smoke over renegade client and probably forgot. Anyway, Mrs. Keating's little boy Val sure was glad to hear from the girl he left behind. And don't get in a snit next time. No harm ever comes to the rascals of the world.

This is my first time in London, and I'm spotting Burbage on every street corner, sometimes gassing with Nell Gwynne. The Brits are great, they crack me up. I hang out in Piccadilly in the pouring rain and check the accents. I con my way into a theater every night. And sometimes I picture you and me under the same umbrella. Kinda raunchy, huh?

Great about Continuum. *Tell Woody 'hello.'*
V.

Sheila Devlin to Val Keating
Lawrence, Kansas—June 8

Val,

Thank you for your letter, I think. Oh, Val, how could you write to me like that? How could you be so casual, so totally inadequate*? I've been in agony. Yes, agony. I haven't slept, couldn't eat—Val, I've been* dying. *And you finally write to me like a kid from camp, like a sailor who's left port, like God knows who, but not you. Not* Val. *Not the man who held me naked in his arms and made such love to me and listened while I poured out my life and seemed to love me—love, need, want, cherish— Did you, Val?*

Has everything changed? Are you too kind to say it, but, for for your own reasons, you want out? A simple yes or no is all I need. And for the love of God send me your phone number, or call collect.
S.

Val Keating to Sheila Devlin
London, England—June 15

Sheila Devlin,

What are you doing, woman? Tearing us apart? You are in my arms. Now. Always. As long as you want. Jesus, what happened?

No, I don't write love letters. I don't even talk love letters. Remember the first day? We had lunch and walked in the Park? You notice I spent the whole day quoting Shakespeare? Not so dumb. He said it all, and better. Better than a goddam kid at camp.

I'm living in a bed-sitter. The phone is downstairs in the hall, padlocked. Also, I'm broke. Theo shells out expenses when you get home, not in advance. Remember when I told you not to get mixed up with the poor people?

Think it over, baby. Maybe you don't need a guy who—you said it—is totally inadequate.
V.

Sheila Devlin to Val Keating
Lawrence, Kansas—June 22

Val,

Forgive me. I was so hurt and miserable. I must have suffered brain damage. Write me any kind of letter. Send me your laundry list, autographed, but send me. I'll control my basically crappy disposition and wait sweetly till you get home. And when the hell is that?

This little household is in full swing. A veritable beehive. Starting at dawn, my mother cleans the house. She scrubs and sweeps every visible surface while she sings hymns at full voice. Frequently she calls to me, "You won't forget we need butter, will you, dear?" Meanwhile I am typing in my room. My new book. The one that's due at the publisher's next month. If my door is closed, my mother starts tap-tap-tapping. A closed door has always been a challenge to my mother.

Downstairs, Woody is drafting letters in longhand to every man, woman, and child he has ever known in the theater. If he cannot reach an address book or a Who's Who, his voice carries to the second balcony, "Sheilah-h-h! If I might trouble you?"

My mother scurries off to the hospital and I grapple

196

with lunch. *Woody is accustomed to sweetbreads and soufflés, but learning to love baloney. The afternoon is gone in a flash, Sheila typing up Woody's letters and his rewrites of the play. For dinner I do the baloney in a new and tempting way.*

So you see, my beloved, while you lounge around Piccadilly and drop in at the theater, your loyal slaves are working on your starring vehicle. We shine the wheels and polish the brass and hope the results will please you. I don't want you to worry that it's hotter than hell's kitchen in Kansas in the summer, or that a writer needs privacy to write. Don't feel that I have disrupted my entire life for you and your frigging play. And please, please don't thank me.

On reading over this letter, I realize I have not been as sweet as advertised, but one of the neighbors has dropped in and my mother is whinnying from downstairs, "Sheilee-ee! Companee-ee!" so to her I go. No time for rewrites. I send you my eternal love and my total exasperation. WHEN ARE YOU COMING HOME?
S.

Val Keating to Sheila Devlin
London, England—June 30

Honey,

Who turned up in my favorite pub last week? Piper York from K.U.! Hollers and hoots, and then she drove me down to her family's wigwam in Kent, forty-nine rooms and grounds like a national park. Pheasant for dinner and four veg, brandy and see-gars to follow. Parents are neat folks and Finley, the third gardener, has been to Nebraska! Piper puts me up on Lord Kitchener, who she says is a marshmallow and I say is three stories high and one hostile piece of horseflesh. So, man, it's a long way down and believe me a long walk home. The next day we go fishing and I'm a smasheroo in comparison.

I know Woody wants a big name for the play, but I hope Piper is drifting through his head. She's a smart kid, and she has talent like a dog has fleas.

Got to go now and take a new client to the Ritz for dinnah, dahling. Rawther clessy, what?
V.

Sheila Devlin to Val Keating
Lawrence, Kansas—July 8

Val,

I'm happy for you, dining at the Ritz, riding to hounds, slaughtering helpless salmon and swilling brandy. Did you get my letter? In it I said I am ruining my career, living on sliced baloney, and screw you, John Peel. WHEN ARE YOU COMING HOME?
S.

Val Keating to Sheila Devlin
London, England—July 15

Beautiful baby,

I bet you've had it with Kansas, but hang in, kid. We're fighting the good fight. Together. We said we'd get this play to Broadway, and that's what we're doing.
CALLING YOU THIS SATURDAY NIGHT. STAND BY.
V.

Transatlantic Telephone Call
Val Keating to Sheila Devlin
London, England to Lawrence, Kansas—July 23

"Hello, honey?"

"Hello."

"Are you okay, honey?"

"I'm fine. How are you?"

"It's raining here and I'm on a street corner. You'll have to speak up."

"I said I'm fine. Don't they have indoor telephones?"

"We've been to the flicks!"

"Who's we?"

"Piper. She says to say 'hi.'"

"Thanks. Val, when are you coming home?"

"She says how's Woody and how's your mother?"

"They died. Bubonic plague."

"That's funny. I thought you said . . ."

"I did. When are you coming home?"

"Piper says she'll play it for nothing."

"Big deal. WHEN ARE YOU COMING HOME?"

"Week from tonight! Nine o'clock!"

"Val!"

"You have a key. Wait for me."

"I'll wait! Forever!"

"So long, baby."

Click.

Sheila ran downstairs to Woody, reclining in the midst of letters, playscripts, and set designs.

"Woody! I have to go east! Val's coming home!"

"Val who?"

"Woody, can you manage?"

"Kind of you to ask. Actually, if you could wait two days, we'd go together."

"Oh."

"Plays are not put on by long distance, you know."

"But your leg."

"With you for my seeing-eye dog, I can make it." He swung his leg to the floor and leaned on her shoulder, making his way to a big chair.

"I've done what I can from half a continent away. Now I have to *be* there, nailing down the money, courting a producer, booking a theater for the love of God!"

"It's only July."

"'Only July!' she says. What twist of fate has surrounded me with idiots? Don't you know every theater in New York is booked at this moment? has been for months? *years?*"

"We'll find one."

"Ah, Sheila, have we been foolhardy to embark on this gigantic enterprise? Remember, my dear, we can still retreat with honor from the battlefield."

This was the familiar retreat-with-honor speech. Woody used it to rally himself and his troops. Sheila carefully lifted his leg and placed it on a chair.

"Now Woody, we never sound retreat. We press on, flags flying. I'll wait two days."

"You're a fine girl, steadfast and true. Hand me that clipboard. Now we're aiming for a late November opening, perhaps a Thanksgiving turkey. God forgive me, I didn't say that." He raised his head and stared at the Kansas evening outside. "Remember autumn in New York? There's a nip in the air. The fat cats are coming in from the Hamptons, and you see fur-bearing ladies on Fifth Avenue. Old geezers roasting chestnuts on the corner. The sunset spilling red on all those glassy buildings. And, over on Forty-fifth Street, God willing, there's a *line* at the box office." He spoke softly, prayerfully.

Sheila chimed in, "I see a line around the block!"

"So that's November. God Almighty, you mean to say from now till then I'm going to be living in some flea-bag hotel off Broadway? eating in Joe's Bar and Grill? French fries with everything? hamburgers, swimming in grease. The stomach heaves."

"You'll be on an expense account."

He slapped the clipboard. "On this budget? You jest. Ah, Sheila, how did we ever commit ourselves to this formidable undertaking, this—" Fending off another retreat-with-honor speech, Sheila plunged in.

"I wish I could help, but . . ."

"Ah you, sitting up there in Westport, Connecticut in your pleasure dome overlooking Long Island Sound."

"I have a chicken coop, overlooking the town dump!"

". . . a plethora of bedrooms, cavernous and cool . . ."

"Three! One with no bed! And my daughter in the other one!"

"Kerry will be in Boston, working at my friend's gallery."

"What? You didn't tell me!"

"Letter came today. Are you pleased?"

"I'm grateful. You still can't come."

"How sharper than a serpent's tooth."

"I need the other bed! For Val!"

"What is this obsession with beds? I shall be happy to sleep in a manger, a solution not without precedent."

"Woody, you *can't come!*"

"I shall pop into town in the morning on the train, spin the wheels of our joint fortune." He leaned heavily on the phrase. "And return quietly, peaceably in the evening. The kind of life style, the *only* kind, that will give me courage for this . . . this almost overwhelming project."

"Woody, I have to be alone! I'm a writer!"

"Not any more, my dear. We'll give you a title. How about production assistant? And bless you, my dear." He reached for her hand and kissed it.

For one delirious moment, Sheila thought of rebellion. She would tell Woody he could not come, tell him she was finished with this penal servitude, typing his letters, wooing his investors, mailing off his scripts to the far corners of the globe. But Woody looked up from her fingertips and she caught a glint in his eye. He had planned this for weeks. He knew as well as she did if she lost Woody, she'd lose the play and yes, perhaps lose Val. Woody was in charge here.

"Yes, Massah," said Sheila and rose to her feet. "I'm going to bed. But before I crawl whimpering between the sheets, I'll pray for you, you scheming, conniving, shameless bastard."

She stalked out of the room to the sound of Woody's
" 'Night, you lovely creature."

Sheila's head had barely touched the pillow when
her mother came tap-tap-tapping and rushed in breathless, round-eyed.

"I've been talking to Sherwood!"

"Yes, Mother."

"He tells me he's going east with you, to stay with
you, in your house!"

"He conned me!"

"But Sheila . . . how simply . . . wonderful!"

"Think so?"

"You've changed your mind! All the years I've been
begging you to let me come, and you wouldn't! Now you
see your precious privacy is not all that important and
you're letting Sherwood come, men being twice as much
trouble, of course."

"Mother, I didn't *want* him to come!"

"I must tell you I've been watching Sherwood like a
hawk. He no longer writes to that actress person. I've
decided to forgive and forget. Sheila, I've set my cap for
Sherwood Pell!"

"No, wait, Mother."

"Isn't that exactly what my clever daughter told me
to do? I shall marry him, dear, after the play, of course.
But in the meantime, I shan't let him of my sight!"

"How do you mean, exactly?"

"I mean me, too, me, too, me, too! I'm coming *with*
you!" She came to the bed and hugged her daughter.

"Mother, no! My house is *small!* We can't *all* live
there!"

"Nonsense, dear. In Moscow they live seven to a room! You'll have me to do your cooking, your marketing, your cleaning, so you can just be typing away! Isn't it simply perfect? Oh, Sheila, I'm so *happy!* I think you're the most wonderful daughter in the whole, wide world! I used to think you were cold—standoffish—but now, we're so close, aren't we? Like peas in a pod!"

She rose and placed a hand on Sheila's head, almost like a blessing.

"Sleep well, my beautiful little baby girl."

She tiptoed out, closing the door softly, silently behind her.

Sheila flopped back in the bed and contemplated life, liberty, and the pursuit of happiness. Her life had been given over since early May. She'd lost her liberty in a bloodless coup. Her pursuit of happiness was what got her into all this trouble in the first place. Falling in love was as dangerous to the human species as waging war. And that's what Woody's play *Continuum* was all about. She was up to her neck in a self-fulfilling prophecy. Never mind. Val was coming home.

O N THE DAY of Val's homecoming, Sheila was up at
daybreak. The *ménage à trois*, now transplanted to
Westport, Connecticut, had already fallen into a pattern:
Woody commuting to New York, Sheila locked in with
her typewriter, and Muriel cheerily bringing order out of
her daughter's five-room chaos.

Sheila's house was becoming hospital-clean. And
Sheila's kitchen a *Woman's Day* dream of pies baking and
jam cooling in jars on windowsills. Sheila was becoming
accustomed to shining floors and windows penetrable to
the naked eye. A house with sprigs of wild flowers in
every room and a ringless bathtub was not entirely to be
despised. But she would gladly have exchanged it all for
one touch of Val's hand, the sound of his laugh.

She lay back in her cool and ringless tub and
focused on one fact: Val would be home tonight. She
would wait for him at his apartment. He would loom
through the door, grinning and holding out his arms to
her. She would melt herself into him, feel the bones of
his body, smell his breath and his skin and his hay-pile
of hair. They would make love and make love and make

love. He would tell her she was beautiful, tell her about London, tell her—

She scrambled out of the tub, in a fever to make nine o'clock come faster, faster. An endless day stretched ahead of her, but the night would be endless, too.

Sheila put on a dress, not jeans, and joined Woody and Muriel at a card table under the trees. Muriel had dug up a flowered cloth—where, her daughter wondered?—squeezed fresh orange juice, and perked the coffee. She patted Sheila's hand—"This is the day, isn't it?"—and Sheila had to admit her mother had a nice sense of occasion. Muriel tucked a pillow under Woody's leg— "Let me comfy your leg"—and poured the cream into his coffee as slowly and reverently as a high priestess. Men can stand a lot of coddling without feeling foolish, Sheila thought. Her mother was a woman out of another age, a woman born to be a "good wife." Living must have been much simpler when that was enough.

Muriel drove them to the station and waved them off. Sheila and Woody walked down the platform together, like any other Westport working couple, Woody playing the slightly older but dashing husband who carried his cane with a jaunty air and tucked the *Times* under Sheila's arm. Nobody would have guessed that Sheila was a woman in turmoil, a writer who could no longer write, a woman so in love, so yearning for night to come that she would have pushed the train to New York.

They boarded and found seats miraculously together. Sheila stared at the *Times* while she tried to make sense of her life. After all, this newspaper succeeded in reducing the agonies of the planet to six neat columns of print per page, day after day. Surely she should be able to capture her own life on the blank page of her mind and look at it and say, "Yes, this is what's happening."

Her life since last spring seemed to have gone out of control, but Sheila reminded herself that "an airplane is a machine that almost doesn't fly." The fight with Kerry would someday be repaired, the child having called from Boston, polite but short of funds. Sheila's work was at a standstill. She had produced not one viable chapter since her singing bird of a mother had moved in. But Woody was coming home each night with another investor signed up and a warm welcome-back-to-Broadway ringing in his ears. In short, life was not unbearable, nor was it the rose garden that nobody had ever promised her. The worst part was Theo.

Theo had not called, and would not accept Sheila's calls. She must be angry, disapproving of the affair with Val. Between them Theo had always been the expert on men, Sheila's disastrous marriage having reinforced her position. But how could she cut Sheila off like this? Sheila resolved that today they would be friends again.

At Grand Central Station Sheila gave Woody a quick kiss and ducked into a phone booth. She dialed Theo's office, disguised her voice, and gave her name as one of Theo's most successful authors. When Theo came on the line, Sheila spoke in her normal voice.

"Hi. It's me."

"Sheila! You rat!"

"Rat? How about you? Refusing my calls for weeks! Hanging up on me. Theo, what the hell is happening?"

"Sheila, I'm going to hang up now."

"No! Godammit, Theo, this call cost me a quarter and you can listen to me, not talk, just listen."

"Oh, shit."

"You and I've been friends since second grade. Are you going to tell me that's *nothing?* Are you going to trash those thirty-some years like they never *happened?*"

Sheila listened for a click, but it didn't come. She cleared her throat and reached for the black box in front of her and held it and pulled herself closer to the phone.

"Remember when I gave you my best turtle and you told me what Slimey Smith kept in his strongbox?"

Silence.

"I showed you my letter from James Dean and you told me about the pip. We drank one thousand frosted chocolates and we stole a quart of strawberries from the Happy Day Fruitstand. We double-dated and I always switched if you wanted to. You were the maid of honor at my wedding and I took you for your abortion. I think you are beautiful and smart and funny and if you never want to see me again"—Sheila was sobbing by now and could hardly get the words out—"then that's perfectly goddam fine with me, but you could at least tell me, for crissake, why? Just tell me. I'm not stupid. Why, Theo . . . why?"

Theo was crying, too.

"I can't . . . I can't *talk* . . ."

"I'll see you at Gino's at one o'clock and you'd better be there and for crissake bring the Kleenex."

They hung up.

Sheila spent the morning buying flimsy underwear

and a diaphanous garment she called her "après-screw."
She arrived at the restaurant to receive Gino's kiss on her
trembling hand and followed him to the "always table."
She fastened her eyes on the door until Theo came
striding in: tall, athletic, and arrogant. The girl had
style. Short, pale-blond hair—a new shade—wide
shoulders and the same nineteen-inch waist; a simple
black dress that cost several back teeth even on Seventh
Avenue, and that proud, flowing walk, angular and
graceful as a giraffe. She came directly toward Sheila,
who sprang up, and they embraced without a word.
Finally, they both spoke at once.

"You look great."

"You look gorgeous."

"Love your hair. What's it called?"

"Urine by moonlight."

They both screeched and fell laughing on the
banquette together, but when they ran out of laughter,
they didn't know where to begin. Theo drank from her
waterglass and Sheila bit her hangnail. Theo spoke.

"All right. When's he coming home?"

"Tonight."

"Splendid."

"I missed him."

"Naturally."

"He's been working hard over there."

"I pay him."

"Theo, don't you like Val?"

"Like him? Who could resist? All that craggy
charm? That boyish candor? That voice." She stopped,
and Sheila finished for her.

"A voice that would light a candle across the room."

"Oh, very *good*."

"Theo, I'm so crazy in love with him! I've been dying to talk to you. Theo, why did you cut me off?"

"Now just one frigging minute! *You* cut *me* off, old girl! You fell into bed with a man I sent to have lunch with you! You flew him out to Kansas and carved out his future without one goddam word to me, your 'best friend.' You proceed to sit out there in Kansas—with your *mother*, for crissake—do you write to me, phone me, send me a carrier pigeon? Certainly not, but my office phones are ringing off the hook with calls for Val Keating, which brings me the news you are not deceased! Don't tell me I cut you off, you rotten kid! Here. Have a Kleenex."

Sheila felt her eyes brimming. She dabbed away as the waiter came to take their order for drinks and pasta.

"Oh, God, Theo, I'm sorry . . . I didn't realize . . . How could I be so dumb? I guess, when I fall in love, I lose my mind. I become . . . incompetent."

"Remember, you said it. 'Incompetent.'"

"I didn't mean—"

"Yes, indeedy. I'm looking after you on this one, Sheely. After all, I'm responsible for this *misalliance*."

"It is not!"

"I was the half-wit who sent Val here for that fatal lunch. I should have known better. This unemployed actor . . ."

"I'm working on that!"

"This swaggering kid from Nebraska . . ."

"A kid of thirty!"

"Sheila, I'm going to save you from yourself."

"So that's why you sent him to England! For my 'own good!' My God, it's like having another mother!"

"Not exactly."

"But my real mother thinks he's the second coming! And he is! Oh, Theo, be happy for me! I'm in love, and I'm eighteen, and I feel . . . an infinite . . . felicity."

"*No.* No, I won't be happy for you. Sheely, this is the wrong guy at the wrong time. He's too young and too poor."

"He'll get older. Richer, too."

"Val isn't finished yet. He's becoming. Who knows what? When I met him, he was devouring five plates of party food at a sitting. He was starving. That's what the theater did for him. Now, he's halfway to being a literary agent. Maybe a good one."

"Val is an actor! He'll be a major star!"

They stared at each other across the deadlock. The arrival of their drinks filled a terrible pause. They raised their glasses to each other and sipped and sipped again.

"Ah-h-h."

"Yeah. Liquid comfort."

"Look, Sheila . . . " Theo looked into her glass for words, she who was always so sure. "Sheely . . . I have no child, no husband, no cat. These guys that parade through my life—they're the best available at the time. But you—well, you've always been there. I can hardly believe what's happening, to make me say things like this. But I'm saying them. In this whole frigging world, you're the one I love . . . I trust you . . . you make me laugh . . . I want you to be happy."

Sheila was nodding, too moved to speak, and dropped her head for a second on Theo's shoulder.

"Sheely, for God's sake, trust me. You're in love. With you, that's out of your mind. I know what's good for you. Drop Val, drop the play, pretend this never happened. Go home and finish the book before the publishers have my head and *cool off*. Give it a month, a year, what's the difference? You *will* get over it. Don't you believe me?"

Sheila slowly shook her head.

"Sheely, tell me something. Don't you ever hear a small voice, the one that says 'Look out, watch this man. He's disaster?'"

"I hear something like that. Sometimes."

"Well?"

"Val and I are so different. He's so happy it's ridiculous, and I'm always wearing this crown of thorns, you know. But Theo, he doesn't care. He loves me . . . and I'd shoot myself in the stomach for him."

"You are a mental midget."

When their lunch came, they ate it pretending their friendship was the same as ever, and perhaps it was. Theo asked about Kansas, Sheila filled her in about Woody and what it was like being midwife to the birth of a play.

"Uncle Woody's quite attractive, huh?"

"Oh, Theo, he's going to marry my mother!"

"M-m-m," said Theo.

They stood outside in the June sunshine and hugged each other good-bye.

"I missed you so much," Sheila said. "Don't ever dump me again."

The midday traffic on Lexington was roaring by. Sheila could hardly hear Theo's answer as she strode away. Was it "Not until next time" or "See you next time," or what? She watched the tall, swinging figure out of sight, glanced at her watch, and closed her eyes for a second. In seven hours she would be in Val's arms. Two double features and a frosted from now.

SHEILA PRESSED THE buzzer for Val's apartment, and pressed again—suppose the Zen Buddhist had failed to vacate?—then climbed the five flights past a United Nations of smells: cabbage, garlic, and fish. She let herself into the apartment and found a state of chaos. Empty food cartons littered the floor. A large branch from a tree nailed above the bed had shed its leaves on the dingy pillow. A dead rose drooped in a milk carton on the sooty windowsill. The telephone dangled its severed cord from the arm of the big chair. The tropical fish were sulking at the bottom of their tank.

She fed the fish. They popped to the surface and snapped and whirled away, and popped, snapped, and whirled again without ever bumping into each other. Sheila sat on the foot of the bed and contemplated a squashed cockroach at her feet. The room had been so clean when she came here with Val. She herself had become accustomed to her mother's spotless environment. How could she contemplate an amorous reunion in such squalor? She sighed and set to work.

After two hours of washing, sweeping, and bed-making, Sheila hung from the ceiling three huge paper fish she'd bought at a Japanese store and draped her filmy, seductive après-screw across the bed. By now, the window was a black rectangle; nine o'clock had come and gone. Wearily, she fell into the big chair, anticlimax flooding over her. She slept.

She was in his arms. He was kneeling in front of her chair, folding her against his chest, kissing her face and lips and eyes, and rocking back to look at her.

"Oh, Sheila, honey, where've you *been?*"

When she realized she was not dreaming, she threw herself at him with such force that he fell backwards on the floor, pulling her down on top of him. She kissed him and stared into his face, raked his hair, felt his warm body through his shirt, his big hands spanning her back and pressing her body against his. In all the times she had imagined their being together again, nothing had ever been like this. Her desire for him was consuming, overwhelming. She rolled herself off and scrambled to her feet to stand looking down at him.

"Last one naked's a rotten egg."

"Oh, Jesus, honey."

He lay still.

"Val—what's wrong?"

"You won't believe this." He sat up then, crossed his feet, rocked forward, unfolding his long body, and stood up. Suddenly, he looked gaunt-faced and hollow-eyed.

"We've got a problem."

"For God's sake, *what?*"

"There's this woman downstairs—"

"*What* woman?"

"She was on my plane, asked me to help her. She lost her reticule."

"Her *what?*"

"Money, credit cards, the works."

"You mean, she's coming up *here?*"

"What could I *do?*" He showed her his dog-eared, empty wallet. "Let her sleep on the street?"

"*Why the hell not?*"

"I told her to give us five minutes and time's up. God, honey, I'm sorry." He was moving toward the door, looking back mournful as a bloodhound.

"If you let that woman in here—" But Val had stepped out into the hall. He gave a long, low whistle down the stairwell and the answer came back in an old woman's croak.

"I'm comin', Sonny. Gor blimey, 'alfway to 'eaven, are ye?"

Val came back leaving the door open. He held out his hands, palms up like a man who had lost control of his life. Sheila went for him, pummeling his chest in fury. He caught her wrists.

"Honey, I couldn't help it! You got to *believe me!* Honey, time out, huh? We got company!" Sheila's pounding slowed to a halt as she turned to see a figure in the doorway.

An ancient crone stood there, draped in rusty black, her hat a giant toadstool. She peered through milk-bottle glasses over a bulbous nose. A few grey hairs straggled down to lie limply on the small, mangy animal that circled her neck. Her wasted body bent forward in a question mark. The hand that trembled on the crook of the blackthorn cane was gloved in an intricate pattern of hand-embroidered warts. The figure tottered toward Sheila and stopped within a musty-smelling inch. The head drooped sideways on the stem of the neck so the fishbowl eyes could look up into Sheila's face.

"S'help me, yr lydyship, Oi'm a bird without a nest, so I am."

"Well, you're not nesting here, Piper York, so get lost."

Piper reeled back, cackling with a hag's laughter. But gradually the cackle changed and deepened into the bubbling merriment of a young girl. She yanked off her hat and the grey hairs with it, shaking her dandelion head. She peeled off her putty nose and shrugged out of her black robes and stood in her blue gunny sack of a dress. All the while Piper was chattering happily in her lilting English voice.

"You simply cannot imagine . . . how *hot* it is . . . to be old! But I wasn't half bad, was I? My auntie's garret in London supplied the wardrobe and the cane belonged to my great-Uncle Twitchell. The grey hairs— would you credit—came from the tail of my first spaniel, who died valiantly in battle with a hedgehog. As for the eyeglasses . . ." She broke off, looking around the room for the first time, noting the paper fish hanging from the ceiling, the gossamer dressing gown spread across the bed.

"I'm afraid I'm the ghost at the feast. Val, I really must scamper off now. . . ."

She started retrieving her garments from the floor where she had flung them, but Val grabbed her arm.

"No, you can't go."

"Why can't she?" Sheila hardly recognized her own voice, cold and icicle sharp.

"Because she hasn't got a red cent for a hotel. I told you, she was robbed in Heathrow Airport!"

Piper chimed in. "My reticule was hanging on my wrist. Beaded black, perfectly in period. This wretched little swine jostled me in the crowd, cut the strings, and ran for his life! I chased him, of course, and I nearly caught him, but he went to ground in the men's loo!"

"It's a fox-hunting expression," Val put in helpfully.

"Thanks, Reynard."

"The good thing was," Piper went on breathlessly, "my auntie had pinned my passport and my air ticket inside my dress!"

"How fortunate."

Val felt the need to explain again. "The auntie's kind of soft on Piper." And he put his arm across Piper's shoulders in brotherly affection. Brotherly? The arm rested there. Five minutes earlier that same arm had held Sheila, welding their two bodies together. Sheila watched the arm hoping it would wither and fall off.

Val dropped the arm. Piper's eyes went from one to the other, trying to read their faces.

"Please—don't be angry with Val. It's not his fault! I stowed away on his plane!"

"You . . . stowed away?"

"In my old-lady get-up! Otherwise, if he knew it

was me, he'd be angry and probably have me chucked off the aircraft before we even left Heathrow! So I stayed in character—heh-heh-heh." Briefly she bent over and took a few rickety steps and straightened up again, "until we'd cleared the Irish Sea!"

Val joined in, eagerly, impetuously.

"So then she comes tottering down the aisle to where I'm sitting, this hag with a voice like a crow, and she tosses me a line from the play! *Our* play!" He came to Sheila and touched her hand, but it was too little and too late. A Judas touch. "Not missing a beat, I come back with the next line, and then I do a take, and a double take, and I'm staring at this old witch, and we're running lines together! Lines from a play that's never been outside of Lawrence, Kansas! Can you imagine? I felt like I'd jumped my track! I get up out of my seat and I grab her, and I shake her." Here Val stopped to demonstrate and Piper's small head bobbed back and forth, "And I said something dumb like . . ."

"He said, 'Where'd you *come* from?' " They laughed at the memory of the private joke, which seemed to Sheila more private than joke. They fell against each other, laughing. Val finally recovered.

"And then I saw through the glasses into the eyes. Piper has blue eyes but special blue, very dark. *Navy* blue. You ever notice? Anyhow, that's when I knew it was Piper. Pretty good makeup, huh?"

"I've seen better on Halloween."

Val dropped his hands and the fun went out of his face. Piper came between them.

"Oh, Sheila, he was so angry, you can't think! He tore me off a strip! But don't you see, there wasn't anything he could *do*, was there?"

"Several things."

"You mean murder me and toss me to the sharks?" She was like the trick candles on a birthday cake, always lighting up again. The child was laughing delightedly.

"But don't you see? I *had* to come! You do understand, don't you?"

The child's face was close to Sheila's, the porcelain skin, the dark pools of the eyes.

"I'm trying not to."

Piper turned to Val. "She's witty, isn't she?" Then she came back to Sheila.

"You know the oldest saying in the theater? 'Be in the right place at the right time.' I had to *be* here! Woody must be casting by now! I want that part so much, Sheila. I'd commit murder for that part. Oh, please—say you understand?"

Sheila looked at the child, who no longer looked so childish. She looked like a young woman, old enough for her first love affair with an 'older man.' Sheila ran the tape in her mind, the whole unlikely scenario: Piper dressing up in her auntie's garret, Piper chasing a mugger through Heathrow Airport, Piper and Val cavorting in the aisles of a jumbo jet, ancient crone and dashing young actor. Was the whole complicated charade invented by two people who could not bear to be parted? Or was it one of the crazy things that happens in "real life?" For a fraction of a second, Sheila balanced on a tightrope, ready to fall on either side. Piper was still standing there, looking innocent, pleading for Sheila's sympathy.

"Do you understand, Sheila?"

Val had been pacing like a wounded animal, but now he growled the fatal words.

"She wouldn't know. She's a writer."

Ah. Now it was out in the open. Two against one. Two fun-loving, dedicated young actors against one grim and humorless puncher of typewriters. If an infidelity had been committed—and perhaps she would never know—*this* was the real infidelity. "She wouldn't know. She's a writer." So it was them against her. Sheila was alone, more alone than ever in her life. But she wouldn't let it show. Never let them see. She collected every shred of herself, and launched into battle.

"Of *course* I understand! And of course you'll get the part! You're going to be a *super* actress! They'll pull you through the streets in a tumbril. But in the meantime, darlings"—she smothered a languid yawn—"where the hell are we all going beddy-bye? In this one tweeny-weeny little bed? Want to try it on for size? C'mon!" She leapt onto the bed, bounced once, and patted the mattress on either side of her. "I must tell you I snore, and occasionally walk in my sleep. If you two are sleep-walkers, we might need starting times, as in golf! I'm going first!" She left the bed and started sleep walking, hand washing bloody hand, as she auditioned for Lady Macbeth. "'Out, damned spot! Out, I say! Blah-blah-blah. Here's the smell of the blood still; all the perfumes of Arabia will not sweeten this little hand. Oh-h-h-h.' " With a blood-curdling scream, she reeled and fell to the floor.

"I say, you're *good!*" said Piper.

"Child's play, my dear," said Sheila, dusting herself off.

"Come on, we'll go up to your house," said Val. "Leave Piper here."

"Kerry is sleeping at my house," said Sheila. "My mother is sleeping at my house. Woody is sleeping at my house. Of course, you and I could sleep standing up in the broom closet. Want to?"

By now she was on her feet again and stood facing Val without a hair's breath between them, as if in a broom closet.

"I—I forgot."

Sheila paced. "Now wait a minute. Three people, one bed. It's the cannibals and the missionaries, isn't it?"

"I have it!" She made a dive for her purse and pulled out her wallet. "One thing about writers, they're *rich*. Dull, unsympathetic, but *rich*." She extracted a packet of crisp bills, the ones she had planned to spend on an extravagant meal and a pair of gold cuff links for Val. She slapped the bills into Val's helplessly outstretched hands. "Now you go find a nice hotel and take those navy blue eyes with you." She gathered up Piper's black garments and stuffed them into her arms. "You put her to bed, or put both of you to bed, as the case may be. But if you do come back, don't wake me up, will you? Think of yourself as an actor between engagements."

She had found his backpack and now she slipped the strap over his shoulder.

"There. Just in case you decide to stay."

Val shrugged off the strap and flung the pack against the wall.

"I'll be back."

He grabbed Piper's hand and swung her out the door, slamming it behind them.

Sheila stood motionless and listened to their footsteps diminishing on the stairs. Then she whirled and yanked down the paper fish from the ceiling, one by one. She squashed them under her arm and whipped her après-screw under the other. She let herself out and closed the door silently. When she heard the front door of the building close, Sheila started, very slowly, down the stairs.

Sheila never cried. It was her mother who was famous for weeping. Besides, a person who cried while going down stairs would probably fall and break her neck. She held onto the railing, just in case.

AT TWO-THIRTY that morning, Sheila slipped into her narrow bed in Westport, gently heaving her daughter to one side. Kerry groaned, gasped, and sat bolt upright.

"Mother! What are you doing?"

"Sleeping."

"But, what *happened?*" Sheila's back was a wall of silence and Kerry lay there, her brain seething with possibilities. But in the morning, there was no escaping the questions. In a small house with one bathroom, biology establishes a rigid traffic pattern. Muriel was leaving the bathroom as Sheila went in.

"Sheila, you came back! What *happened?*"

"Mother, shall we *not* discuss it?" and Sheila slipped in. As she slipped out again, Kerry was waiting in the hall.

"Hey, what's the plot, Mom?"

"Forget it, okay?" and Sheila marched on back to the bedroom.

As Kerry left the bathroom, Woody was waiting, eyes averted as chivalry demanded. Kerry, who loved spreading any news, good or bad, confronted him.

"Woody, you won't believe what happened!"

"Thank you, I can count," and Woody went in.

Kerry rushed to tell her mother in great delight. "Hey, Mom, Woody's been counting the flushes!" but Sheila stayed silent under the sheet. She knew very well that Kerry was inviting her to share the joke, perhaps even to make up. But she had wrapped herself in misery. Longing to be touched, she remained untouchable.

Face to the wall, Sheila heard Kerry slicking on her blue jeans, then a zip and a snap. She heard her rustling into her shirt, then two swishes as she tied the shirt-tails into a double knot in front. She heard a bare foot squeak on the floor as the child turned to pick up—a sneaker? Sheila knew without looking that Kerry was slipping on a shoe while standing on one leg like a stork. Then came the other shoe and Sheila pictured that fluid folding and unfolding of the long, smooth limbs. Now she must be dressed. Two footsteps and Kerry was at the foot of the bed. She stopped. She must be looking down at her mother, waiting. Oh, God, how they would talk, laugh, cry, hug. Sheila stopped breathing. *Please, let her come.* Neither one moved. Neither one spoke. The silence was forever. Then Kerry left the room.

Sheila lay there, plumbing the depths of her sorrow until there was nowhere else to go. Coffee smells drifted into the room. Sheila could hear her mother and her daughter laughing together as if nothing had happened. Business as usual. We don't know and we don't care about each other's pain. Then came the unmistakable smell of banana pancakes. Sheila had had no dinner the night before. The thought of the pancakes was a torment.

225

How humiliating to feel hunger in the midst of her searing grief. The tyranny of the body. She flung herself out of bed and into her ugliest bathrobe and slippers. She shuffled toward the happy voices in the kitchen, Woody having "joined the ladies" and all three faces turned toward her expectantly.

"I prefer not to answer any questions, about anything. Pretend I'm not here. Is that understood?"

"Why, of course, dear," said her mother, and turned back to flipping pancakes.

"Pour your mother some juice, Kerry, in *case* she drops in," said Woody deadpan.

"Hope she does, y'know?" said Kerry. "Mom's not bad in the morning. My roommate *snarls* until second period."

"Your mother has always had a sunny disposition," said Muriel. Sheila heard the palpable lie but gave no sign.

Kerry brought juice and poured her mother's coffee. Woody looked at the ceiling and pronounced, "Sheila's a smart girl, talented, pretty." But Muriel eagerly overlapped him. "My daughter is beautiful and kind and good."

Sheila thought she must be dead and listening to these eulogies from her coffin. How comforting they would be if she were not beyond comfort. The phone rang. Kerry and Muriel looked to Sheila, who shook her head. Kerry ran to the hall and yelled an enthusiastic "Hello!" and the other three froze, hanging on every word.

"Sheila Devlin's house but she's not home . . .

Piper? Where *are* you? New *York?* How come? . . .
You *did?* . . . He *did?* . . . She *did?* . . . Piper,
tell me everything!. . . Yeah . . . Yeah . . . yeah
. . . yeah . . . yeah . . . Got it. Call you back."
She hung up quickly and came back to the kitchen.

"That was Piper York."

"We are not hard of hearing," said Muriel.

"You want the whole, gruesome story?"

Muriel turned apologetically to Sheila. "I always
believe in hearing both sides, dear."

"Here's the short version, folks. Piper stows away
on Val's plane, dressed as an old witch. She's been
ripped off at Heathrow, so Val brings her to his flat.
Mother thinks they're having it on and flips her lid.
Sends Piper to a flophouse with Val and slams out of
there. That right, Mother?"

"If you *must* know—"

"Geez, Mom, you really blew it, didn't you?"

"Why, Sheila, don't you trust that nice, honest
young man? Shame on you!" said her mother. Sheila
would have risen and stalked out, but Woody spoke up.

"Val—and little Piper York? That teen-age pixie
playing dress-up? Oh, come now, Sheila!"

"Piper thinks you need a brain surgeon," said
Kerry.

"My dear, I'm inclined to agree," said Muriel.

Sheila looked from one to the other, unbelieving,
and they looked back, accusing. She would leave this
room, suddenly filled with enemies. But Kerry blocked
her way.

"Come to think of it, what's so surprising? You did

exactly what I'd have pegged you to do." She turned to the others like a lawyer working the jury. "My mother makes up her mind and she walks out. Does Val get to defend himself? Does Piper? Forget it. My mother listens to *nothing* from *nobody*. I mean, my mother is a hanging judge! Am I right?"

Kerry turned to Muriel at the stove, to Woody leaning against the refrigerator. Nobody disagreed.

"I rest my case," said Kerry. Sheila found the silence unbearable.

"Mother, Woody, are you *agreeing* with her?"

"Kerry, you mustn't be harsh," said Muriel.

"I said do you *agree* with her? Look, two minutes ago I was beautiful and kind and good. *What the hell happened?*"

"We thought Val had jilted *you!* And you let us think so, didn't you? You made fools of us all, comforting you, fussing over you. Sheila, how *could* you?"

Sheila turned to Woody, her last hope. "Woody, you understand, don't you?"

"I understand you came out to Kansas a few weeks ago and went after my play like a barracuda. And you got it. Now, when Val, who happens to be my leading man, commits a real or imagined infidelity, you're going to have your lovers' quarrel and the play be damned, is that it?"

Before Sheila could answer, Kerry plunged in.

"Listen, I went out to Kansas to ask her, to beg her, to let me to to Italy this summer. *Nyet.* No discussion. Over and out." Kerry pointed at her mother. "Y'know what's wrong with you? You have no mercy!"

"Kerry, don't point," said Muriel. "You see, dear, I feel a tiny bit of sympathy for your daughter. How many years have I begged you to let me come here? For a tiny visit? On trial? Well, I'm here now and it's not so terribly bad, is it?"

"Yeah, it's hell on wheels!"

"Writers are so self-centered. If you'd ever worked in a hospital, trying to keep everybody happy. . . ."

Woody sat down opposite Sheila and pinned her with his look.

"Did it ever occur to you, in the midst of your jealous pique, that I have abandoned my academic career and crossed the continent to live in a suitcase and panhandle up and down Broadway looking for a producer for this play you *pretend* to admire?"

"I do!" Sheila heard herself croak.

"Ah, but you're in love! When women fall in love, they no longer *think*. They *feel!* They desire! They lust! A woman in love can create the world or destroy it! She is as wanton as a child, not to be trusted . . . I trusted you, Sheila."

He rose and walked away from her. Sheila, stunned, looked over at Kerry, an avenging goddess in the window, at her mother fussing with the percolator, and back to Woody in his elegant dressing gown, his hand trembling with rage as he lifted his coffee cup. Sheila pushed away from the table and stood facing them all.

"With a family like you, who needs friends or lovers or a kick in the arse from a blind horse?"

She left them.

She went to her room and shut the door quietly behind her. She shuffled through papers, hoping she could work, but her head was throbbing with echoes. "Hanging judge" . . . "barracuda" . . . and worst of all, "I trusted you."

She felt condemned, and by the three people closest to her in the world: her mother, her daughter, and Woody. How could they be wrong? . . . But, oh, God, how could they be right?

She sat, staring out the window. This moment, right now, she would always remember. The morning that everything changed. The morning she found out. Found out what? She could hardly put it into words. Found out herself. She felt ugly and sick and alone.

She saw the side yard; a row of spindly evergreens, two wooden chairs that needed painting, and long, early-morning shadows zigzagging across the chairs.

Then Woody came out with his *Times*—she had forgotten it was Sunday—and settled in one of the chairs. Kerry followed him and they talked. It was like a movie with no soundtrack. Kerry showed Woody a catalog, perhaps from his friend's art gallery where Kerry had been working. Did she like it? Was she happy there? Muriel joined the other two and admired the catalog. They were all talking. Then Kerry stretched out on a towel to sunbathe, picking a sunny stripe between tree shadows, and Muriel sat beside Woody shelling peas into a large blue bowl. Woody showed her something in the *Times* and they both laughed. Muriel passed the paper to Kerry, and she laughed.

Then nothing happened. Woody went on reading,

and Muriel shelling and Kerry sunning. They were there with each other, complete without her. Was this Coventry? Or some terrible play she was condemned to watch, in which nothing would ever happen? Three people sat there on the grass and the shadows slowly grew shorter and a summer morning went by for nothing, while time died of loneliness and boredom.

Sheila snatched a train schedule from her desk. She threw open the window and called, "Kerry, drive me to the station, please?"

They rode in silence until Kerry said, "I guess I blasted you this morning."

"You and who else?"

"Are you hurting, Mom?"

"Are you?"

"Yeah."

"We'll talk when I come back."

"Deal."

Sheila let herself into Val's building without ringing. She climbed to his floor and stood in front of his door, gathering her courage. She knocked, and waited for a lifetime. Val opened the door and he was almost the same, so tall and gaunt. But she had never seen his face in despair before. A question came into his eyes and he moved toward her, closing the door behind her. His hands rose slowly to hold her face while he searched for something in her eyes. She met his look, then dropped her head against his chest. His arms slowly came around her. They swayed together from side to side. He groaned, and rested his cheek against the top of her head.

CHAPTER

19

THE LOVERS DREAMED away the weekend, making love and murmuring together, strolling the hot city streets, returning to feast on cold bird and a bottle in Val's apartment.

On Monday morning, real life returned: Val must go to his office and Sheila to Westport. He walked her to Grand Central Station, where they stopped many times to cling to each other as they crossed the vast rotunda. He boarded her train with her and stayed on, grasping the rack above her seat and looming over her until the last possible second. Finally he dashed out the door and started walking along the platform beside the moving train. Now he was jogging, now running. As she caught her last glimpse of him, he was plunging an imaginary dagger into his heart and reeling into his death agony. Sheila stared out the grimy window. She had never been so happy, nor so bereft in all her life.

She was thankful to find her house empty: Kerry had returned to Boston, Muriel was marketing, and Woody doing his rounds in Manhattan. Sheila pulled her work around her like a cloak and let the day go by. That evening Val telephoned. Theo was sending him to Canada to prospect for new authors. To Canada? Why? When? For how *long?* How *could* she?

Sheila tried again to hear Theo's last words as they had parted after lunch, words garbled by traffic noises. She should have known. No words of Theo's were ever garbled by accident. Even then she was planning another separation, for Sheila's "own good." Oh, Theo, perfidious friend. The call ended in frustration as Val ran out of change for the pay phone.

Sheila returned to the dinner table and a fallen soufflé, but was not allowed to sink into despair herself. Muriel said it must be lovely in Canada now, so cool, and Woody briskly added, "He'll be back when we need him. *If* we need him."

"If?" Sheila winced, "What do you mean?"

"I've found a stage manager, costume designer, sound man. Also, production manager, light man, treasurer. I've found half the money."

"Half?"

"Using every contact I ever had, rounding up former investors from everywhere short of the grave, exactly half."

"But you'll get the rest!"

Woody shook his head. "Investors have backed too many turkeys, too many good plays that never earned back production costs." Woody uncharacteristically wolfed his soufflé and rose to pace the small kitchen, u-turning at the refrigerator like a swimmer doing laps.

"So now they're looking for a preproduction movie sale, costarring Buddha and the baby Jesus."

233

"Sherwood!"

"The fabulous invalid has finally done herself in, may she rest in peace." He picked up a copy of his script. "Ladies, what am I offered? A dollar? Half a buck? Come now, the paper and the binder must be worth two bits! I'll even give you a receipt! Watch!" He wrote on the flyleaf in his flowing hand. *Received $.25 in full payment for four years of writing, forty years of learning how. Signed, Sherwood Pell.*

He glared at them. "All right, where's the cash?"

"Woody, stop it!" Sheila slapped a quarter from her jeans pocket onto the table. "We'll get the money!"

"Yes? . . . From . . . where?"

They stared at each other, both longing for the answer, then heard Muriel's sweet, lilting voice.

"If you really and truly need more money—"

Sheila and Woody chorused, "We do."

"What about the third Musketeer?"

"You mean—Uncle Fritz?"

"Who else could I mean? I suppose you were too young to remember when your father and Uncle Woody and Uncle Fritz were the 'Three Musketeers.' Don't you remember when they used to walk across campus together, scarves flying in the wind? What a sight they were! People turned to stare. People said 'There go the Musketeers!' "

Muriel was gazing out the window as if she could still see the three cavaliers, then brought herself back to the present. "Fritz would be happy to help you out."

"Nonsense, woman. Fritz is an arbitrager, the king

234

of the LBOs. He has not the slightest interest in the theater!"

"I'm sure he's still interested in his old friends."

Muriel managed to look modest, but totally confident.

"Mother, do you *hear* from Uncle Fritz?"

"Only the occasional Christmas card, dear. And of course a black pearl on my birthday, the foolish boy."

"A what?"

"I must have almost a necklace by now. I have told him to stop, of course. I have never, believe me, never done anything to lead him on. But in this case, I'm sure he would be happy to help out his oldest and closest friends. I believe dear Fritz has become extremely wealthy. A 'living legend,' as they say."

"I believe he lends money to banks," said Woody.

"Why . . . are we . . . sitting here . . . *talking?*" Sheila asked.

"One could, I suppose, make inquiries," said Woody loftily.

"Mother, I'll spring for a phone call to New York!"

Muriel called Uncle Fritz, who was "expected back from Teheran." She left her name and number.

At 3:00 A.M. the phone rang. Muriel, whose bedroom was closest, groped her way to the kitchen. The booming voice of Uncle Fritz could be heard equally well by Sheila, second to arrive at the phone and leaning close to the receiver.

"Muriel Devlin, you she-devil, how the hell are you? Fine? How can you be fine when you call me for the first time in this goddam century and say it's urgent? I thought sure you had a terminal disease! Listen, you want to make a deathbed confession, I'm your man! I always was your man, remember? Hey, Murie, are you as beautiful as ever? Don't answer that. I'll be the judge. Now you get your sensational fan-tan down here and we'll have breakfast together. Popovers and gooseberry jam, remember? All *right*. I'm sending my driver for you, seven A.M. sharp at your house. What? What directions? If my driver can't find the Devlin house in Westport, Conn., I won't just fire him, I'll have him arrested. See you later." Click.

Muriel and Sheila stared at each other.

"Wow," said Sheila.

"Uncle Fritz was always a *definite* man," said Muriel with a slight smile and a toss of her head.

"Was he a *real* friend of yours, Mother?"

"Mercy, what an hour to call," was Muriel's evasive remark. "We must get back to bed!" Woody had joined them by now, impeccably bathrobed and combed. Woody would be black tie for an earthquake.

"Ladies, might I ask—"

"Mother's having popovers with the living legend!"

"And with you, dear." She patted her daughter.

"Me? Are you crazy? Mother, he could be our angel! *You* have to talk to him! *Alone!*"

"If I go alone, my dear," said Muriel with soft finality, "I do not go at all!" She swept from the room.

Sheila turned to Woody.

"Woody, he's mad for her!"

"Always was."

"You mean they had an affair?"

"One will never know. But your father was wearing his *Hamlet* sword when he told Fritz to leave town."

"*Why?*"

"Fritz and Muriel were locked in the church overnight after choir practice. I believe there are cushions on those pews."

"*Woody!* All right, now tell me everything. What's an arbitrager? What's an LBO? What did Fritz teach at KU?"

"Economics, of course."

They stayed up so long, while Woody educated Sheila in corporate takeovers, that the sun rose and a limousine drew up outside, measuring itself against the length of Sheila's house and winning by a monogrammed license plate in the rear. The chauffeur was a black belt from Beijing who selected Händel's *Wassermusik* for the stereo and they flowed into town. They drew up in front of an elegant townhouse in the east Seventies. Their driver did an end-run in front of them, opened a wrought-iron door, and pressed a series of buttons in the vestibule to disengage the burglar alarm. He waved to the closed-circuit television. "It's me, boss. You have *two* ladies, very fine," and let them into a glistening marble hall. He ushered them into a tiny elevator lined in velvet and closed the door. They waited, feeling like forgotten jewels. Finally, they rose five flights and stopped. The door was flung open by a big man in a blue jumpsuit who folded Muriel in a mammoth bear hug.

"And who's this little lady? Could this be Sheely-baby, all grown up? Come on, Murie, I always wanted you to see this!"

237

He pulled them down a hall and into a sunlit forest. The top floor of the house was a glassed-in garden. Muriel gasped at the sight of the trees, still dripping them from their morning's watering; the brilliant, half-hidden patches of flowers between rock ledges; the tiny red-yellow-green birds swooping among the branches. On cue, the birds started to sing.

"You like it, Murie?" He put his big hand on her mother's shoulder. She turned her flowerlike face toward him.

"It's—it's paradise!"

Uncle Fritz glowed and led them to a glassy table piled with fruit and beaded pitchers of cold juice. He seated Muriel as if she were made of glass, speared her a gleaming slice of melon, and poured steaming coffee into her cup. Muriel was a child at her first birthday party. She put both hands to her mouth and looked at Fritz with dancing eyes. He chose the most towering of popovers and spread it liberally with gooseberry jam. Muriel laughed happily and fed him the first bite. Sheila looked around her.

Here in this enchanted bubble, Uncle Fritz controlled the weather, told the birds when to sing and the popovers when to pop. A man who could do all this and doted on her mother would surely help produce a play. An off-Broadway play. A fine play written by his old friend and former Musketeer. Sheila leapt into the future. Val would become rich and famous and they would live together almost happily forever after.

"What do you do, Sheely-baby, when you're not horning in on your mother's dates?"

Uncle Fritz was leaning toward her, a humorous face, well fed, as sensitive as a charging bull.

"I write novels and castrate people who call me Sheely-baby." She raised her fruit knife and twirled it in the sun.

"Holy God Almighty, she's her father's daughter!"

Uncle Fritz roared with laughter, his fist hit the table, and the silverware jumped. Sheila kept her own face smiling, "saucy" he would probably call it, but behind the face she was sober. Don't blow it, Sheila. The rest of your life could depend on how you handle this man with the sharp eyes and beautiful fingernails and a key to Fort Knox.

Fritz had turned back to Muriel. "Y'know why I never had a child? Can't stand 'em. Leaky, drooling little bastards. But if I could have a full-grown one like her— say, is she up for adoption?"

"Oh, Fritz, you are so *amusing!*"

He turned back to Sheila. "Would you believe I had three wives? Number One died when you got your first two-wheeler. You went ass-over-tea-kettle the day of her funeral." He reached for her right hand and gently circled her wrist with his fingers. "Mended real nice, didn't it?" He withdrew his hand. "So then Number Two walked out on me with her golf pro. Number Three left me for a school teacher! Tell me, Sheely-baby, what do women want anyhow?"

"Maybe they want names instead of numbers," said Sheila, keeping her voice gentle. At this moment, Uncle Fritz looked so vulnerable. He was shaking his head very slightly, like a bear with a toothache.

"Not stupid—are ya?" He wiped his mouth on a huge linen napkin. "And now, ladies, if you have enjoyed my unworthy food and drink—as they say in the People's Republic of China, where I'm due next week— why, we'll move on out of here."

He offered Muriel his arm and walked them to the elevator. He stood facing the gate, the women behind him, and spoke to them over his shoulder as they descended. At the fourth floor he said, "That's my gymnasium, fully equipped. Shape up or ship out, right?" At the third floor, "My bedroom. Restrain yourselves, girls." At the second floor, he flung back the gate and they filed out into the living room. It was cavernous, running the length of the house and sparsely furnished. But the walls were crowded with paintings, each lighted and glowing against dark-paneled walls. At the far end of the room in a bay window stood a huge concert grand, a stretch Steinway. Fritz waved to it, saying, "Give us a tune, Sheely-baby." He pulled Muriel down beside him on a nearby sofa, thus insuring that the vastness of the room would lie between them and their chaperone, Sheila.

Walking the mile to her instrument, Sheila reviewed her repertory of three pieces that had not changed since she was ten years of age. She decided to open with the *Rustle of Spring*, close with the *Ride of the Wild Horsemen*, and sandwich in the *Minuet in G*. She sat down and ripped off an arpeggio, instantly humbled by the sonority of the instrument. This little concert would be the greatest desecration since the sack of Rome, but she plunged in.

She soon found she was able to take long pauses, making *ritardandos* where the composer had never intended them, during which she would pick up snatches of the conversation on the sofa.

"Ah, Murie, all these years . . . never called me, never dropped me a line, except 'Thank you for the pearl.' You leading a wild life out there? scandal of the town? . . . You, Murie, a widow? . . . Don't con me, girl. You wouldn't be a widow if you buried ten husbands . . . I know you, you've been carrying on behind my back. Philandering . . . Come clean, admit it!" Sheila could hear indignant protests from Muriel, then more of the same from Fritz. By now the wild horsemen had ridden twice and Sheila had, pianistically, nowhere to go. She played the last few measures *fortissimo* and rose to take a bow. The audience applauded lightly and Sheila made the trip back, pulling up a chair to join them.

"Uncle Woody sends you his best."

"How is the old coot?"

"My mother's going to marry him."

"Like hell you are!"

"He doesn't know it yet, but she is!"

"Woody's not your style! He's a fancy-Dan! Great guy, but fancy. Murie, you soft on him?"

"Oh, Fritz, at my age . . ." Smiling and dimpling, she managed to look forty. "Woody's a fine man. He's a full professor now."

"Don't give me full professor! You got the hots for him, yes or no?"

"Don't you shout at me! And don't use that rude language!"

Muriel rose in agitation and tap-tapped down to the end of the room, hankie to her lips. Sheila put a restraining hand on Fritz's arm.

"Wait. She's upset."

"She can't do it! She's making a big mistake!"

"Think so?"

"She's waited ten years! *Why now?*"

"Woody's written a play, a good one, Broadway material. But you can't find investors these days."

"So?"

"So they'll go back to Lawrence, Kansas, and get married. Don't you see, she feels sorry for him."

"Just like her. Sacrificing herself. Christian charity. Hogwash."

Muriel had seated herself at the piano and was limbering her tiny hands, lifting her pretty chin. She played the opening measures of *Afternoon of a Faun,* forgetting the F sharp.

"That is one pretty little woman."

"Yes."

"I'd have married her long ago if I'd known the exact situation. If I hadn't been married to Number Two . . . no, after her and before Number Three . . . well, anyhow . . ."

Muriel's wasp-waisted figure was outlined against the window. She looked small and womanly, the light bouncing off her famous red-gold hair. There was a long, very long pause.

"What's it cost to get the curtain up nowadays?"

"Woody's raised half the money already."

"The first half's always the easy one. How much?"

"Oh, a million, plus the overcall," said Sheila, tossing it off.

Fritz whistled.

"What's that to you, the corporate raider from Lawrence, Kansas? You made that much last week when you finished your leveraged buyout of IBM."

"BMI for Chrissake," he corrected, but he looked astonished and amused.

"You made ten times that last spring when you sold that dumb bottle company."

"Oh, yeah, 'Crystalclear.'"

"You sold that stock back to the public at thirty times what you paid for it in your LBO five years ago! And even then, you used the company's own assets as collateral!"

"Not bad, huh?"

"How about last December when *Acquisitions Monthly* said you were a walking Christmas tree, with real gold for tinsel."

"Say, wait a minute, girl, where are you getting your info?"

"From Woody, of course."

"Woody?"

"Woody knows every move you've made since you left campus. He subscribes to the *Wall Street Journal, Barrons,* and *Fortune.* He has a file on you."

"*Why?*"

"Because he's proud of you. You're his friend. He remembers when the Three Musketeers walked together and fished together and argued all night long together. Woody doesn't love many people, but he loves you."

"I'll be teetotally damned."

Sheila glanced down the room at her mother and realized she was starting the *Faun* on his third *Afternoon*. Time to wind it up, for better or worse.

"Tell me one thing, Uncle Fritz. How many friends like that have you made since you came to the upper east Seventies?"

Fritz spread his empty hands, wordlessly.

"Uncle Woody needs you all right now. You'll coproduce with him. I know the golden rule: never use your own money. But you have your syndicate, ready to jump when you tell them. You form a limited partnership. You become an "angel," Fritz, and you fly over that crazy wonderful world called the theater! Win, lose, or draw, you have one wonderful time! What do you say, Uncle?"

The sound of the piano stopped abruptly, and Sheila realized Muriel had heard every word. Fritz stood looking down at Sheila, then over at Muriel, and his eyes began to twinkle.

"Don't just stand there, Sheely-baby." He took a card from his wallet and handed it over. "Call my lawyer. Tell him to be here in an hour or less."

Then he strode down the room and scooped up Muriel in his arms.

CHAPTER

20

U NCLE FRITZ, not given to dawdling, took Woody
to lunch the following day. After seven minutes,
according to Woody, seventeen years fell away. They
were friends again, enjoying the attraction of opposites:
Fritz the operator and Woody the observer. That same
afternoon, before leaving for the People's Republic of
China, Fritz signed a mailing to his syndicate. A date
was set, shortly after his return, for the backers' audition
to be held in his own vast living room, but called an
"investors' party," since Fritz said a party might be all
they'd ever get out of this particular leveraged buy-out.

The party went off with gusto. A stage was
improvised at one end of the living room and a few
spotlights concealed behind the rented greenery. Val
flew down from Canada and Piper turned up an hour and
a half early. Their scenes together were connected by
Woody, who gave a brief synopsis of the intervening
story. At the end, he stood before the backers and said,
"Ladies and gentlemen, that's a small sample of our play.
Thank you for coming." The investors, who had never

lost a nickel by following Fritz on every deal, applauded heartily and signed up for one, two, or five units each.

Many of them, over champagne and caviar, asked, "That little Piper York going to get the part?" Even Muriel cornered Woody with the same question. "She's so *sweet*, Sherwood." Piper herself followed Woody silently around the room, her big dark eyes imploring him. And Fritz, disclaiming any knowledge of this "acting business," told Woody to sign her up. "The kid's a knockout." Sheila watched this tidal wave forming. Then Val came to share a handful of nuts with her. Tossing one into his mouth, he said, "Piper can do it. Tell Woody, huh?" and he went off to charm the investors.

Sheila supposed Piper was talented, having long since ceased to be objective on the subject. And if she opposed her now, would it be a hangover of the terrible night those two came home from London together? The night that was followed by "the morning of the long knives?" Sheila swallowed some small nameless tidbit from a silver tray and hoped she would not be asked. But sure enough, Woody joined her and asked if she thought the kid could handle it. After a long sip of champagne, she looked Woody in the eye and said, "In a breeze." Woody nodded and patted her arm, and somehow she knew he had already planned to give Piper the part. He tapped his glass for silence and made the announcement: Piper York would play the lead opposite Val Keating in *Continuum*. Applause followed. Piper threw her arms around Woody and then around Val and then, surprisingly, around Sheila. That night, before he

246

returned to Canada, Val took Sheila to his apartment. They were alone and in love and happy. She didn't want to waste any time in sleeping, but he talked her to sleep, reciting Robert Burns: "And I will come again, my luve, Tho 'twere ten thousand mile!" In the morning when she awakened, he had returned to Canada.

Fortunately, as "production assistant" Sheila was kept busy night and day. Up till now, the play had been a chimera in all their minds. Now it was a juggernaut, starting to roll. She rented a small office on Forty-fifth Street for Woody and acted as runner with costume sketches and set designs. But most of her time was occupied by the auditions Woody held in a small, vacant theater. He was casting the parts of Mother, Father, and Friend. Word that Woody Pell was casting a new play traveled on the wind. Actors gathered by the hundreds to read for the three remaining parts.

On the first day of casting, Sheila sat—pad in hand—next to Woody as one by one the actors, young and old, talented and terrified, filed onstage to read from a script they might never have seen before. A single bare lightbulb hung center stage, but Woody had contrived to have the house lights at half, so the actors were not staring into a black auditorium. He came down to the edge of the stage to speak quietly with each actor before his reading, and, for the sake of variety, kept selecting different scenes from the play. But in spite of his efforts, the business of casting was a long and grueling exercise. The male stage manager would sometimes find himself reading opposite a male actor in a love scene, and the tension would be momentarily relieved by ripples of laughter. Dozens of actors were disappointed for every one asked to come back tomorrow. Sheila thought of Val and prayed he would never again be subjected to the "cattle call."

Finally, the roles were assigned, but Sheila found there was never time to celebrate one event before they were breathlessly headed for the next. The studio of the set designer was suffering a "work stoppage." The actor contracted to play Father had a bid from Hollywood. Play production, Sheila decided, was a hydra-headed monster: for every problem solved, two more sprang up. Meanwhile time was telescoping. Opening night was bearing relentlessly down upon them. Woody moved to a shabby-respectable hotel in town and Sheila kept a toothbrush at Theo's, where Val's name was forbidden by mutual consent. While Val himself was up there charming the Canadians, Sheila barely had time to long for him. Muriel was happily commuting by chauffeur for tea at the Palm Court with Fritz. Suddenly this fast-forward piece of time was over, and it was the first day of rehearsal.

The actors arrived promptly and stood about on-stage, acting casual but serious. Val loped in, panting as if he had run from Toronto, hugged Sheila, pumped Woody's arm, and tossed his backpack into the wings. Woody said quietly, "All right, people, shall we get started?"

He sat at the end of a bare wooden table center stage, motioning Val to a chair at his right, Piper to his left, and Sheila close behind him with her pad. The others took their places. Woody's calm tone seemed to emphasize the sense of occasion in the air.

"Suppose we read right through the play, get the drift of it. You're probably wondering what it's all about, aren't you?" There were wry smiles and head-shakings. "That's good. We'll all find out together. And people, I'm going to get the play on its feet by the end of the week." The actors nodded, knowing this would mean no more books. "One more thing. Please listen to each other. *Really . . . listen . . .* All right? . . . Curtain . . ."

He nodded at Piper, and her clear, young voice spoke the opening line. Woody nodded to the stage manager to note the time and the reading began.

As it progressed, the actors seemed to struggle to become an ensemble, to adapt to each other's timing. Father's style was old-school, while Friend was a method actor, who threw in heavy pauses and read more for himself than others. Val and Piper, in their scenes, read smoothly, the others glancing up involuntarily at the first sound of Val's exceptional voice. Sheila delighted in the sound and counted the hours till they would be alone together. But after the reading, Val rushed off to see his agent. Sheila reminded herself that an actor who has just landed a leading role has little time for anything else, adding "Big deal!" under her breath.

But the real separation from Val was an imaginary line called the "footlights." After the reading, Woody started blocking the play and Sheila took her place "out front" where she belonged. Even Woody, unless he was illustrating a particular piece of business for an actor, remained out front watching and listening. The stage belonged to the actors now. The footlights bounded that small, magic world where only actors live and the rest of the world is audience. Sheila had made it possible for Val to be up there on that stage, and now he was as remote from her as if he lived in another element.

Or was it only in her mind? When they all went out to lunch together—Woody and the cast, often Bill the stage manager—they went to the closest greasy spoon where the waitress soon learned to save them a large table, bring pots of coffee quickly, and hold the French fries on Woody's burger. They all told theater anecdotes, getting laughs and vying for laughs. Actors who had worked together were blood brothers. Actors who had been out of work together shared an almost equal consanguinity. No, it was not only in her mind. Actors lived apart, and Val, if he succeeded, would, too. Well, what did she want, a CPA?

After lunch, she and Val would walk back to rehearsal together.

"Hey, buy you dinner tonight," Sheila said.

"Geez, honey, I said I'd run lines with Piper."

"She *knows* the lines."

"Sure, but she's antsy. After all, this is the big time."

"I'm busy tonight anyway. Playing bezique with Lord Olivier."

"What's bezique?"

"*One* of the things he knows and you don't."

"Yeah. Listen, you think I'm doing all right? So far?"

"You'll do."

It seemed an actor ran on his vanity and that vanity needed constant nourishment. One day Val turned up at rehearsal wearing a new shirt. It was lavender. Sheila contrived to sit next to him at lunch.

"New shirt?"

"Gift from my leading lady. Like it?"

"I find it pusillanimous."

"Uh-huh, I like it, too."

It was hard to reach Val these days. Of course, there were nights when they went to his apartment. The play was a forbidden subject and Val became again the funny, lanky lover who knew all her secrets and loved her anyway. Knew her moods and laughed her out of them. Knew the country where she lived, even if he couldn't follow her there. He was the love of all her life. She prayed she would never forget it.

But then, the next day, Val and Piper would do their five-mile run together at lunch hour, and return in a glow of ostentatious good health. They claimed it was a time-saver, they could run lines together while running.

"How did Sarah Bernhardt ever learn her lines with only one leg?" Sheila wanted to know. Val roared with laughter. But generally he was very serious these days. Whenever Piper's name was mentioned, Val praised her work. She was maturing, growing *into* the part. Didn't Sheila think so? Sheila always managed to agree.

And, indeed, she did agree. The child had grown up to the work. Her performance was at times so naked, so poignant that Sheila found it hard to watch. She and Val played together with such intimacy, such exquisite

251

timing that Sheila's heart ached to see them. Offstage, their conversation was sprinkled with lines from the play, forming a language of their own, a language foreign to Sheila. She was angry, hurt, and excluded, but remembering the "morning of the long knives," she would toss off a remark in Italian and leave them to it.

Halfway through the rehearsal period, there was a change in the mood of the company. One or two people dropped out of lunch, then everyone started lunching separately, in twos and threes. People were whispering in corners backstage and the Equity representative was constantly asked for an appointment, for the airing of petty grievances. Woody remained patient as always, but the performances were sometimes ragged, sometimes lifeless. The company was no longer a company but a collection of inimical strangers.

Sheila took Bill, "the best stage manager in the business," for a cup of coffee.

"What's happening, Bill? Everybody's gone sour."

"Hard to say. Actors. Jesus. Like Thoroughbred horses."

"Come on, Bill. What is it?"

"There's a member of the cast might be on the sauce."

"What else?"

"That character woman's mourning the death of her cat."

"Go on."

"S'help me, Sheila, I don't know. I'm going to get out of this racket and play the horses."

That same afternoon, Val told Sheila that Piper wanted to talk to her.

"Me? Are you sure?"

Yes, he was sure. Sheila went backstage after rehearsal.

"Hey, you want to talk to me?"

Piper nodded and they walked in silence to the greasy spoon. Piper chose a booth in the back and sat facing Sheila. If a child of nineteen could look haggard, this one did. Sheila had put it down to nerves, but this was a look of anguish.

"Piper, are you all right?"

"Oh, yes. No, not really. I mean, I have a slight difficulty. Val commanded that I talk to you. I told him it would be frightfully boring for you."

"So far, I'm not bored."

"It's so silly, because nothing you could say would make the slightest difference." She gave a small, tattered laugh and caught her breath.

"Piper, please, tell me. What's the matter?"

"Nothing, actually. Except everything, if you follow me. Oh, God, I should never have asked you to come!"

"Piper, breathe deeply. We have lots of time."

Sheila ordered two coffees and two vanilla ice creams. Fattening, but a favorite of Piper's. "You're very good in this play, Piper."

"That's too bad, because, you see, I have to leave."

"You *what?*"

"If I leave now, Woody will have time to replace me. I know zillions of people who'll do this part, who'll bleed and die for this part. So . . . no harm done, don't you agree?"

Sheila looked at the child's pleading face and tried not to believe what she had heard.

"Piper, you're *leaving the cast?*"

"I'm leaving. You can't change my mind." She jutted her chin forward, a direct descendant of Winston Churchill.

"Why . . . are . . . you . . . leaving?"

"Because . . ." At first the words wouldn't come. Then the waitress set down the ice cream and Piper attacked it with her spoon, eyes cast down, every spoonful punctuating another painful rush of words. "Val and I . . . when we're working . . . we're perfect . . . we're a bird . . . one bird, with two wings . . . and we *fly* . . . we leave the ground . . . we elevate . . . can't you *see* it? Are you *blind?*"

Suddenly the child raised her head and the deep blue eyes, glistening with unshed tears, were searching Sheila's face.

"I see it."

"But then . . . when we come offstage . . . he *leaves* me . . . he tears his body . . . out of *our* body . . . he goes away . . . to *you!*" The child's face was distorted with grief. Sheila reached to touch her hand, but the child pulled away as if she'd been burned.

"Don't you *see?* . . . I . . . *love* . . . *Val* . . . *Keating.* I can't stand it! Not any more!"

She clenched her small fists against her ravaged face.

"Piper, I know! I understand, about the pain."

254

"Don't comfort me! *I'm leaving!*" Sheila looked at the small, furious person facing her and realized it was true. This child could bring disaster down on all their heads.

"Piper, you are not leaving this play."

"And who's to stop me?" The Churchill look again.

"You will. Because you know you'll never work again in this country and maybe not in England."

"I don't care! I shall be a registered nurse!"

"Chicken-shit! You've wanted this all your life! Now you have it! And you're going to *quit?*" Piper turned her face away, but Sheila reached and roughly turned it back to her. "You could do that to Val and Woody and all of us? Piper York, *don't . . . you . . . dare!*"

"Don't talk to me!" Piper stood up. "I never should have told you! You're smug and superior and—and practically perfect, aren't you?"

The child was edging out of the booth. In a moment she'd be gone.

"Wait! Piper, please don't go!"

"'Parting is such sweet sorrow.'" Mocking, Piper perched on the edge of her seat and cupped her chin in her hand.

"Piper, how do you think I feel? You're an actress. Play my part. Be me. I'm sitting at rehearsals, day after day. I'm watching you two up there onstage. Yes, you're a bird in flight. Yes, you're so beautiful together you break my heart. You break it every day, Piper."

"But . . . he loves you! He told me so!"

"You know what people say about Val and me? They say he's too young and too poor. If he does this play,

255

he won't be poor any more. But you know something terrible? He'll always be too young."

"Oh . . ."

"I've never said that to a living soul before. He's too young." Sheila looked down at the ice cream melting in its silvery dish. Her throat ached and she couldn't trust herself to speak. She tapped the table between them and forced herself to look Piper full in the face.

"Do what you want, actress. I have to go now."

Sheila snatched some bills out of her wallet, and blindly left the place. She walked in a daze toward the theater, her mind echoing the words she had spoken to Piper. Val was "too young." Too young. Too young. How long had this tolling bell been in her mind? How long had she refused to listen to it? Was it true? She couldn't bear it. Not now. Some other time. She arrived at the theater and thankfully plunged into the feverish process of a play being born.

The next day, Piper showed up for rehearsal. Val caught Sheila's eye across the footlights and bowed his head in gratitude. Sheila nodded, and the rehearsal began.

CHAPTER

21

B Y SOME MYSTERIOUS telepathy, the actors knew that catastrophe had been averted. The company regrouped itself. They rehearsed with a high seriousness, no time for clowning and small jokes. They were on the home stretch now, headed for the first preview. Every time an actor went up in his lines, he knew it must be the last time, ever.

Sheila refused to think about Val and their future together. So many unanswerable questions were lying in wait for her that she gave all her energies to the play, hiding away from her own uncertainties. The gathering momentum of the production played into her hands: Val was so busy with rehearsals, interviews, and fittings that they passed each other at a run, calling out, "Hi! You okay?" or sharing bites of a hamburger during rehearsal break. The play had taken over their lives, and Sheila was, in a strange way, grateful.

The company moved to their own off-Broadway theater: the Lambs. No more rehearsing in dance halls and rehearsal studios. They took possession of their little theater with its tidy three-hundred-sixty-four seating capacity. They tested its acoustics and noted its sight lines. Here the verdict would be delivered. Was the play a hit or a bomb? A sleeper, or a great sluggish beast that would lie there on opening night and never, never come to life? Sheila heard snatches of the actors' hopes and fears as she moved between dressing rooms backstage. Actors were a resilient lot, and they were committed now. Mother moved her new cat in, complete with feline latrine, indicating a long run.

The machinery of the production went into high gear. Bill the stage manager was holding his understudy rehearsals. Bits and pieces of scenery began to arrive. A wig or a wooden horse had the power to spark a whole day's work. The Chinese-style "stage-hands," actually dancers in black leotards, began to work in symbiosis with the cast, spreading a shimmering blue river just in time for the fording, or building a mountain range of ladders two seconds before the crossing of the Alps. To Sheila, the whole play was coming alive. But a glance at Woody's face reminded her of the painful contrast between theater as the public saw it and theater from the inside. The obverse of this "glamour industry" was anxiety redoubled by exhaustion. Woody had aged ten years.

He had started smoking again and surrounded himself with coffee containers half full of drowned cigarette butts. He was pale, with a tremor in his hand, and he seldom saw the glowing autumn days outside. Conferences with actors were sandwiched between business meetings with Fritz and sessions with his general manager. The director's prompt book became an exten-

sion of his right hand. He rarely took the time to eat a
civilized meal. The theater had turned an elegant
university professor into one more frenetic Broadway
gambler, staking his future on a handful of actors and a
few thousand words. There was only a week remaining
until previews. Sheila wondered whether Woody would
make it.

The first run-through went reasonably well, though
Bill was shaking his head over the playing time. "Two
and a half hours! They'll miss the eleven-oh-seven to
Scarsdale!" But Woody had made many cuts during
rehearsals and intended to make no more. "We'll go with
this." Yet Sheila could feel, sitting next to him, his
confidence draining away. Listening to the same words
repeated day after day was a form of torture, even (or
especially) to the author of those words. Later, as Sheila
and Woody brooded over a lunch counter, Woody pointed
to the pedestrians passing on the street.

"We need *them!* An audience! We're stale! Sheila,
I've got to have an audience!"

"You'll get one. Next week!"

"I want it *now!*"

Regrettably, Woody had an idea. For the next day's
run-through, he imported a busload of fifty students from
St. Barnaby's School of Nursing. The young girls sat
there, many of them having their first taste of live
theater. They ate candy bars and whispered and filed out
looking sullen and confused. Sheila listened to their
comments in the lobby.

"What's it *mean?* . . . Listen, who knows?
. . . Theater makes me feel cruddy . . . Yeah, me

too . . . They should've had music . . . Yeah . . . Let's grab a flick . . ."

That same day, Kerry had come to town for the weekend and begged to be allowed to attend rehearsal. She sat with Sheila in the fourth row of the orchestra, just behind Woody. During the intermission she asked Sheila, "Listen, Mom, what's this play *about* anyhow?"

"It's about the difficulty of men getting along with women," Sheila replied.

"Or *vice versa*," Woody hissed over his shoulder and annihilated them both with a look of pure misogyny.

The next day Woody arrived at rehearsal seven minutes late and the cast sprang to attention. He stopped rehearsal in the middle of the run-through and spoke to Val. Usually, when Woody gave the cast his notes he had no comments for Val except perhaps "Nice bit in twenty two. Keep that." He had called Val "an actor in his gut. He reaches into himself till he finds the character and he drags him up." But now, today, Woody was asking Val to change his entire characterization. The cast listened in stunned silence.

"This is a serious play, Keating, but not funereal, I hope. I want you to play *against the lines*, Keating. You follow me? Let them think they're watching a comedy, eh? Give it a try, there's a good chap."

Val "gave it a try," but the emphasis of the whole scene changed, the other actors were unsettled and Val himself, for the first time, was acting from the outside. Woody even committed the directorial sin of giving Val "line readings." Val, reduced to a mimic, became wooden. Sheila could see that a carefully balanced performance, built up over the weeks, was in mortal danger. Now Woody was speaking to Val again. "Fine, just fine, Keating. Now take it again, please, from the top. And settle into it, right?" But Val announced that he had a photo session and costume fittings. The cast almost audibly sighed with relief. "Get you tomorrow, Keating," said Woody, obdurate, and continued the rehearsal "working around" Val. Sheila sat in her orchestra seat, dull with foreboding, then found her way to a phone and caught Muriel in Westport.

"Mother, you have to come to town. I need you. Take down this address and bring dinner for three and a toothbrush. Muddy, will you do it?"

"Of course, dear. I always enjoy a nice picnic."

Sheila gave her mother the address of Theo's apartment, knowing Theo to be out of town with her new man, and returned to rehearsal.

When Sheila invited Woody to dinner, he resisted, but feebly. Early evening found them embracing Muriel on the sidewalk and riding up to Theo's apartment. Muriel was looking pink and pretty, chattering on about plays and movies and art galleries she had visited with Uncle Fritz. She wore a new dress that made a virtue of dowdiness, flaunting a wholesome Kansas look that was startling, so far from its native habitat. Woody was gripping the picnic basket and staring straight ahead like a zombie. Sheila took her mother's hand for a moment. "You're a little engine that could, you know it?" They reached Theo's floor and filed into the cool, shadowy apartment.

While Muriel made for the kitchen like a homing

pigeon, Sheila led Woody to a huge marshmallow of a chair and pushed him down, letting the tranquil grey and white spaces of the room work on his fragmented spirit. When Muriel brought a platter of fried chicken and sandwiches, mother and daughter began telling stories of the old days in Lawrence, Kansas. They remembered Tom Devlin's voice student, so in love with him that she wept real tears as Melisande to his Pelleas. They remembered Uncle Fritz hooking a fish in the River Kaw and heaving his rod upward, the fish hitting Woody squarely in the face. Woody smiled, and his face ironed out. But when Muriel stood to collect the plates, the spell was broken. Woody dropped his head in his hands.

"Little old Lawrence, where are you now?"

Sheila jumped into the opening she had been waiting for.

"Where's Lawrence? Right there in Kansas, heartland of America, comfy and cozy, safe as churches!" She sprang to her feet and stood over him as if she could breathe life and faith back into him. "Woody, you *did* all that! Faculty meetings, campus politics, talented amateurs! You had to come back here, to Broadway, where you belong!"

"Did I indeed? Did I have to leave a secure and *profitable* way of life to come to this snake pit of a city and make a fool of myself in front of God and *The New York Times?*"

"The play's going to *work*, Woody."

"One week from tonight I shall be crucified. The audience will bark like seals, drop their umbrellas, and rattle their shopping bags. They'll waddle out of there muttering, 'Haven't I got enough trouble at home?' and tell their friends to go to the Ice Follies. And the critics—ah, yes the critics—they'll polish off the adjectives that kill: 'ponderous,' 'obscure,' 'pretentious.' They'll say 'Sherwood Pell has returned to us from Kansas in a vehicle, alas, as cumbersome as a covered wagon.' Or try this—'*Continuum* tells the story of the human race for three centuries. It seems only half that long.'"

"Woody, that's enough!"

"No, no, I have many more."

"Sure you do. It's fun to torture yourself. We've been locked up with this play for weeks. You're sick of it. I'm sick of it. You *said* this would happen. You told me people get so desperate they'll ask the cleaning lady up in the balcony, 'Hey, how did you like the second act?' Woody, you're exhausted, burnt out. But listen to me, Sherwood Pell, *don't you screw up our play!*"

"I beg your pardon."

"You spent four years writing it, making it say *exactly* what you think of life on earth. Life is painful, isn't it? Oh, sure, there's love and lust and double chocolate shakes. But there's always the pain. Is it knowing we're gong to die? I just know life has a terrible, wonderful secret at the center, like honey way inside a flower. And—oh, hell . . .'"

Sheila, pacing the room, saw her mother's puzzled look, and Woody's face, inscrutable, and the large, cool room around her waiting for her to solve the riddle of the universe and she felt foolish, suspended, inadequate.

"Woody, do *not* pretty up this play. It is *not* the

263

goddam Ice Capades. Don't go for laughs, and leave Val Keating the hell alone. *Continuum* is a *grand* play. It is highly serious. Woody, have courage. I love this play. I beg you to believe in it the way I do. Don't cut it. Don't change it. Just . . . bring up the curtain."

Embarrassed, she turned away from his impassive face. She stood in the window, looking down into the street. The room was so quiet the doorman's whistle was like a scream. Then Sheila heard her mother's pleasant, everyday voice.

"You know, Sherwood, one of the investors told Fritz he thinks your play is a major theatrical event."

"Which investor?"

"He said you bring grandeur back to the theater, and eloquence and—oh, you know, all those other things."

"What other things?"

"And he said—well, he said you belong . . . in the company . . . of the immortals."

A pause. Woody's face gave nothing away. He nodded.

"A man of keen discernment."

He rose from his chair, squaring his shoulders and buttoning his jacket over a trim waistline. He walked with a springy step to give Muriel a quick kiss.

"I've missed you, you lying hussy."

He touched Sheila's arm. "Ladies, I bid you goodnight. I value your peerless friendship."

He turned to go and Muriel moved to see him out. But Sheila stopped her, knowing Woody would prefer a clean exit.

Later, as Sheila and Muriel lay in darkness in Theo's twin beds, Sheila stretched her arm across the empty space between them. Muriel heard the rustle of the sheets and reached to grasp her daughter's waiting hand.

"Are you happy, dear?"

"Happy?" Sheila gave a bleating laugh. "What's happy?"

Muriel flung back the sheet and came to sit on Sheila's bed. "Sheila, what is it?" Sheila wrenched the words out of her throat, the second time she had ever said them.

"He's too young for me!" In the dim light, Sheila could see her mother's astonished face.

"Too young? Too *young?* That's the silliest thing I ever heard in all my born days!"

"Ten years."

"Ten years! And if people had a particle of sense wouldn't the man be always younger? Isn't it a well-known fact that men die first, and isn't the entire world crowded with widows whose husbands were older? Wasn't your dear father nine years older than me? And don't I wish every day of my life it had been the other way around?"

Her mother always spoke with an Irish inflection when she spoke of Tom Devlin and now Sheila could almost feel her father's presence in the room. Muriel's eyes were glistening with tears and anger.

"You're a foolish, ungrateful girl! When the good Lord has provided you with a fine, decent man you start complaining that he wasn't born at an earlier time. Now

265

you stop thinking such ridiculous thoughts, you hear me, Sheila?"

"All right, Mother, all right."

"My dear child, can't you be happy for the love of God?"

"I'm happy, I'm happy." Sheila was crying and Muriel wrapped her in her arms like a child and rocked her and crooned over her. "There now, there's my baby girl. Your father used to say 'Sure she's never content unless she's miserable, that one.'" They laughed together and dried each others' tears.

When Muriel had returned to her own bed, Sheila lay staring into the darkness. Could her mother be right? She remembered when her mother had always been right. She realized with mild surprise that she was fond of her mother.

CHAPTER

22

THE NEXT DAY Woody said nothing more to Val about "playing against the lines." By tacit consent, Val went back to the performance he'd been creating and Woody offered only an occasional "All right, Keating, keep that." The rest of the cast seemed more willing to work for Woody than ever before, perhaps relieved to find him human, as subject to the fear of failure as they were themselves.

In this last week of rehearsals they were developing a style, a manner of playing together that lent continuity to the shifting of time and place inherent in the script. Woody was moving now from one part of the theater to another as he watched the performance, Sheila tailing him pad in hand. Afterwards, in giving the cast his notes, he would still say, "It's not quite theater-size yet, people." Those actors who had worked more in front of the camera than behind the footlights would nod their understanding. There was always the unspoken wish, "If only we had an extra week of rehearsal time . . . an extra day . . ." But ready or not came the technical rehearsal, which was rough, then the "dress," recalling the overworked superstition about "bad dress, good performance." Three preview nights went by with the intricate timing of Chinese "stagehands" and fluid lighting changes not quite perfected. At last, for better or worse, it was opening night.

Actors scurried between dressing rooms, exchanging presents and good luck wishes. Sheila came to Val's dressing room an hour before curtain time bearing a huge box, but he was gone. One wall of the tiny cubicle was lined with his costumes, a shelf above holding a wild array of hats: a plumed hat and a high silk hat, a tasseled cap and a shining silver helmet. Taped to the wall was a printed chart of his costume plot, since this production did not afford him the luxury of a dresser. A few telegrams were pasted to his mirror, signed by nobody she knew. A coffeepot purred on a hot plate in the corner. Sheila put down her box and poured herself a cup to quiet the tremors in her stomach, then wished she hadn't.

She could feel Val's presence in the room, but it was a different presence: it was Val Keating, actor. She was surrounded by the trappings of his future life, his masquerade costumes, his makeup, all the deceptions that would help him to become somebody else. This actor-person was a stranger to her. She fingered a velvet coat and smelled its strange, dusty smell. It smelled of the stage, when the curtain first rises, not of Val who had held her naked in his arms. She had spent days, weeks seesawing on the question of their ages. But Val was not only too young, he had moved into another world. *How could she marry a man like this?*

He had flung his shirt across the back of a chair. The collar was frayed and buttons missing, but when she buried her face in it . . . *How could she NOT marry a man like this?*

Val burst in, wearing his first-act doublet and hose and took her in his arms. "You been here long? I was giving Piper her dumb present, a little gold horse—'Lord Kitchener'—He's the nag that—"

"I know. How do you feel?"

"Geez, great. How about you?"

"I'm glad you have a sink for throwing up."

"Ah, baby, come here. Sit. Okay? Now put your head back and leave everything to the nice doctor. Think peace. Think quiet. Think happy." He gently, rhythmically massaged her forehead and temples.

"This is ridiculous. *You're* opening and *I'm* sick."

"Figures. You found me a play and got me a production. Who's got a better right to throw up for me?"

"I think I feel better."

He came around her chair and squatted in front of her.

"You look sensational." Sheila was glad of the month's mortgage she'd spent on her black body-bag.

"I brought you a present. Open that big box over there."

"Geez, honey, what is it, a Buick?"

He opened it and took out a vast ten-gallon hat.

"In case you get a swelled head."

He slapped it on his head, topping off the doublet and hose, and walked bowlegged around the room, shouting, "Heigh-ho, Silver! I'm gonna git me a hoss!

269

I'm gonna git me a silver-studded saddle! I'm gonna git me a muzzle-loadin' flintlock rifle!" He paused for a split second in his outlandish costume, his arms flung out and legs bowed around his imagined steed, and Sheila felt her love for him flooding over her. Then he came toward her, his voice suddenly soft and loving. "And I'm going to git me a bride, a beautiful, sassy, smart-as-a-buggy-whip bride—all mine." He dropped on one knee and swooped off his hat. "I mean it, honey. We're going to get married."

"Oh, Val."

"Go ahead, say 'yes,' honey."

"I—I can't." She couldn't bring herself to lie to him.

"What do you mean you 'can't'?" His face had gone from joy to bewilderment.

"Look, we have to talk later."

"No, *now*. What's wrong? What happened?"

"Nothing. Val, it's almost curtain time."

"Who gives a shit? Honey, aren't you going to *marry* me?"

"Val, don't ask me *now!*" He shook his head.

"I always thought we'd get married . . . I was sure . . . as soon as I got some money . . . we love each other . . . don't we? Look, are you trying to tell me . . . did you, all of a sudden, quit loving me?"

"No! Oh, God, *no*, Val."

"Jesus, you scared me." He dropped his head in her lap. Looking down she put a hand on his shaggy hair and could find nothing to say that could be said on opening night with people shouting in the hall outside and Val not made up yet and a voice coming over the P.A. system: "Half hour, please. One half hour, everybody." All the months of loving him and wanting him had finally brought her to this incoherent moment. He raised his head. He was grinning again.

"I got it. You have to wait till after tonight. If we're a flop, I'll still be poor, right? I jumped the gun, didn't I?"

"I don't *care* about poor!"

"We have to care." He rose to his feet. "In a couple of hours we'll get the word. Radio critics, then the early edition of the *Times*, second string. Then we'll know. And we're going to be a hit. I'm not going to let you down, Sheila."

"You couldn't." She rose to go, and faced him, looking into his eyes. "You're a prince of players. I'm very proud of you." They stood for a second with the length of the small room between them and footsteps outside the door and the coffee pot growling as it reheated itself.

"I love you, Val."

Woody knocked and entered. "Came to say drop dead, Keating." The men shook hands. Val put on his cowboy hat and, backing away from her toward his makeup table, flicked the brim.

Sheila made the round of all the dressing rooms, the snatches of the actors' talk falling around her like a snowstorm. "Best of luck . . . thanks for everything . . . loved the flowers . . . no, not nervous, only paralyzed . . . my rabbit's foot . . . my four-leaf clover . . . my cat has a fur ball, bad sign . . . zip

271

me up, will you? I'm going to pee in my pannier . . . Jesus, what's my first cue? . . . if she steps on my line again . . . do I look all right? . . . I wish I had listened to my mother, 'Teach school,' she said . . . I'm going to be a prostitute and rest my mind . . . this wig has fleas . . . who took my shoe . . . what time is it? . . . See any critics? Oh, God, there must be an easier way . . . All right, suck in your gut, folks, William Morris is watching."

Sheila found her way out front, down a half-flight of stairs and into the side aisle of the orchestra. She saw rows and rows of faces, the small house nearly full, thank God. She caught a glimpse of her mother between Kerry and Uncle Fritz, all laughing and chatting like *tricoteuses*—how could they?—and continued on to the back of the house to stand beside Woody. They leaned together on the plush-covered railing and watched the house fill up. Woody's face was composed, but as white as his shirt collar, his cheek pulsing as he clenched and unclenched his teeth. He checked his watch and muttered, "I told Bill to go up at eight-oh-five."

"I have eight-oh-three," Sheila said. They waited the endless two minutes, Sheila reciting her social security number under her breath. The house lights started to dim. The audience gave one final rustle like a large animal settling down and then was quiet. Sheila touched Woody's arm and he put his cold hand over hers. The curtain rose.

Sheila, having seen the play times without number, saw it this time with the audience, feeling every reaction with them. They were puzzled and quiet, held in

272

suspense for that first agonizing five minutes while they decided whether they had wasted their money or not. After the first laugh—Piper had a patter speech and danced away with it—they settled down. Not bad. Val made his first entrance. At the sound of his voice, the silence deepened and the heads turned to follow his every move onstage.

When the first shift in time took place and Val appeared as his own son, they were startled. A few whispered questions in the dark, a few head-shaking no-answers. But Val knew how to take the audience into his confidence, beguiling them. Sheila thought of Olivier as Richard III, playful, sharing his game with them. Only a churlish audience would refuse to play. This audience did not refuse. They were his.

Continuum was a love story slipping down the generations, seeking always the essence of a thing people learned to identify as "love," seeking its fixed, immutable center. This gift of love brought mortals close to the angels, endowing them with insight and pity and a terrible capacity for pain. Of course, an audience was always reluctant to feel pain—"Haven't I got enough trouble at the office?" In this play, they were asked to feel pain and joy at once, to laugh at a quixotic character tumbling from his horse, even though they knew he tumbled mortally wounded. They stayed with it. Sheila wanted to embrace them all. By intermission, she was almost sure the play was working.

She and Woody went out to the lobby to sip their villainous orange drink, separating to eavesdrop on the audience comments.

273

"So I told her, twenty percent off, you call that a sale?"

Sheila moved on to another group.

"Lizzie's fine. She had her tummy tucked and her tubes tied and married her son's roommate."

Sheila moved on. Finally, one group was discussing the play.

"That actor Keating is hot for that little actress. Those two could start a fire."

Sheila returned to the theater to lean on the railing and grind her teeth. Woody joined her saying, "See that man over there in the dark glasses? That's the Shubert organization."

"What's it doing here?"

"Prospecting."

The second act went well. The applause at the final curtain was loud and long. Sheila looked toward Woody who had never yet uttered a hopeful word about the play's future.

"They like it," she said brightly.

"Friends, relatives, and backers," he said grimly. "If *they* didn't like it, we'd be closing tonight."

They joined the sardines packed into the halls and dressing rooms backstage, Val's cubicle being largely filled by his co-workers from Theo's office, one of them plastered against him like a wet sheet in a high wind.

"Why didn't you *tell* us you were an actor? I played Third Witch in . . ."

Val clapped his hand over her mouth before she could say *Macbeth* and waved to Sheila, who gave him the victory sign. Sheila and Woody made their rounds, congratulating the actors. "No notes tonight," Woody said and the actors, half in and half out of their costumes and high on applause, groaned in mock disappointment.

When Sheila returned to Val's dressing room, it was even more crowded than before. He waved to her and put on his ten-gallon hat and saluted. But he was fenced in by a solid wall of women. Where did they all come from? They had a claim on him. He was an actor now. She stood and watched him for a moment. He laughed at their jokes and shrugged modestly at their compliments. He was all charm. She mouthed the word "Sardi's" and elbowed her way out.

She found Woody and they made for the stage door. Outside, a dozen young girls stood in clumps, waiting. Some of them held autograph books. One blocked Sheila's way and asked, "Are you anybody?" Sheila answered, "No, nobody."

Woody took her arm and announced "She's a celebrated writer who *never* gives autographs!" and he started to pull her away. But Sheila stopped. "Who're you waiting for?"

"Val! Val Keating!" came the reply.

Sheila muttered, "My God, they're younger than Kerry."

"Don't worry, next week, the latest rock star," said Woody and pulled her away.

They walked west on Forty-fourth Street to Sardi's for the opening night party and climbed to the Belasco Room on the third floor. In the entrance hall was a huge blowup of the *Continuum* poster, showing Val and Piper tumbling down three centuries. The room itself was suitably dramatic with red carpet, dark paneling, and tall windows. Sheila scanned the photographs that lined the walls: Lily Langtry, Otis Skinner, Maude Adams. All the names that had been lovingly handed down to Sheila from her father were suddenly real people who had once posed for the camera as Val was posing now. Sheila stood in one of the windows and looked down past the huge neon "S" of Sardi's, at the Broadhurst and the Shubert and Shubert alley, jostling with people. She looked back at the room, every table bright with flowers and a small band tuning up in an alcove. People would not be bored while they waited for the ax to fall. If the play were about to fail, it would fail with a bang, not a whimper.

CHAPTER
23

MURIEL AND KERRY arrived at the party together, Uncle Fritz staying downstairs to greet the backers. Sheila led her mother to a table in the corner. "The chief mourners will sit here."

"Now, Sheila, it's going to be just fine, and what do those critics know about it anyway?"

"Enough to close it on Saturday night," Sheila answered.

Kerry looked around her, taking in the music and flowers. "Like a wedding that could turn into a funeral, huh?"

The cast arrived and staked out their table. Friends and investors drifted in and clustered around the bar for a tranquilizer. Val came, hugged Sheila, and started roaming the room, a patch of forgotten makeup behind his left ear. Sheila sat, folding and refolding paper napkins into shapes unknown to origami. And so began the long wait for the first reviews.

When Fritz joined them to carry on his running flirtation with Muriel—"How's my little Kansas sunflower tonight?"—Kerry touched Sheila's arm.

"Mom, you busy? I mean do you have to go and save the American theater or anything?"

"No, I did that." Sheila covered the long, slim hand with her own. "I've missed you so much."

"Yeah, I was counting up. I been an orphan since last April."

"I know. Oh, baby, this play has taken over my life. I couldn't help it. Did you understand?"

"Yeah. I was frosted for a while, during the Italian period."

"Is it over? I didn't know."

"Italy's over, but London's where it's at."

"Oh, I agree."

"Whitney's going to London next summer."

"Whitney?"

"Whitney worked at the gallery with me this summer in Boston. I was going to tell you. Now he's back at school. Williams. We don't cohabit. He's into theopathy."

"I don't—"

"He's deeply religious. He's working on a sculpture forty feet high and it's called 'Doxology.'"

"What's it made of?"

"Iron fence. Whitney's short, but very muscular, you know?"

"Sure, heaving that fence around."

"So I'm going to London with him, if it's part of God's plan." Kerry's young face suddenly took on a look of peace and piety that Sheila had never seen on her daughter before. "And not to worry. I'm working three jobs and Whitney's uncle has a loft in Soho and we take our sleeping bags."

"Right."

"Listen, I'm really glad we had a chance to talk and I've got to go check in with Piper. Wasn't she totally celestial?"

With a quick hug, Kerry rose and took herself off. Sheila watched the tall figure cross the room and thought to herself, "So endeth six months of maternal guilt and self-recrimination. Amen."

Uncle Fritz, too, was watching Kerry's athletic stride. "So that's another of the Devlin girls. Backbone of the nation. Is that one smart like her mother and gammy?"

"Smarter," said Sheila.

"Don't kid me, Sheila-baby. They don't come any smarter than my sunflower here." His arm went around Muriel's shoulders and gave her a sudden squeeze that jerked her head sideways. "Listen, I'm going to get you ladies some liquid refreshment. This party needs a little shot in the arm, right? So what did you think of your play tonight, Sheila-baby? Kinda heavy stuff I'm telling you. Is that what the public wants these days? Personally I'll take an old-fashioned musical, with plenty of girls and a couple of laughs. But listen, if this thing goes over, I'll make a bundle. If it's a turkey, it brought me my little bride." He gave Muriel another squeeze, but she was ready for him, stiff-necked. "So either way, how can I lose? Now don't go 'way, girls."

Uncle Fritz rose and left them.

"Did he say 'bride'?"

"Yes."

"Mother, you're not going to *marry* him?"

"I haven't said 'yes.' Then again, I haven't said 'no.'" Her mother smiled mysteriously.

"Well, say it. *No.*"

"No? And then what? There's heaps of women would like to marry your Uncle Fritz. They make a line three times round the block. So I go back to Lawrence and clean my house and cook my dinner and talk to the birds, I suppose."

"But Mother—What bout Woody? I always thought . . ."

"It so happens your Uncle Sherwood has never asked me to marry him."

"Never?"

"Never, never, never." Her mother looked away, then turned her lost look back to Sheila. "What do you expect me to do? Ask him myself?" She fixed her eyes on Woody, four tables away, and spoke very softly. "Sherwood, will you be my husband? We could live in your house or my house. No matter. You'd tell me your opinion about things when you came home for dinner. You do enjoy my cooking, don't you? So many things I haven't fixed for you yet, dishes that might be too rich for a man with a broken leg, not taking any exercise. I know my nutrition, you see. You won't find yourself in the hospital, your veins chock-a-block with cholesterol. No indeed, with my cooking, you'll live to be a hundred and they'll have to take you out and shoot you."

She gave her little laugh and leaned forward still

further, her chin pointed at Woody, as if she hoped he might hear without hearing. "And Sherwood, I'm not so stupid about the theater as you might think. You could read me a scene you'd written while I was doing the mending. Would you believe I can still turn a collar on a shirt? Darn socks? Make our own soap? . . . Oh, you have no idea what an old-fashioned wife . . . I . . . could be . . ."

She trailed off and sat, looking down at her hands lying idly in her lap. Sheila put her own hand between them.

"Muddy, he'll ask you. He's—he's taking his goddam time!"

"Yes, isn't he? Eight years, and don't swear, Sheila." Her mother sat up very straight. "You see, I've waited long enough. I won't go back to Lawrence and wait any more. Living alone is for hermits and crabs and hermit crabs!" She smiled at her small joke. "I must have somebody to do for. Sheila, you write books. I do for somebody."

Sheila saw Uncle Fritz bearing down on them and had just time to say, "Okay, but not him, you hear me?"

"Now how's about a small libation all around? Belly up to the bar, girls!" His large hands were wrapped around three drinks and a smile wrapped around his broad, jack-o'-lantern face. He hooked his foot behind the leg of an empty chair and pulled it out while setting the drinks down on the table, hauling a dish of nuts from one pocket and bread sticks from the other. A good man on a camping trip, Sheila decided, but Muriel was not a camper.

Uncle Fritz began describing to Muriel the Seychelle Islands where he would take her on their wedding trip. The Seychelles had frigate birds, he said, and jet black parrots and a dark blue robin with white wings that exists nowhere else in the world. Muriel was smiling and shaking her head like a woman being offered the rarest of jewels and refusing them, but not for much longer.

Sheila rose, unnoticed, and went to join Val at the actors' table, Woody presiding at one end, Val at the other. When Val reached for her hand and pulled her down beside him, Sheila wondered what she had been doing away from him.

The actors were betting on which notices would be good and which ones bad. Mostly they were predicting scathing pans, like children scaring themselves with ghost stories. Woody was the best at this game, tossing out phrases like "yawn-provoking" and "Titanic tedium." Val and Sheila looked at each other with wan smiles, wincing at the gallows humor.

Suddenly Ben, the press agent, appeared, threading his way between the tables toward the center of the room. He held up both hands, the band played a short fanfare, and there was instant silence.

"Ladies and gentlemen, I have Frank Rich for you."

"Frank Rich . . . Did he say *Frank Rich?*" The actors turned to one another, incredulous.

"That's right. Because our famous director-playwright Sherwood Pell is returning to Broadway after an absence of ten years, *The New York Times* sent its first

282

critic to one of our previews. His review will appear in tomorrow morning's early edition." Ben waved a computer printout. Val whispered to Sheila, "Here we go, honey. If we get Frank Rich, we've got it!"

Ben started to read.

" '*Continuum* is a rich theatrical experience, covering three centuries and containing not one dull five minutes.' " Ben paused for a fraction of a second and the cast burst into cheers and applause, releasing the tension of many weeks. Ben held up his hand. " 'In one magical evening, a man and a woman battle their way from then to now, showing once more why men and women cannot live together and cannot live apart. If you ever wanted to see the human race reflected in a mirror—and that's why we go to the theater, isn't it?— you will find this play funny and heart-breaking and true.' "

More applause. Val looked down at Sheila. "Honey, we're in!"

Ben continued. " 'Val Keating, playing the Everyman of the piece, is an actor to recall the young Olivier, a gifted artist with a voice like music. Keating has all the makings of today's matinee idol, the homely good looks and self-deprecating charm. But Keating also has an indispensible attribute called *fire in the belly*.' "

Here the cast interrupted again with whistles and catcalls, until Val rose and took a bow, facing the wrong way, and sat down again. " 'The actress who plays his wife-mistress down through the ages is a British nymphet, a sprite who can cross the stage like a puff of smoke. Together these two bring back to the theater something that has been lacking for years: tender, hot-blooded passion.'"

The cast hooted and stamped. Piper flew from her chair to embrace Val, who rose and twirled her in his arms. Under cover of the *pas de deux*, Sheila slunk off to the ladies' room, which thank God was empty. She sank into a chair facing a mirrored wall and stared. The play she had worked so hard for was a hit and Val Keating was a star. But she wanted to walk through that mirror and into another world. Any other. She dropped her head down to the cold glass shelf. The door swung open and Val stood there.

"Val! You can't come in here!"

"I'm in. What's wrong?"

"Go away."

He came and pulled her to her feet. "Hey, the play's a hit. Now we can get married."

"No."

"Why the hell not?"

Two women came in and stopped in their tracks. "Well, excuse *us!* My God, it's Val Keating! Listen, don't rush off. We're backers and you're going to make us a mint!" Turning to Sheila they said, "And are you . . . just a friend?"

Sheila crashed out of the room with Val behind her. He caught her arm and pulled her behind a screen where folding chairs were stacked and pinioned her against them.

"Now look, honey—"

"Val, everything's different now! You're going to be

rich and famous! Listen!" Ben's voice could be heard again.

"I have Stuart Klein for you. 'The star that dazzled Forty-fifth Street last night was more like a comet. His name is Val Keating and he's headed for Hollywood and a lot of glory.' Hey, Keating, where are you?"

"Val, get *out* there!" Sheila pushed him out and watched him saunter back to his table amid cheers. Sheila skirted the table and found a place next to Woody, whose "sardonic wit" was likened to that of George Bernard Shaw. When the tumult had died down, people got up to dance. A waiter handed Woody a business card. Sheila held her breath while Woody read a note on the back.

"Remember the spy from the Shubert organization?" She nodded. "Seems we might be moving to the Plymouth. Just over a thousand seats. A Broadway house, you understand. One of the best."

"*Woody!*" She threw her arms around him and he patted her shoulder. She drew back and looked at his wintry smile.

"Woody, can't you for once *rejoice?* blow your top? What are you—a sore winner?"

"It's Christmas afternoon, isn't it? We got everything we wanted. Now what do we do?"

Sheila could not admit how well she understood. The tension of months had gone and in its place there was only emptiness.

"You see, I've burned my bridges. I can't go back to Lawrence, I can't stay here in this slaughterhouse of a city. I'm the Flying Dutchman. I have no home."

Sheila could see Muriel across the floor. Fritz was leaning over her, an arm around her shoulders, holding her hand in both of his. Anger flared up in Sheila.

"You think home is a place, don't you? Well, it isn't! Home is a *person!*" She willed him to look across the room, but he was toying with his drink, morose. "A loving, waiting, wanting person! And if you don't know that, you can just keep on flying, Dutchman!"

The band had doubled the decibels and Val pulled her to her feet. He spun her away and then stepped back to look at her.

"All right. When do we get married?"

"Don't rush me."

"*Rush?* What've we been doing for six months? Now the play's a hit and I've got a contract! I'll get a checking account! I'll be respectable!"

"I don't want you respectable! I want you poor!" He looked at her dumbfounded. "You had two shirts and a tankful of fish and I loved you! How do I know I'm going to love a big star, a sex symbol with screaming fans and 'fire in his belly?'"

He spread his great hands, bewildered.

"I'm the *same!*"

"You wait! You'll be on talk shows, wearing a gold chain and sneakers! You'll give interviews and be charming! You'll sell salad dressing with your picture on it! You're going to be disgusting!"

"You're out of your skull!"

"You'll live in Hollywood! You'll have a heart-shaped swimming pool and give *parties!* Half the time you'll be on location! Burma! The Outer Hebrides!

Hoboken! I'll need an appointment to see you, once a year!"

"That's a lot of garbage! Big star—Hollywood— salad dressing—you don't believe that stuff!" He actually shook her. "Now look. I'm from Nebraska. We don't fool around! My mother and father never kissed until they got married, except in the daytime! I don't believe in all this bed-hopping! You and I are going to get married, or—"

"Or what?"

"Don't make me say it, honey." He held her close and they swayed with the music. Sheila felt they had come to the edge of a chasm and looked down. She was terrified, facing for the first time, head on, the possibility of losing him forever.

A manicured hand tapped Val on the shoulder.

"May I have this dance?"

There stood Theo in hemorrhage-red with black hair and a smile.

"Well, dears, I'm here to say congratulations and you win. I'm an investor, so it's a pleasure to be wrong. Now then, when's the wedding day?"

"Hi and shut up," said Sheila.

"I see," said Theo. She wedged herself between them. "Dance with me, Val, and explain everything." She moved into his arms, laying curled fingers across the back of his neck. Sheila turned away with one quiet word. "Vulture."

As she was leaving the dance floor, two bare arms came around her waist from behind and a voice spoke in her ear.

"Don't turn round, please or I shall lose my nerve and I really must tell you this. A big theater person just said I should be nominated for a Tony award. I want you to know because you kept me from haring off . . . I must have been bonkers . . . I shall remember you . . . most fondly . . . in my forthcoming"— (giggle)—"memoirs!" The arms loosened their hold and Sheila turned in time to see Piper dancing away, blowing a kiss over her shoulder. Sheila watched the girl move out of sight and thought, "There goes an actress for life."

Sheila wandered aimlessly until she saw Woody and Uncle Fritz flanking her mother at a far table. Muriel was turning one way and then the other, enjoying her moment. Sheila joined them, taking her place beside Uncle Fritz and set out to divert him.

She praised his courage in backing the show, his discernment, his tenacity, and his tailor. Uncle Fritz leaned back in his chair and basked, like a man taking the sun, then said, "Woody's making a play for your mother. You tell him to lay off. I always was a better fisherman!" He clapped Sheila's back and roared, "What's your poison, Sheely-baby?"

"Cyanide with a twist," said Sheila.

Uncle Fritz trotted off to the bar, a Percheron in a business suit. Sheila looked across his vacant chair toward Woody and her mother. Muriel was heaping praises on the play. "So grand, so emotional! I was so tired when it was over I felt three hundred years old!"

"You don't look it," said Woody. With one deft finger, he drew an errant lock of hair back from her cheek, for Woody a gesture of unbridled passion.

The dance floor was crowded now, the conversation at nearby tables more raucous, every living soul at the party knowing he had something to celebrate, having hitched his wagon to a winning star. Sheila scanned the room for Val, but could not find him. Suppose he had left? What would she do with the rest of her evening? What would she do with the rest of her life?

A beautiful woman was floating toward their table, her frothy garments foaming in her wake. Her head was held high on a swan's neck and her arms spread wide to encompass, apparently, Woody, who rose and stepped toward her. Immediately, he was inundated by a wave of shimmering blue-green and a voice as seductive as the singing of whales. Sheila was embarrassed to be listening, but listened.

"My darling Woody, embrace me! Oh my God, you are so beautiful, so elegant! I had forgotten how I adore you. And your play! All three hours of it! A triumph of passion over posterior! Kiss me again and tell me you missed me unbearably!"

"I was able to bear it, Addie." Woody swam out of her embrace and turned to introduce Sheila and her mother. Addie introduced a half-dozen young men behind her—"My claque, they follow me everywhere and I lo-ove it!"—and then turned the headlight of her attention on Sheila.

"*Not* Sheila Devlin the writer! But I can't face an evening without the latest Devlin by my bed! How can she be such a brain and beautiful, too?" Then it was Muriel's turn. "*This* is the mother of *that?* Ridiculous.

They're sisters. Woody, what a harem you've been collecting in my absence!"

She chose a seat center stage, facing the dance floor and overlooking the room. Somehow Woody was seated beside her and Fritz, returning with drinks, was settled on her other side. The claque dragged over extra chairs, fussed over Muriel, and told Sheila archly how she had caused them sleepless nights. With her supporting cast disposed, Addie began her monologue.

A natural-born Scheherezade, she told wild stories of her life in India, accompanied by her dancing hands that glittered with watery jewels. Gradually Sheila realized it was Addie alias Adorée who had betrayed Woody years ago, walked out on his production, and run off with her Indian Raj, only recently dead. It was also Addie alias Amanda, who had corresponded with Woody, her urbane and witty professor. Woody claimed he had known all along that Addie was Amanda, while Addie insisted she had identified Woody after his second letter. After all, how many professors at Midwestern universities can call themselves a mortal loss to the Broadway theater? The banter stopped abruptly when Addie turned to face Woody with her great, glittering eyes and said, "Woody, I want back in the theater."

"Do you, Addie?"

"I'm richer than cream now and I'm still a draw. How about you and I buy us a theater and call our own shots?"

There was a pause.

"Very kind of you, Addie. But in this life, I fear, there are no second chances." He gave her a look with a razor's edge he had been honing for ten years. He pushed back from the table, rose, and went to stand behind Muriel's chair.

"My wife and I have other plans."

Muriel looked up. Woody bent down and in full view of the multitude, kissed her on the lips. "Come along, my dear, I believe this is our dance."

Sheila saw her mother rise like a sleepwalker and fall into Woody's arms. He steered her between the tables. When they reached the dance floor, he whirled her away.

Sheila, watching them, felt her heart rejoicing. Her mother's face was radiant and the Seychelle Islands be damned. Woody's face was always illegible, but his arm was tightly circling her mother's waist. Perhaps a misanthrope had need of a perpetual jollity to work against, to whet his appetite for the world's impending ruin. Sheila felt absurdly sanguine. Her own life might be a shambles but there was a shaft of hope for those two. Muriel would provide the grain of sand so irritating to the oyster that he goes on to produce a pearl, or another play as the case might be.

A waiter tapped Sheila on the shoulder. "You telephone? Please?" Sheila went in the direction indicated and Val's large hand reached out of a phone booth and pulled her in. When he swung the door closed, they stood pressed together, her face to his chest, his hands on the wall behind her.

"All right, cookie, what's the *real* reason?"

"Oh, shit."

"Hurry up. We could smother in here." Sheila

struggled vainly to get out. "Godammit, Val, you don't have to know *everything!*"

"Just one thing. Why won't you marry me?"

She looked up at his face, distorted by the strange angle and blurred by their closeness and felt a panic of claustrophobia. "You jerk, you're too young for me!"

He looked at her, totally uncomprehending. "Too young?"

"You're thirty! You know how old I am?"

"How *old* you are?" he repeated with the open mouth of a slow learner.

"Old, old, *old!* Kerry's nineteen! I was twenty-one when I had her! You moron, can't you *add?*"

Deadpan he said, "So you're forty."

"Yes! Forty! Ten years older than you! *Ten years!*"

"So . . . *what?*"

"You have fans my daughter's age! You and Piper set the stage on fire! She wears a barette! You are *young!* and you'll never catch up with me! So forget it! Let me out of here!"

"Oh, God, honey, is that *all?*" He was laughing and kissing her, pushing her against the wall of the phone booth. Sheila felt herself getting weak and the lights getting dim. Perhaps she was fainting. No, she was still standing and the lights were still dim. She saw the whites of Val's eyes rolling sideways as he noticed the lights, too. He pulled open the door.

The hall they were in was dark, also the main room beyond. Val stepped out, dragging Sheila behind him, and walked back to the party. In the dark room people were singing and a glow of light came from the far end where Muriel and Kerry were carrying between them a huge platter with a birthday cake blazing with candles. They set it down on a center table in time for the last words of the song: "Happy birthday, dear Va-al, happy birthday to you!"

Kerry called to Val, "Come on, you have to blow!"

Val still held Sheila firmly by the hand as they approached the table. She whispered, "Is it your *birthday?*" He glanced at his watch. "After midnight. Sure is. Hell, I'm thirty-one!"

Sheila looked at her mother's beaming face. "Mother, how did you *know?*"

Muriel said, "We peeked in his personnel file," and winked at Theo. People were calling to Val. "Come on! Make a wish and blow out the candles!" He turned to Sheila. "Do I get my wish?"

"You rat!"

He whispered, "Honey, now it's only nine years! Makes all the difference, right? Say yes, honey!"

She looked at the circle of faces around them. Muriel was nodding and smiling; Woody nodding judiciously; Kerry nodding quickly, eyes dancing; Piper nodding, even Piper. The candles were guttering. Somebody called, "Bad luck if you don't blow!" Sheila stared at Val. His face looked older in the shadows thrown by the flickering candles, much older.

"Yes."

Val blew out the candles, then he kissed her.